Please return on or before the latest date above.
You can renew online at *www.kent.gov.uk/libs*
or by telephone 08458 247 200

'You, my dear wife, are a brazen wench.

'I have been seriously deceived. I thought you as innocent as a new-born lamb. I knew as soon as I looked at you that you were something special. Just how special I am now beginning to realise.'

Lavinia's soft perfume mingled with the warm-smelling hay, sending his senses reeling. Once again his lips found her throat, and the force of passion building inside him threatened to crumble the wall of his restraint. Taking her hand and gently placing his lips on her palm, he sighed before looking at her, his eyes smouldering.

'I have missed you.'

'Have you? I'm glad to hear it.'

'You do realise that this wasn't part of our agreement, don't you?'

'Yes,' she breathed.

'I find seducing you extremely pleasurable. Despite our agreement, my dear wife, I find I cannot treat you with the impartiality I should.'

'Do you mean you regret our arrangement?'

'No. I will say that I have decided to take our marriage a stage further—that I have a far better arrangement in mind.'

Helen Dickson was born and still lives in South Yorkshire, with her husband on a busy arable farm where she combines writing with keeping a chaotic farmhouse. An incurable romantic, she writes for pleasure, owing much of her inspiration to the beauty of the surrounding countryside. She enjoys reading and music. History has always captivated her, and she likes travel and visiting ancient buildings.

Recent titles by the same author:

CONSPIRACY OF HEARTS
AN INNOCENT PROPOSAL

CARNIVAL OF LOVE

Helen Dickson

MILLS & BOON®

First published in Great Britain 2001
Large Print edition 2001
Harlequin Mills & Boon Limited,
Eton House, 18-24 Paradise Road, Richmond, Surrey TW9 1SR

© Helen Dickson 2001

ISBN 0 263 17189 2

Set in Times Roman 14½ on 15 pt.
42-0701-85130

Printed and bound in Great Britain
by Antony Rowe Ltd, Chippenham, Wiltshire

Chapter One

1789

The Italian May was surprisingly warm, and through half-closed eyes Lavinia looked up into the Saracen blue sky, which was a canopy of ever-changing hues. The sun's warmth had an invisible, embalming quality and she sighed languidly, apathy and inertia calling the tune, the lull and gentle rocking of the boat cradling her nerves as she listened to the gentle splash of the oars and the lap of the water against the hull.

She was content to forget the passage of time as Giuseppe, clad in the scarlet and black livery of the Scalini household, guided the black-gilded boat slowly among a host of other vessels passing hither and thither on the San Marco Canal, some of them sailing too close and approaching too fast for comfort at times.

Basking in the heat, the city of Venice rose out of the calm waters of the lagoon like an exquisite, elaborately adorned crown, seeming to float in the iridescent haze which skimmed the surface of the canal.

Virginia creepers unfurled their leaves as they climbed the peeling and stained stuccoed façades of convents and palaces like huge fishing nets hanging out to dry. It was a city full of candle-lit palaces and churches built on water, shuttered and secretive, magnificent and ancient, its towers and crenellated buildings soaring at random.

'Isn't this just perfect,' Lavinia murmured to her companion Daisy Lambert, where they lounged side by side on silken cushions under a gold-fringed scarlet canopy. Daisy's mother, after consuming a little too much wine earlier and finding the heat of the day too much, had fallen into a light doze across from them.

They were returning from a visit to the Lido, which extended along the mouth of the lagoon. There they had strolled along the spit of sand, gathering seashells and picnicking at noon, before heading back to the house of Signor Leonardo Scalini and his wife Valentina in the Castello area of Venice.

The Scalinis were an old family of merchant stock. They had become close friends over the years with Mrs Lambert's husband, who had been a merchant. Venice, being a key trading centre where spices, silks and other Eastern luxuries were exchanged for necessities of the West, was where he had spent much of his time, before being struck down by some kind of undulant fever—which Mrs Lambert was certain he had contracted from the noxious vapours rising from the canals—eighteen months ago.

The Scalinis, wishing to relieve Mrs Lambert's sorrow, had invited her and her daughter Daisy to stay at their home for a while. The invitation had been extended to included Mrs Lambert's niece, Julia, who was the widowed daughter of her late brother. Julia's half-sister Lavinia, and Lavinia's betrothed, Robert Feltham, had also been invited.

Before coming to Venice they had visited Rome and Florence, but Lavinia loved Venice most of all. She was overawed by its decaying elegance; despite being weathered with age, it retained a certain patina of charm. The moment she had set foot on one of its hundreds of small islands—like writers, poets and artists throughout the ages who had been drawn into its mesmeric aura—she had embraced it at once, feeling it close around her like a warm blanket.

Daisy, two years older than Lavinia, sighed languidly, stirring on the cushions to feel the warm sea breeze on her cheeks, and to gaze at the hundreds of small boats and the uniformity of the gondolas in funereal black spread across the water. It was a rich kaleidoscope of colour, an amazing spectacle of life and gaiety, against the backdrop of the city.

'I only hope Giuseppe is in no hurry to reach the house,' Daisy murmured. 'I feel rather like Cleopatra must have felt on being rowed down the Nile on her royal barge. I could stay on the canal all afternoon. We've been in Venice two weeks now, and I can't for the life of me think why we haven't been to the Lido before today. We must go again before we leave.'

'The reason we haven't been before is because there's been so much else to occupy our time,' breathed Lavinia, watching in fascination as bare-chested men swooped up and down the rigging and busied themselves on the decks of the large sea-going vessels, ranged along the Giudecca quayside to the left of their boat.

They had both taken to the sightseeing and social whirl that Leonardo and Valentina had plunged them into with enthusiasm. Their hosts, eager to make their stay in Venice as pleasurable as possible, had seen to it that they visited the opera houses and the theatres, and had taken them to the grand houses of their many friends where they dined in style.

'I only wish we had been here for the end of the Carnival—instead of spending so long in Florence,' said Lavinia with regret. She would have loved to take part in the Carnival celebrations, which spanned the winter months to the eve of Lent. 'Valentina says it's such an exciting time to come to Venice, the Carnival being a riotous affair, when Venetians don their masks to hide their identities as they indulge in revelry. The merriment goes on night and day, with pageants and parades and masked balls.'

'I can well imagine. But Valentina also says that the anonymity of the mask gives free reign to fantasies, roguery and all manner of licentious behaviour. Little wonder Robert chose to spend so much time in Rome and Florence before coming to Venice,' Daisy said drily, referring to Lavinia's betrothed—a man she had little liking for. Robert was confined to his bed after eating something which had disagreed with him, and had been unable to accompany them to the Lido. 'His disapproval of such wild and decadent behaviour—when all social distinctions are thrown to the wind and men and women become truly incognito, from the Doge down to the meanest beggar—would have sent him into a fit from which he would never have recovered. Had we arrived during Carnival time he would have chaperoned you every step of the way.'

Lavinia smiled. What Daisy said was true. Robert, who was certainly not lacking in moral restraint and regarded any kind of frivolous entertainment with severe disdain, would not have allowed her to partake in the festivities. Not being one to indulge in flamboyant display, a sightseeing tour of the city and its many beautiful churches and treasured works of art were more to his taste.

'Perhaps you're right, Daisy. Poor Robert. If only he would let himself go from time to time. Still, we do have the costume ball to look forward to.'

Valentina and Leonardo had arranged to take them to the ball, which was to be held at one of the palaces along the Grand Canal. It was an important social event to celebrate the twenty-first birthday of an Italian nobleman's son, and promised to be an exciting occasion. However, because it did not coincide with Carnival time—much to the young man's regret—he had decided that it would be a costumed ball with all the extravagance of the Carnival.

'It will give us the chance to dress up and wear Carnival masks,' Lavinia continued, 'and there's to be champagne and music and dancing till dawn. Even Robert would not be so ungracious as to turn down such an invitation as that. I think Sir John and Lady Evesham and their daughter Sophia have been invited, too. You remember, Daisy...we were introduced to them by Valentina at the theatre the other night.'

Daisy wrinkled her nose with obvious distaste. 'Yes. I remember. Sir John and his wife seemed quite nice, as I recall, but I can't say I liked Sophia much. She has a mean, peevish look about her, and she is so plain it's hardly surprising no suitors were forthcoming when she made her debut a year ago. Her parents thought she might stand a better chance if they exhibited her around Europe. Valentina has invited them to call on us but I can't remember when. No doubt we'll see them at the ball.'

Both girls were looking forward to what promised to be an exciting and glittering occasion, and Lavinia had already chosen her costume, having found it in a chest holding a wide variety of Carnival clothes which Valentina kept for such occasions.

'What will you wear, Daisy? Have you made up your mind yet?' Lavinia asked, idly watching a colourful, boisterous group of travelling players, singing and clowning, float by on a barge to perform on the Lido, one young man entertaining them on his guitar, the melodic notes of a love song and their laughter trailing behind like ribbons.

'No, I haven't decided. It's between the lilac and the red velvet.' She turned her head and looked admiringly at her companion. 'But no matter what I wear, I will not look as splendid as you, Lavinia,' she murmured. Being small and with a tendency to put on weight, Daisy envied Lavinia her slender shape and delicate features. With hair like spun gold and eyes turquoise blue and as vivid and deep as the Venetian lagoon, her friend really was quite lovely. Everywhere Lavinia went heads would turn and admiring eyes would follow her.

'Nonsense, Daisy,' countered Lavinia, looking warmly at her friend, having become extremely fond of Daisy during the months she had known her. This trip to Europe had thrown them together, and they had both been relieved to discover that they got on well. Daisy threw herself into whatever it was they were doing with such enthusiasm, which was one of the characteristics which made her such a stimulating companion. 'You will look very nice in either—but if you want my opinion, with your colouring and dark hair, I think the red suits you best.'

'I think you're right,' Daisy replied, knowing she would bow to Lavinia's eye for colour and sense of good taste in the end. 'I wonder what Mr Feltham will say when he sees you in your costume, Lavinia. Considering how brusque and high-handed he always is towards you—and how he is always telling you not to lend yourself to gossip—I'm surprised he allowed you to choose it without his prior approval.'

'I know,' Lavinia replied, remembering the moment when Robert had told her he would trust her this once to choose something suitable to wear for the occasion, as if he had been bestowing a vast favour on her. 'But there's nothing provocative about it. It's not revealing in any way, so Robert cannot disapprove.'

Having seen Lavinia's costume on her in all its simple, triumphal glory, Daisy wasn't so sure about this and gave her friend an arched look. What Lavinia didn't know was that the fluidity of the white silk outlined every curve of her body when she moved. It shimmered and made her look as though she were floating on air, and was far more revealing and alluring than if she were going to the ball stark naked. Robert Feltham might cut a fine figure, but he was a man who shunned frivolity and excesses, and Daisy would take mischievous delight on seeing the horror he would be unable to conceal when he saw what his betrothed was wearing.

Content to bask in the pleasant warmth, a lengthy silence fell between them, but Lavinia suddenly became alert, her eyes widening in alarm when she saw that a barge being rowed at speed was coming perilously close to their own. On a gasp, she scrambled to her feet, shouting to Giuseppe, who was facing away from the oncoming barge. Turning quickly, he saw to his horror the barge bearing down on them and tried to steer the boat out of its path, but it was an impossible task.

Waving an arm, he ordered Lavinia to sit down, but it was too late. The barge collided with their own, which then rammed into another. When the bow of their boat rose, to her horror Lavinia found herself unable to maintain her balance, and was cast into the water.

Gasping for breath, she flailed and floundered about wildly, but she was unable to swim. Her heavy skirts pulled her down and she felt the cool water close over her head. Gripped with terror and panic, she was certain she was about to drown. After bobbing up to the surface she was immediately dragged down once more, having hit her head on the hull of a boat—whether the Scalini boat or someone else's, she had no way of knowing—but the sharp stab of pain exploded inside her head.

From somewhere a long way off she could hear her name being called above the roaring in her ears. With her mouth full of water she was unable to breath and felt as though her lungs were bursting. Looking up, she could see the underneath of a mêlée of boats and a brightness which seemed to dim by the second as she sank further and further. A red haze was beginning to cloud her vision. Gradually a sense of peace and calm began to descend on her as the world as she knew it and her consciousness both began to recede; at that moment death seemed almost certain.

Just when she thought all was lost she was conscious of someone beside her, coming between her and death, condemning her to live. Grasping her arms, he pulled her towards his naked chest and held her in a paralysing grip. As he swam with her to the surface she saw the bright light coming closer, larger, until she burst through its centre and felt the warm sun on her face once more, finding it strange that she was unable to move, that her body didn't seem to belong to her any more.

'Hold on to me,' said a man's voice in English, which seemed to come from far away. 'We'll soon have you back on board the boat.'

Instinctively Lavinia obeyed, unable to do anything else. The stranger held her close, with arms wrapped round her like a vice. Hands reached out of the boat and took hold of her, pulling her up, her rescuer lifting her with what seemed to be superhuman strength. Half-drowned, she was hauled over the edge and into the boat where she collapsed, motionless, face down on to the bottom. The air was rent with voices, Italian and English, all talking at once.

'You're safe now,' she heard Daisy say, but she couldn't move. Everything seemed so far away and her body felt like lead.

Lavinia became conscious of someone's hands moving urgently over her, tearing her dress down the back in an attempt to loosen the lacings of her tight bodice, before kneeling at her head, raising her arms and placing his hands on her shoulder blades, his fingers spread out over her bare flesh as, with a rhythmic movement, he began to pump the water out of her lungs in an attempt to revive her. Pink-faced, all Mrs Lambert, who had been woken by the commotion, and Daisy could do was watch as the man paused and lifted one of Lavinia's eyelids, which flickered at his touch.

Eventually she began to cough and splutter as she tried to rid herself of the water which had almost consumed her, labouring to drag breath into her tortured lungs. The pain in her head, which had momentarily disappeared, returned to torment her with a savage vengeance.

Seeing that she had regained consciousness, the man ceased his pumping and gently turned her over on to her back, wiping back the veil of wet hair and looking down for a moment in silent contemplation at the pale, heart-shaped face which was fragile and fine-boned, her lips shell pink and perfect.

'You'll be all right now,' he murmured. 'You're out of danger.'

With one arm flung above her head, Lavinia's eyes fluttered open to see a darkly handsome face, bronzed by the sun, bending over her, out of which looked a pair of questioning, clear blue eyes, which shone as bright as jewels. Black brows were puckered together in frowning concern.

'My—my head,' she managed to whisper.

Lavinia's rescuer, who seemed to have taken charge of the incident whilst the others looked on in anxious shock, took her face gently between his lean fingers and turned it to one side, brushing back tangles of her hair to reveal a small gash just above her ear, from which a thin trickle of blood oozed.

'You must have hit your head on the boat when you came up beneath it. The wound is superficial and I don't think any permanent damage has been done— but no doubt your head will ache for a while.' He smiled down at her, his teeth dazzling white between his slightly parted lips, making an instant appraisal of the lovely young woman sheathed in wet clothes whom he had just fished out of the canal. She was a golden girl, slender as a wand, and had been as light as thistledown when he had lifted her up into the boat. 'You were lucky not to drown.'

'Which is thanks to you.'

His eyes went to her bodice which only just covered the soft curve of her breasts. 'Your dress is ruined,' he apologised. 'I had to act immediately, and because it restricted your breathing I had no alternative but to tear it.'

Lavinia managed to summon up a smile and answered him in a weak voice. 'It is nothing. I owe you a great debt, sir. I am truly sorry for any trouble I have caused you.'

'It wasn't your fault. It was lucky I was standing by the rail of the ship and saw the boat career into your own, casting you into the water.'

'And you immediately jumped in to rescue me,' she whispered, trying not to let her eyes dwell on his athletic physique, on the wet, powerful muscles of his tanned chest, which tapered to a narrow waist and gleamed beneath the hot sun.

'Something like that.' He grinned. 'You had a close shave, it's true, but you're safe enough now.'

Meeting his gaze, Lavinia saw that his eyes were lively, with a hint of humour in their depths, and shining like a light out of an otherwise dark countenance. His hair was short, jet black and gleaming. It curled vigorously, and droplets of water dripped off the ends and ran slowly down his lean face. Stark black brows were slashed across his forehead and his mouth was wide, his chin indented in a firm, thrusting, arrogant jaw.

The stranger's masculinity was obvious and complete and, despite his bare chest and feet, there was a certain refinement in his well-defined handsome features. She wondered at the character behind them, sensing strength, impatience and steely determination.

Lavinia was curious to know the identity of this man whose prompt action had saved her life.

'Thank you for saving me. But for you I would be lying on the bottom of the lagoon.'

By this time Daisy had recovered sufficiently from the shock of Lavinia's tumble into the water and had gathered her shattered wits about her.

'You gave me such a scare, Lavinia,' said Daisy softly, kneeling beside her and placing a cushion beneath her head in an attempt to make her more comfortable, disturbed by this handsome stranger who had jumped into the water from a nearby sea-going vessel to rescue her friend, his only article of clothing being a pair of tight black breeches, which clung to his masculine body in such a manner that she had to avert her maidenly eyes.

The stranger got to his feet, continuing to gaze down at Lavinia. 'I shall leave you now that I can see you are sufficiently recovered and in capable hands.'

'Thank you, sir,' said Mrs Lambert. 'We cannot thank you enough. We'll get her straight home where she will be put to bed and the physician sent for.'

'I would advise that. Do you have far to go?'

'No. But who do we have to thank?'

He smiled crookedly. 'Maxim Purnell at your service, madam. And you are…?'

'Mrs Esme Lambert. This is my daughter, Daisy— and the young lady you so gallantly rescued is Miss Lavinia Renshaw.'

Maxim inclined his head slightly, his eyes settling on Lavinia propped up on the cushions, gazing up at him intently. 'I am happy to make your acquaintance—although I wish we had met in less traumatic circumstances.'

The offending boat that had collided with their own went on its way after much irate shouting and gesticulating between the oarsmen, and others, which had been alerted to the crisis and stopped to watch, also carried on about their business.

Lavinia struggled to sit up when her mysterious rescuer disappeared over the side of the boat, watching in fascination as he ploughed his way through the water back to his ship with powerful strokes, his black head bobbing up and down and his strong shoulders gleaming as they broke the rippling surface of the water.

On reaching a rope ladder hanging down the ship's side, Maxim effortlessly hoisted himself up before vaulting on to the deck, where he turned and looked in Lavinia's direction, calmly watching her boat continue on its way. The incident had brought a moment of relief from his own troubles, and he would welcome many more such incidents if it gave him the opportunity of making the acquaintance of women as lovely as the one he had just plucked from the lagoon.

It was the tense situation in France that had brought Maxim to Europe, his anxieties compounded by the deepening political crisis in that country. The growing unrest had produced panic and was badly affecting markets throughout Europe. Public order had also collapsed in many regions and, like everyone else, he was very much afraid that open insurrection could be transformed into revolution.

Owning warehouses in ports in France and Italy, warehouses which were filled with commodities he shipped to various countries in the world in his own vessels, he had come to see the heightening crisis at first hand, and to order the emptying of those warehouses should his worst fears be realised and revolution did break out in France. Its possible implications could prove disastrous.

A jovial, middle-aged man by the name of Tom Player and in the same state of undress as Maxim, came to stand beside him. Knowing that Tom was in Venice at this time unloading a cargo from the Levant, Maxim had arranged his journey so that he could spend a few days in the ancient city and see this old friend. Having witnessed the incident and been faintly amused by it, Tom clapped his companion good-humouredly on the back.

'You haven't been in Venice forty-eight hours, Maxim, and already you are plucking damsels out of the lagoon. Who is she, did you ask?'

'Of course. She is English and her name is Lavinia Renshaw.'

'Will she be all right?'

'Yes—although I only just reached her in time.'

His friend glanced at him sideways, a wicked gleam glinting in his eyes. 'And was she worth getting wet for?'

Maxim grinned, his blue eyes gleaming wickedly. 'Well worth it.'

'And is there a chance that she might show her gratitude?' Tom asked meaningfully, his weatherbeaten face wrinkling with lines of humour and a wicked twinkle dancing in his eyes.

'No, Tom, you old rogue. I could tell at a glance that the young lady is much too refined and chaste for what I know you are implying.'

His friend chuckled. 'Same old Maxim—giving nothing away. How many ladies have you left dangling for your favours back home, eh?'

Maxim frowned, his expression suddenly serious. A muscle moved spasmodically at the side of his mouth and his voice was rough with emotion. 'Just the one, Tom. Just the one.'

Tom looked at his friend in taut silence, knowing precisely the woman he was referring to. All at once Maxim seemed like a man being stretched beyond the limits of endurance. 'So, it's still Alice, is it?' he scowled, nodding slowly with understanding. 'So— the wench is still chewing away at your gut, is she?'

'She is, and her teeth get sharper the more she chews.'

Alice Winstanley was the daughter of a small shipping merchant—and mother of Maxim's three-year-old daughter. Alice was charming and pleasing to the eye, but she was as greedy and as ambitious as her father had been before his demise over three years ago—and in Tom's opinion she was as immoral as sin.

Tom sighed deeply. 'I remember the time when you took up with her and I tried to warn you about her, knowing through my long acquaintance with her

father—and her mother being my cousin an' all—
what she was like. I recall how you would swear and
curse at me for speaking out against the girl who
roused such intense feelings in you. So she still won't
marry you.'

'Not without a grand title. Whatever there was between us was over and done with a long time ago,
Tom, when I became aware of the unsavoury depths
to her character that I couldn't possibly know about
on first meeting her. Her hold on me is stronger than
it ever was because of Lucy, and she damned well
knows it. Nothing and no one has claimed my heart
like that child has done. I would give her anything
she wanted—even the moon if I could reach it. I
curse the day I made Alice aware of the title—for
she has given me no peace since.'

'And is it not within your power to acquire the
title? After all, it is yours by right. You are the next
Earl of Brinkcliff. All you have to do is go and see
your uncle and reconcile your differences. He's been
hankering after a meeting with you since your grandfather died—to affirm you as his heir.'

Maxim tensed and looked straight ahead, his fists
clenched by his sides and his mind locked in murderous combat against the idea of going to his uncle.
When his grandfather had been alive, the old man
had turned his back on the elder of his two sons,
Maxim's father, disinheriting him and banishing him
from his home because he had dared to defy him to
marry the woman he loved, a woman his grandfather
had deemed unsuitable to be the Countess of Brinkcliff, chatelaine of Brinkcliff Hall.

On his death the inheritance had passed to Maxim's uncle, Alistair Purnell who, hounded by illness throughout his life, had never married. Feeling a belated sense of regret for the long estrangement and wanting to make Maxim his heir, he had written him frequent letters in an attempt to mend the breach. But Maxim could not forgive what his grandfather had done and, because Alistair had done nothing to right the wrong done to his father when he had been alive, he considered his uncle's conduct over the whole affair no better.

'It's not as easy as that. It's too damned complicated and you know it,' he growled between clenched teeth. 'Out of sheer spite Alice is determined to stand against me on this—regardless of the shame she not only brings on Lucy but also on herself.'

'Since when did Alice Winstanley possess the capacity to feel what would cripple any other mortal?' retorted Tom with biting scorn.

'I have no illusions where she is concerned, Tom. Had it been any other decently bred young woman she would have hidden her condition and married me instantly. But not Alice. Maybe if her father had not died around that time, he would have succeeded in persuading her to marry me. But one way or another, while ever I have breath in my body, I'll fight to gain custody of my daughter—to have her live with me permanently.'

Tom gave him a questioning stare. 'Why, has something changed? I thought Alice and little Lucy were living with you at your London house.'

'They were—have been for the past twelve months or more—until this mess with France blew up. When Alice knew I was coming to Europe, in a fit of anger and resentment at my refusal to allow her to accompany me—for she was convinced my trip to Europe was one of pleasure and not of business—she went to live with her stepmother, taking Lucy with her. I have to do something, Tom. I have watched my daughter grow from a babe in arms to a sturdy three-year-old. I am the centre of her everyday world, and she attaches herself to me like a shadow. I will not lose sight of her because her mother is too stubborn and too ambitious to bow to reason. Nor will I be held to ransom by Alice.'

'I can't begin to conceive what kind of life you'll have married to a woman of Alice's ilk—and I certainly don't envy you—but if you intend making an honest woman of her and keeping Lucy, then you'll have to swallow your own pride and let bygones be bygones. What is past is past. It's the future you have to consider. Go and see the old man. He's been trying to make amends for what your grandfather did to your father for years.'

'It's too late for that, Tom.'

'Better late than never. And how do you know it wouldn't be what your father wanted? You know I have no liking for Alice, Maxim, but I think you'll have to give her what she wants in the end. It's the only way you'll get to keep your daughter.'

'Maybe you're right. But much as I want Lucy with me, I have no great desire to saddle myself with Alice for the rest of my life. If there is any other way

I can obtain custody of Lucy, then I will find it. For some time before I knew Alice was to bear my child, our relationship was cooling and I had decided to end our affair, but when Lucy was born I knew I could not banish the perfidious bitch to obscurity or cast her memory aside. She doesn't love Lucy as a mother should love her own child. She sees her as nothing more than a means to an end. Aye, she is callous and ambitious—and treacherous into the bargain.'

'You loved her once, Maxim.'

'Maybe I did but, whatever it was, it wasn't meant to last.'

Shaking his head Tom moved away, leaving Maxim to do battle with his conscience and to mull over what he had said, hoping that in the end common sense would prevail. Tom, who had captained Maxim's father's one and only ship plying coal from Newcastle to London—an old barque Maxim's father had purchased with a few gold coins after his split from his father—now captained a much finer vessel, one of a fleet of ships owned by Maxim, which flew his flag and carried cargoes from all over the world.

From an early age it had become clear to Maxim's parents that he was a highly intelligent child with an insatiable thirst for knowledge. With the help of his mother's family, he had been sent to a school in Westminster and afterwards to Cambridge to finish his education. But in the meantime he'd had to suffer the loss of both his parents, whose entire fortune was wrapped up in the three-masted sailing ship.

Possessing a shrewd and clever brain, on finishing his education Maxim had attacked life with a single-

minded determination. Immediately putting his mea-
gre inheritance to use, he had sold the vessel and
gambled on a series of investments which had paid
off. Learning fast, he survived and prospered—in
fact, it was as if he could do no wrong. He had embarked on new ventures, buying land in England and
America, land which yielded its riches of gold and
tin and coal. Tom had laughed with admiration, telling him that his father would have been immensely
proud of his son who had turned out to be a brilliant
businessman of the first order, a man who had obviously been born with the Midas touch.

Maxim thrived on taking risks and was forever
driven by the thrill of the wager, always winning and
becoming richer by the day, his wealth bringing him
untold luxuries, but no apparent happiness. At best,
he was a fiercely proud and private man, guarded and
solitary, a man accountable to no one. At worst, he
was a man with a wide streak of ruthlessness and an
iron control that was almost chilling. He could be
cold, calculating and unemotional, which was how
his business adversaries thought of him.

Where his grandfather and his uncle, the Earl of
Brinkcliff, were concerned, Maxim was as hard and
unforgiving as his father had been before him, but
Tom knew that Alice had found the chink in his armour by providing him with a daughter outside wed-
lock—although a son would have given her more le-
verage in persuading Maxim to become reconciled
with his uncle. How long would it be, he asked himself, before Maxim lost the battle to stand firm
against his uncle and went to see him?

Deep in thought, Maxim continued to watch as the boat carrying Lavinia Renshaw went on its way. The incident which had just occurred had left its effect on him, and he had a strong desire to see her again. Her pale features and those incredible turquoise-coloured eyes amidst the mass of corn gold hair had drawn him like a magnet.

Unbidden, he remembered the last time he had seen Alice, when she had flounced out of his house in anger. Things had been thoroughly unpleasant between them for so long that not for one moment had he considered going after her. Alice was a gifted, ambitious schemer with a highly refined sense of survival, and he didn't give a damn where she went or who with, providing Lucy was not harmed. He was determined not to let Alice and her unreasonable demands cut his heart to shreds. Because of his daughter he had allowed her into his home and his life, but he was damned if he would let her become the centre of it. No woman would ever have that much power over him.

Chapter Two

Despite her unfortunate ordeal, when they reached the Scalini residence Lavinia managed to get to her room where she was bathed and put to bed to await the doctor. The elderly physician praised the gentleman who had bravely jumped into the canal to rescue her, for he had no doubt that his prompt action and knowledge on how to treat people who had almost drowned had saved his patient's life. As a result of the knock to her head, no doubt it would ache for a while but, apart from that, the doctor was sure she would suffer no ill effects.

There was a good deal of fussing and concern from everyone in the Scalini household. Lavinia lay in bed as people came and went, her head so crowded with impressions and suppressed emotions that she was quite bewildered. Julia swept into her room with her usual exuberance.

Over the years Lavinia had learned to cope with her half-sister in her own way, which was largely to avoid her whenever possible. This had been quite simple when Julia had married, but on the death of her husband—who had left her with nothing but a pile of debts—she had returned to live at Welbourne House in Gloucestershire.

On his death two years ago, Alec Renshaw, Lavinia's father, had left his considerable estate to his son, Edgar, who was seventeen and still pursuing his education at Oxford. Alec had granted his stepdaughter a generous allowance—although not as much as she would have liked, which was the cause of much of her complaining and discontent—and that she could continue living at Welbourne House until such a time as she decided to leave. To Lavinia he had left a legacy of thirty thousand pounds, which was to be held in trust until she was twenty-five, or to be made available on her marriage.

Julia, who was eight years older than Lavinia, was outspoken and callous and always undermining Lavinia and taking her to task over something or other. In fact, she constantly made life downright unpleasant for her. With dark hair, flashing brown eyes and full red lips, Julia was a handsome woman. As usual she was dressed in the height of fashion—a gown of the finest silk clung to her figure, showing to anyone who was interested that it was full and shapely. She was such an overpowering person that most people felt subdued in her presence, and she put Lavinia's quietness down to her ordeal rather than her own domineering manner.

'Well, Lavinia? How do you feel? It must have been a terrifying ordeal for you,' she said imperiously, unmoved by what had happened to her half-sister, making it abundantly clear that she had come to enquire about her health out of duty rather than any concern she might feel for her well being. 'It is clear that your rescuer saved your life.'

'Oh, yes, Julia. I owe him a great deal,' Lavinia murmured.

'I hope you have everything you require.' Her eyes did a quick sweep of Lavinia's pale face and slender shape beneath the covers. 'You look well enough, to be sure.'

'I am. Thank you.'

Lavinia looked at Julia, sensing there was something different about her. Her expression was as cool as ever, but there was an excitement behind it and she appeared to be suppressing some inner emotion. Coming to stand close beside the bed, Julia's eyes were inscrutable. Lavinia recalled how Daisy had commented just the other day on the amount of time Julia and Robert spent together, and her friend had laughed when she had told Lavinia to watch for the way Julia fluttered her lashes and how the tone of her voice would change when she spoke to him. Daisy was convinced that Robert was aware of it, despite trying to conceal his feelings behind that marble façade of his. *Why*, Daisy had said, *he puffs up like a mating bird every time she goes near him.* The words had been innocently spoken and soon shrugged off by Daisy, but they had left Lavinia with a feeling of unease, and she found it strange that she should think of it now.

'Your escape was a wonderful piece of luck,' Julia told her, 'but it is over now and you must put it behind you.'

'I intend to. Have you been shopping, Julia?'

'No—not yet. I'm just on my way. Leonardo and Valentina had to go out and so I decided to delay my shopping trip until later—in case Robert should need anything, you understand. Someone had to stay and look after him.'

If it was Julia's intention to make Lavinia feel guilty for leaving her betrothed alone when he was unwell, she did not succeed. Robert was not the type to have anyone fussing around him. Schooling her features into a polite mask, she gave Julia a cool look. 'I expect he was grateful for your concern, but he was not so ill when I left him to go to the Lido, Julia.'

'He may have appeared to be a little better but he was far from it. You really should have put off going to the Lido until he was well enough to accompany you,' she chided.

'We can always go again,' Lavinia told her lightly, determined not to be intimidated by her sister. 'Where is he, by the way? I thought he would have been in to see me.'

'He has been told what has happened and will be in to see you directly—as soon as he has dressed.'

Julia was looking at Lavinia steadily. Did Lavinia imagine it, or was there a malicious gleam in her eyes and a secret, rather smug smile on her sultry lips? A horrible possibility that there might be some truth after all in what Daisy had said dawned on her, and for the first time she eyed her sister with mistrust. It had never occurred to her that Julia might resent her forthcoming marriage to Robert—that she might want him for herself.

With a thin smile on her lips, in a cloud of heavy perfume and a rustle of silk skirts, Julia swept out of the room. Lavinia was left staring at the closed door, glad that she had gone, turning over in her mind the suspicions which had been implanted there by Daisy. But then she shook herself, telling herself not to be ridiculous, and that her tumble into the lagoon must have addled her wits. Robert was an honourable man whom she trusted implicitly.

News of what had befallen Lavinia forced Robert from his sick bed. Of slender build and with thin, greying hair and sharp features, he was not handsome but striking, in a distinguished kind of way. He was also twenty years Lavinia's senior. Everything he did was meticulously thought out and controlled. From poor beginnings, he had inherited neither title nor wealth, yet by hard work and frugal living he had managed to amass a considerable fortune and had purchased a fine property close to Welbourne House.

Lavinia was under no illusion that her legacy of thirty thousand pounds had drawn Robert to her but, feeling there would be no Thomas Dorsy in the future to capture her heart—the young man she had loved with all the passionate ardour of her youth, the man she would have married had he not been killed serving King and country in India—she had accepted Robert's suit. However, she had grown very fond of Robert, and always looked forward to his visits to her home. She saw no reason why they shouldn't be happy together.

Robert entered her room, adjusting his cravat, giving the impression that he had dressed in a hurry. His face was pale and pinched, which was his natural state and had nothing to do with his sickness. He came directly to the bed where he stood looking down at her.

'I trust you're suffering no ill effects from your ordeal, Lavinia?'

He was angry about what had occurred. Lavinia sensed it and braced herself for a ticking off. 'Apart from a headache caused by hitting my head on the bottom of the boat, I am fine, Robert.'

'Good. I am glad to hear it. The doctor says you are to remain in bed for the rest of the day. But perhaps the accident might have been avoided. According to the boatman, if you had not been standing up in the boat at the time, you would not have been thrown into the canal.'

'I know,' she admitted, giving him a wan smile. 'But when I saw the other boat about to ram us, I didn't stop to think.'

'No—which is proving to be a failing in you, Lavinia,' he reproached her harshly.

With growing anger, Lavinia glared at her betrothed from beneath half-lowered lids. Only Robert would make it sound like it was all her fault, she thought crossly. No doubt he blamed her for drawing attention and making a spectacle of herself, as though she had fallen into the canal deliberately. Heated words rose to her lips, which at any other time she would have stemmed, but, fuelled by her thumping head and tired of always trying to keep on the right side of his temper, a rebelliousness stirred inside her that she could not repress.

'Contrary to what you may think, Robert, I did not fall into the canal on purpose. However, it is over now and no serious harm was done. However, with all my faults, I cannot for the life of me think why you want to marry me at all. There is certainly nothing romantic about our relationship, is there?' she said scathingly, astounding herself that she dared voice her thoughts. Warnings of danger that she had gone too far flashed into her mind, but ever since she had regained her senses and looked into the clear blue eyes of Maxim Purnell, nothing was the same as it had been before her tumble into the lagoon.

Robert was looking at her with disapproval, but was also a little nonplussed and surprised by her sudden outburst. 'We are not discussing romance but reality, Lavinia,' he said sharply.

'No doubt Julia has been looking after you in my absence,' she said, making a sudden play of adjusting the pillow behind her head. Catching his sudden frown and the sharp glance of unease he threw her way, her suspicions that hidden forces were at work about which she knew nothing increased.

'She has been both thoughtful and attentive in your absence. But you defied me, Lavinia,' Robert accused coldly, leaving Lavinia with the impression that he wanted to veer the conversation away from her sister.

Again she bristled at the harsh tone of his voice and raised her chin with a touch of defiance. 'I did no such thing.'

'I said I would take you to the Lido when I felt up to it, but you were determined, you and Daisy—who in my opinion is far too high-spirited and friv-

olous—and if this insolent outburst is anything to go
by, her influence where you are concerned is proving
to be far too disruptive. No doubt she found it exciting taking you on some hair-raising adventure.'

'That's ridiculous, Robert. It was merely a trip to
the Lido—and I certainly cannot call my tumble into
the lagoon an adventure. I was almost drowned. I
certainly didn't want it to happen.'

'Nevertheless, after this unfortunate occurrence I
must ask you not to leave the house again unless you
are accompanied by me. Is that understood? No doubt
by tomorrow I shall be feeling a good deal better.'

Despite her annoyance at Robert's unreasonable
manner, Lavinia felt obliged to ask after his health.
'How are you, Robert? Has the sickness left you?'

'I believe I am somewhat restored.' His expression
guarded, he lifted his brows in bland enquiry. 'And
to whom do we have to be grateful for your deliv-
erance from the lagoon?'

'Someone by the name of Maxim Purnell.'

Robert frowned, becoming thoughtful, as if the
name was familiar. Lavinia looked at him curiously.

'Do you know anyone of that name, Robert? Have
you heard it before.'

'I believe so—only in passing, mind. If they are
one and the same man, that is.'

'It's hardly a common name. The man I saw was
tall, very dark—and undoubtedly handsome,' Lavinia
told him boldly, probing to learn more about her rescuer, knowing Robert would find her description of
him annoying and distasteful. 'Tell me about the
Maxim Purnell you know.'

'I believe I might have seen the man once or twice in London, but I can't say that I know him or recall what he looks like. Despite the time I spend in London, I move in very different circles to Mr Purnell. I only know that he's said to be the nephew of the Earl of Brinkcliff, who resides, I believe, at Stannington in Oxfordshire.'

'Said? What do you mean?'

'That nobody knows for sure. What is known is that the Earl is an old man without an heir.'

'But if Maxim Purnell is his nephew, then surely—'

'I have told you that nothing is known for sure, Lavinia,' Robert answered irritably. 'It is rumoured that when the Earl of Brinkcliff's older brother wanted to marry a woman not of their class, their father threatened to disinherit him, believing it would have the desired effect. But the old man underestimated his son because he went off and married her anyway. I believe Maxim Purnell to be their offspring. True to his word, the old Earl disinherited his eldest son—an action which, by all accounts, the present Earl has come to regret.'

Lavinia listened with immense fascination. 'So the man who saved my life could be the nephew of the Earl of Brinkcliff.'

'It's possible. But much good it will do him if he isn't reconciled with the old man.'

'How does he live? What is his profession?'

Robert looked at her coldly, disapproving of the interest the man had aroused in her. 'Handsome he may be, but his social standing is far from impeccable. I do not approve of his lifestyle. I believe the man is an adventurer and a gambler, Lavinia. A professional gambler—successful, too, by all accounts.'

Lavinia's eyes opened wide. 'But if he's as successful as all that, then he must be very good at it.'

Robert gave her a withering look. 'Gambling is not an honourable profession, Lavinia,' he admonished.

'No—of course it isn't, Robert,' she said quietly, feeling well and truly reproached whilst forcing herself to repress a smile.

'But if the man who pulled you out of the lagoon is the same Maxim Purnell, then he appears to be one of nature's survivors to me.'

Lavinia and Daisy had arranged to purchase their masks for the ball the following day, but because of Lavinia's mishap they put it off until the day after. True to his word Robert accompanied them, but when they reached the Mercerie, the main street in Venice which linked St Mark's Square with the Rialto, he and Julia left them, preferring instead to while away an hour or so beneath the tall tower of the Campanile in St Mark's Square drinking coffee at Florian's, giving Lavinia the freedom to shop with Daisy and her mother.

Protected from the hot Venetian sun under pretty parasols, the three of them wandered at leisure, meandering through an enchanting maze of alleyways, squares and bridges. All around them was an amazing spectacle of life and gaiety, full of noise and colour and teaming with people, but it also had a seedier

side, for the alleyways leading off were where cour-
tesans offered their services to all comers.

The many shops were filled with curios and sumptuous goods from the East, and caged nightingales
sang sweet melodies above the heads of the crowds.
They found the mask shop Valentina had recom-
mended almost immediately, and Lavinia became so
absorbed in her task of selecting one to go with her
gown for the ball that she failed to notice the tall
man standing a little to one side, who was watching
her with studied interest.

The whole window of the mask shop was festooned with beautifully created masks on display.
Lavinia gazed at them in wonder, undecided which
one to choose. There were all colours—silver, white
and bronze—some sequined and decorated with ribbons and pearls. Some were elaborately adorned with
soft feathers, others with delicate tissue and gold leaf.

'Come along inside, Lavinia,' said Daisy breath-
lessly, her eyes as wide as the empty eye-hole sockets
of the masks looking back at her through the window.
'We must try some on.'

'Yes, yes, Daisy—but look,' gasped Lavinia, dragging her back as she was about to move away. 'See
that one in the centre—the gold silk with sequins and
beads.'

'Yes, I see it. Oh, Lavinia, it's adorable,' she enthused. 'But Robert would never approve. It's far too
costly and elaborate for his taste. You know he never
spends a guinea when a shilling will suffice.'

Lavinia looked a little downcast on being reminded
of Robert's miserly ways. It was as if a cloud had

suddenly descended on her. 'Well, what of it?' she replied with a hint of rebelliousness in her tone. 'It would certainly go with my dress.'

'That's true. But you would have to dig deep into your pocket to pay for it—or perhaps I should say Robert's, considering he's paying for it. Which is strange, don't you think, when he clearly thinks that any item of luxury to be some kind of sinful indulgence?'

There was just a hint of scorn in Daisy's voice when she spoke of Robert which Lavinia noted and decided to ignore. The man she had chosen to marry would never meet with her friend's approval, so there was no point arguing. 'I suppose you're right,' she admitted with a wistful sigh, gazing at the forbidden mask with longing. 'Although it is perfect, isn't it? Still—it's going to be hard enough for Robert to accept the dress without adding to his vexation by appearing in something he would consider too expensive and frivolous by far. Let's go inside and look for something else.'

An assistant welcomed them into the shop which was full of people and crammed with masks of every description. There was a strong aroma of paint and glue emanating from the workshop at the rear, where masks were made from clay moulds for the nobility and general public alike.

Watched over by Mrs Lambert, both girls excitedly tried on one mask after another. The majority was made from papier mâché, but there were others made from leather and canvas, all skilfully made and exotically trimmed. They delighted in the anonymity to be achieved by the wearing of something so small, the masks creating an atmosphere of secrets and mysteries, the empty eye holes giving them a sinister air.

Inside that small shop the many faces of the Carnival came alive to them. Some were grotesque, some comical and others tragic. Some were linked with characters of the underworld, while many of them represented characters from plays performed by bands of actors who travelled through Italy. The most familiar of these Commedia dell'Arte characters were Harlequin, Columbine and Brighella, and the long-beaked clown Pucinella.

'I had no idea there were so many different kinds,' gasped Daisy excitedly. 'There are so many to choose from I shall never be able to decide.'

Eventually Lavinia chose a plain white oval mask, thinking it suited her and would go well with her dress. Mrs Lambert was trying to help Daisy make up her mind between a red silk mask or a black sequined half-mask, and it was proving to be extremely disconcerting for Daisy, who always found it difficult to decide on anything when presented with a choice.

While she was waiting Lavinia couldn't resist the temptation to try on the mask that had caught her eye in the window. The assistant was only too willing to oblige and handed it to her before turning away to serve a gentleman.

Lavinia gazed at the mask, fingering it with sheer delight. It was a half-mask, a work of superb craftsmanship, of gold silk and intricately sewn with winking gold sequins and tiny gold beads. Holding it up to her face she looked into the mirror, aware of someone coming to stand close behind her and taking the delicate ribbons in his fingers

'Allow me,' said a voice, low and soft like velvet.

Lavinia's breath caught in her throat when her eyes met those of her rescuer from the lagoon in the mirror, and she was unable to do anything other than watch in astonishment as he deftly fastened the ribbons at the back of her head before leaning forward so that his face was beside hers, his eyes watching her in the mirror in speculative silence before saying quietly, his breath warm on her cheek, 'I think this becomes you extremely well.'

Lavinia expelled the breath she hadn't realised she was still holding, and she turned and stared up at him through the eye holes of the mask. The dazzling charm of his lazy white smile was doing strange things to her pulse rate. 'You!' she breathed. He was so incredibly handsome, with eyes that seemed to look deep into her heart. Until then she had thought she remembered exactly what he looked like—the image she had of him in her mind's eye was that of a man who had just emerged from the lagoon, with black unruly hair and flashing white teeth, wet and gleaming with health and vitality, everything about him exuding brute strength.

This arrogantly handsome man was in such contrast that it was difficult to believe they were one and the same. He was dressed immaculately, his thick black hair well groomed. The dark green cloth of his superbly cut frock coat stretched across his broad shoulders, and the pristine whiteness of his silk neckcloth emphasised his bronzed features. There was a

leashed sensuality about his face, and his finely
sculpted lips were slightly parted in a lazy white
smile as he regarded her.

It was the clear blue of his eyes that told Lavinia
it was indeed the same man who had come so quickly
to her aid and her heart soared. As a result of the
tender care and her day of rest after her tumble into
the lagoon, she presented a fresh and blooming countenance to the man she had every reason to be grateful to.

'I—I did not expect to see you here—or again, for
that matter. Forgive me,' she faltered. 'I—I hardly
recognised you.'

Maxim arched a sleek black brow. 'Why? Because
I appear before you fully clothed? Or can it be that
you have forgotten me already?' he asked on a note
of mock regret.

'Oh, no—no.'

'I am happy to see you suffered no ill effects from
your accident,' he said, smiling a slow, dazzling
smile that swept across his tanned features; its effect
on his face was as startling as the effect it had on
Lavinia's senses.

Maxim felt his heart slam against his ribs when he
looked at her, unprepared for the shock of purely
physical desire that swept through him. Dressed in a
delicate shade of pastel pink, with her golden hair
arranged in delicate curls about her heart-shaped face,
Miss Lavinia Renshaw was eternally female, elegant
and slender, with an air of serene composure. It was
as much a part of her as her magnificent eyes—large,

translucent and deep turquoise, with a darker rim around the iris, which gave them a glowing intensity.

And her mouth—never had he seen or wanted to place his own lips on a mouth like that. Maxim was certain it must have been shaped by one of the famous sculptors whose statues graced the many beautiful churches of Venice. It was chiselled to exquisite perfection, wearing a smile as tantalising and mysterious as the silks and brocades that floated behind the gondolas on the canals at Carnival time.

'I am so grateful for what you did the other day. Your prompt action saved my life. As you see I have made a full recovery, but thank goodness you are such a good swimmer.'

Maxim's cool blue eyes warmed with amusement. 'I've had plenty of practice. However, I don't make a habit of jumping into the lagoon to rescue people. You are the first.'

'And the last, I hope,' Lavinia laughed, looking up at him.

'My advice to you is to learn to swim.'

'I would love to—but unfortunately there are no facilities where I live.' She moved to one side to make room for another customer at the counter. 'I had no idea so many people would be buying masks outside Carnival time.'

'That is because so many tourists—especially the young gentlemen on the Grand Tour—find them ideal gifts to take back to female relatives and friends.' Maxim eyed her quizzically. 'And you? What is your reason for purchasing a mask?'

'We are to attend a costume ball tomorrow night. It's being held at one of the palaces along the Grand Canal.'

'I do know of it. And have you decided which mask you are going to buy?'

Lavinia sighed, removing the gold one and fingering the plain white on the counter. 'Yes. This is the one.'

Maxim frowned, looking at her closely, seeing the unmistakable regret mirrored in her lovely eyes, having heard it in her voice. 'It is not nearly as becoming as this,' he told her, indicating the gold one. 'It is evident to me which one you prefer.'

Lavinia caught her bottom lip with her teeth, an unconscious habit she had acquired as a little girl when she was about to do something she would regret. 'I know. But—'

'But?' Maxim queried.

'If I appear wearing anything as extravagant as this, my—my betrothed will be quite put out,' she explained, wondering why she should suddenly feel so reluctant to mention Robert.

If Maxim was disappointed to learn she was betrothed, he gave no sign of it. 'So—you have an escort to the ball.'

'Yes. Why do you ask?'

He grinned. 'Because I would have asked to take you myself.'

Lavinia's eyes lit up. 'Oh! Are you invited?'

'I am.'

Lavinia was thrilled to know this, and she tried to ignore the dull ache of disappointment in her chest, shocked to realise how much she wished he was to be her escort instead of Robert. A slow, lazy smile swept across Maxim's face.

'Perhaps it's sensible of you to choose a plain mask.'

'Do you think so? Do you mind telling me why?'

'Because it will help stave off the many contenders for your hand that a mask with so much seduction sewn into it with those sequins and beads would be sure to attract.'

Flushing softly, Lavinia handed the mask to the assistant, who shook her head with dismay as she was about to place it in a box, telling her in broken English that the ribbons had worked loose and would have to be fixed. But it was no problem. She would have it done and delivered to her address before the shop closed. After giving the assistant the Scalinis' address—an address the assistant was well familiar with—Lavinia turned back to Maxim. The crush inside the shop made it virtually impossible to move.

'Come outside,' he urged, taking her elbow.

Lavinia turned to Daisy, who was completely unaware of Maxim's presence as she frowned in desperation, her eyes going from one mask to the other, racked with indecision.

'If you would like my opinion, Daisy,' Lavinia laughed, coming to her rescue, 'I think the black will complement your red dress perfectly. The red mask might not be of the same shade and might clash.'

'Do you think so, Lavinia?'

'Yes. I'll wait for you outside the shop. It's so crowded in here.'

After extricating themselves from the crush, Maxim and Lavinia found themselves out in the street, where the crush was almost as great as inside the shop. Holding Lavinia's arm firmly, Maxim cut his way through the crowd like an irresistible force, coming to a halt across the street where it thinned out, but still able to keep an eye on the shop so that Lavinia would see when Daisy and her mother emerged.

'So,' said Maxim, his bold gaze sweeping over her shining hair, a smile of frank admiration gleaming in his eyes when they settled on her upturned face, 'you are staying with Leonardo Scalini and his wife.'

'Yes. Are you acquainted with them?' she asked, managing to keep her expression calm at finding herself in such close proximity with him, but her treacherous pulse was racing twice as fast and her mind was in absolute confusion. No other man had ever had this affect on her before.

'Only slightly. The Scalinis are an old, established family in Venice—and much respected. There are few who have not heard of them.'

'When you jumped into the lagoon to save me you were on board a ship. Are you a sailor?' Lavinia asked, curious to know if he was the same Maxim Purnell Robert had told her about.

He laughed. 'Heaven forbid. No. I was merely visiting a friend of mine, who just so happens to be the captain of that ship.'

'So you are not staying on the ship?'

'No. I am staying at an apartment of a friend of mine in the San Marco area—not far from here. In fact,' he said, taking her arm and drawing her into the street a little way and indicating a rather grand-looking creamy yellow mansion with green shutters down one of the narrow streets, 'that's the building down there.'

'Yes, I see. And are you in Venice long, Mr Purnell?'

'No. A few days at the most, then I have to leave for England.'

'And where do you live when you are in England? Where is home?'

'Kent.'

Lavinia could see Daisy and her mother coming out of the shop and she smiled up at Maxim. 'Here are my friends. I—I must be going. Goodbye, Mr Purnell. I can never repay you for what you did.'

Reluctant to let her go, Maxim moved closer, seeming to tower over her. 'Yes, you can.'

'How?' A nervous quaking jarred through her when she saw how intently he was looking at her.

'By saving a dance for me at the ball tomorrow night.'

Lavinia caught her breath, teetering on the edge of an abyss, trying not to blush at the wicked thoughts that sprang to mind. Maxim Purnell was making her feel things she had never felt before. It was like she was completely helpless, finding herself being pulled to this man by some invisible force she couldn't resist, no matter how hard she tried. 'I—I don't think that would be wise,' she whispered. 'Robert, my betrothed, would not approve.'

'Surely he would not object to one dance,' Maxim pressed, not the kind of man to be put off. 'And Robert will have to give way at some time during the evening. The night will be one of intense revelry when everyone throws off their inhibitions. Robert will find that I will not be the only man wanting to dance with you.'

Lavinia found it impossible to resist his request—and secretly she didn't want to. She smiled. 'Then what can I say? Yes, Mr Purnell, I will by happy to dance with you—with Robert's permission, of course.'

'Of course. Until tomorrow night,' he said, turning to Daisy and her mother and indulging in a few polite greetings before excusing himself and moving off into the crowd.

Lavinia watched him go with unconcealed interest in her wide eyes, and a whole bewildering array of emotions sweeping over her. She had an uneasy feeling that there was something dangerous about Maxim Purnell, that the fine clothes and indolent manner were to lull the unwary into believing he was refined and civilised, when beneath the disguise he was primitive and barbarous, the sort of man who had done and experienced things both dangerous and terrible, things that had hardened him. Yet he was wickedly handsome, she thought. He reminded her of a black panther—sleek, beautiful and dangerous.

Reluctantly she tore her eyes away from his retreating figure and began walking in the direction of St Mark's Square to find Robert and Julia, her steps as light as her fluttering heart.

* * *

Later in the day when the gold velvet box containing Lavinia's mask was delivered to the house, she took it to her room to try it on, accompanied by Daisy. Upon lifting the lid of the box she let out a gasp of surprise, for, instead of finding the one she had ordered, it was the other—the exquisite gold silk which had so caught her eye.

'Oh, Daisy, look,' she whispered, taking it gently out of the box and staring down at it, seeing it had been studded with shining jewel-like objects which winked and shone when they caught the light. Lavinia was sure they hadn't been there before. 'There must be some mistake. I certainly didn't order this.'

Daisy came to stand beside her, her eyes wide with amazement when she saw the mask. 'Good Lord, Lavinia. If you didn't order this, then which one did you order?'

'It was white—plain white—and I couldn't bring it with me because the ribbons had become loose. The assistant promised to have them repaired and delivered to the house. I cannot keep this—Robert will have a fit. It must be returned to the shop immediately.'

'No, wait. What's this?' said Daisy, reaching into the box and picking up a small card from the bed of velvet. 'It just says—This becomes you better. M.' She looked at Lavinia's stunned face in question. 'M?'

'Mr Purnell,' whispered Lavinia, experiencing a shock of quivering excitement mingled with alarm when she realised what he had done. 'Oh, Daisy! He was there when I tried it on in the shop. He told me this mask suited me better than the white. He must have returned and told the assistant to deliver this one instead of the one I ordered, paying the difference himself. But what can it mean?'

'It means, Lavinia, that you have made quite an impression on Mr Purnell. Why else would he send you something so exquisite?'

'But it is quite wrong of him to place me in such an embarrassing position. He should not have done it.'

'You cannot blame him, Lavinia. How was he to know you are betrothed to Robert?'

'Because I told him. You must see that I cannot possibly accept a gift from any man without Robert's approval—especially not such an expensive gift as this. It would be too rash. And see—those sparkling stones were not in the mask we admired. It is either a different mask or they have been added on Mr Purnell's instructions. They cannot possibly be real.'

Daisy studied them closely. 'Well, I'm no expert on such matters, but they certainly look real to me. And besides, I wouldn't say Mr Purnell is the type to buy fake anything—that it has to be the real thing or nothing at all.'

Real or not, the mask had certainly thrown Lavinia into a quandary. 'Oh, what can I do?'

'Accept it. I would,' Daisy said firmly in answer to Lavinia's questioning glance. She shrugged. 'Why not? You're never going to receive anything as expensive or as exotic as this from Robert. Besides, he'll never know if you don't tell him. It's not as though he's going to be asked to pay the difference, is it?'

Daisy spoke with so much force that Lavinia was almost persuaded. She looked at her, feeling herself weakening, aware how dire the consequences would be if she were to accept it and Robert found out. On seeing the unconcealed encouragement and mischief lurking in Daisy's eyes, she knew she would succumb to temptation, unable to believe that a chance meeting with Maxim Purnell could have created such a rebellious change in her. The unconventional event of their meeting would be indelibly and importantly marked for all time if she accepted his gift.

'But—I can't do that. It would be deceitful—wouldn't it?' Her lips trembled into a smile.

Daisy giggled softly. 'Madness, I'd call it, but it isn't as though you intend becoming involved with him, is it? Besides, Robert has his head so high in the clouds most of the time that he will never know. Enjoy yourself while you can, Lavinia. Life will be no bed of roses when you're back in England and married to Robert. At least you will have this wonderful time you have spent in Venice to look back on—to know that for a while you were admired—albeit from afar—by the extremely handsome and exciting Maxim Purnell.'

Chapter Three

Dressed in all their finery, the large party from the Scalini House went by water to the ball. Just as Daisy expected, Robert almost threw a fit when Lavinia presented herself in her white silk dress. If Valentina and Leonardo hadn't come to her rescue and enthused about how lovely she looked, Daisy was certain he would have ordered her back to her room to change into something else.

Robert was so incensed that he failed to notice the expensive, exquisite beauty of the mask his betrothed was wearing, which twinkled with expensive jewels. Valentina raised her eyebrows in surprise as her sharp eyes inspected it closely, but she made no comment other than to smile secretively and say how beautiful it was. But she was curious to know how Lavinia got away with wearing something which her expert eye told her was far too expensive for Robert to have purchased, and she would dearly like to know who had.

The Grand Canal was alive with gondolas and barges ferrying people to the palace where the ball was being held. Light streamed from the arched win-

51

dows of the many grand houses on either side, the moon reflecting its silver sheen on hundreds of roof-tops. Arriving at their destination, the boatman secured the craft to a wooden post and they alighted and climbed the steps. The palace, with its intricate, lace-like façade, was of fifteenth-century architectural elegance, very grand and awe-inspiring, although not as large as Lavinia had expected it to be.

They moved into the ballroom which had frescoed walls and a magnificent carved and gilded wooden ceiling, panelled with beautiful scenes of Venice painted by leading artists of the time. Flowers were bursting out of baskets and vases and music filled the air. It was like a magnificent theatre and no expense had been spared.

Lavinia could not have imagined such a spectacle. It was lavish, with so many people in a variety of dazzling, exotic and sumptuous costumes and bedecked with jewels. Many of the families attending the ball were part of the hierarchy of powerful families which ruled Venice. There was such gaiety and so much colour. It was like make believe, like stepping back to a medieval age, and Lavinia felt absurdly happy as she mingled with the throng on Robert's arm, who had surprised them all by wearing a Harlequin costume. But it was plain that he was feeling ridiculous and finding it impossible to relax.

Lavinia was light-headed, which had nothing to do with the wine she drank as the evening progressed. There was no discretion, only a sense of boldness, of daring and recklessness as the Carnival atmosphere of the ball invaded each and every one of them and took them over. A sense of fantasy and unreality prevailed over the whole night.

She was conspicuous because of the simplicity of her attire among so much flamboyance. She had chosen to wear a dress that was like a shining column of white silk, with long flowing sleeves and a high stiffened collar which framed her face, her only piece of jewellery being a gold brooch at her throat. Her dress was extremely flattering and alluring, showing the curvaceous outline of her body when she moved, and hinting at her small waist and hidden delights.

A white wig, short and softly curled, covered her hair, and the golden mask sent to her by her admirer covered the upper part of her face. The colour, set against the startling white of her attire, emphasised the brilliance of her turquoise eyes.

Lavinia immediately became the focal point of several masked revellers, and she was surprised when Robert raised no objection to her being whirled on to the dance floor by one of them. As the ball gathered momentum her feet didn't touch the ground as she danced with one partner after another, each one totally unrecognisable, but all the time she was waiting in excited anticipation for one man in particular to come and claim her for the dance she had promised him. But as the evening wore on she felt her spirits begin to wane when he didn't appear.

'By the way, Lavinia,' Robert said, having come to stand by her side after conversing with Sir John and Lady Evesham, who were accompanied by their daughter Sophia. 'It may interest you to know that I have heard something concerning the man who pulled you out of the lagoon—Maxim Purnell.'

Lavinia was all attention. 'What have you heard?'

'It would seem he is the same Maxim Purnell I have met on occasion in London.'

'Oh? How do you know that?'

'I have made enquiries. He is not unknown to Leonardo. It is important for me to know to whom I am indebted for saving my betrothed from drowning. Apart from rumours about him being the nephew of Lord Alistair Purnell—the Earl of Brinkcliff—the man remains a mystery and of no consequence. The only thing that is known for sure about him is that he is a common gambler.'

Robert spoke about Mr Purnell with such harsh censure that Lavinia felt compelled to rise to his defence. 'Really, Robert. You cannot hold that against him.'

'You know I consider gambling a weakness, Lavinia, and that I deplore it in any form—which gives me good enough reason to dislike Maxim Purnell. It is extremely galling to find myself indebted to a man of such poor character for pulling you out of the lagoon.'

'Then I feel I must apologise, Robert,' said Lavinia, her voice dripping with sarcasm. 'The next time I decide to fall into the lagoon I shall have to try and make sure that the person who is courageous enough to jump in and rescue me has breeding, good connections and background.'

Robert's eyes glinted hard at her through the eye holes in his mask. 'Don't be flippant, Lavinia. I cannot for the life of me understand what has come over you of late. Your behaviour is so out of character. It does not become you.'

Immediately contrite, Lavinia averted her eyes. Robert was right. What was happening to her? Why, whenever she was alone with him of late, did she feel a temper she didn't know she possessed come to a simmering boil?

'And, seeing that you are so interested in your rescuer,' he went on, 'it would appear that Maxim Purnell was at a ridotto last night—gambling, of course; by all accounts he lost heavily.'

Lavinia knew that a ridotto was where people went to indulge in gaming. Since the authorities had banned public gaming because it was the cause of so many bankruptcies of Venetian families, it still went on throughout the city in private places—palaces, wine shops and coffee houses—frequented by the very men who had made it illegal. For some reason she could not explain, she had not told Robert about her encounter with Maxim Purnell at the mask shop. Now that he had told her about Mr Purnell's losses at the ridotto, she wondered if it had anything to do with him not being at the ball.

Feeling disappointed and deflated, she took a glass of champagne from the tray of a passing waiter, an action which Robert observed with a frown of disapproval.

'That is your third glass of wine, Lavinia,' he commented with reproach. 'One glass is usually considered sufficient for a lady. I have noticed of late that you have acquired a taste for alcohol.'

Lavinia smiled coolly, refusing to let him intimidate her. 'That's right, Robert,' she agreed. 'I find champagne so refreshing—especially in this climate.'

'Nevertheless, Lavinia, I do not like to see my future wife quaffing liquor like a sot.'

Lavinia's eyes opened wide with burgeoning annoyance mingled with amusement. 'Robert! I drink no more than any other woman here tonight—in fact, much less. And I will remind you that I am not your wife yet and have no intention of being thirsty.'

Robert was cut and angered by the jibe. He stared hard at her through the eye holes in his black half-mask, but he was prevented from saying anything else—at that moment Valentina appeared beside them in an elaborate brocade gown and a huge feathered head dress. She enquired if they were enjoying the ball, and Robert was obliged to smile and utter polite words. Lavinia knew how much the effort was costing him.

Valentina, who had strong features and dark Italian skin, was a tall, statuesque woman in her early forties, having lived on the mainland until her marriage to Leonardo when she had come to Venice. Her fluent English could be attributed to her sharp and clever mind and the many English merchants she met through her husband's work.

Robert secretly thought her unfeminine and disapproved of her outspokenness and independence of spirit, but Lavinia liked her sense of fun and no-nonsense manner, and she strongly suspected that Valentina did not possess a high opinion of Robert. But on this occasion Valentina was determined to try and make him smile, and after much persuasion she managed to get him on to the dance floor.

The music had slowed to a waltz to allow the dancers to catch their breath, and Lavinia was standing watching Daisy in her shimmering red dress and her rather boisterous partner, when a man's voice spoke softly in her ear, making her heart beat rapidly.

'Dance with me, Lavinia.'

Startled, slowly she turned and looked at the tall masked man who had spoken to her and knew who it was immediately. Maxim's clear blue eyes pierced her own. He was dressed in one of the most common disguises, La Bauta—perhaps the most frightening and sinister of all. It was comprised of a black silk mantilla beneath a black tricorne hat, the long mantilla covering his wide shoulders. A white bauta mask covered his face, startling and eerie and spectral in its whiteness, the upper lip prominent to allow for eating and drinking.

Without waiting for Lavinia to reply, Maxim took her hand and drew her into the dance and into his arms, sliding his hand around her minuscule waist and holding her close to his firm body, closer than was proper, she thought, but she could not have objected if she had wanted to. Feeling as if she were in a pleasant dream, she placed her gloved hand in his and looked up at him as he whirled her round with a relaxed grace, trying to imagine the expression on the handsome face behind the mask.

'You look ravishing,' he murmured, feeling her close and glad that he'd decided to attend the ball after all.

Maxim's late arrival had nothing to do with the fact that he might be bemoaning his losses at the ridotto the previous evening—which was what Lavinia had suspected. Realising the futility of pursuing a woman who could never be anything more to him than someone he had met in Venice, a woman who was betrothed to someone else, Maxim's indecision about attending the ball at all was more to do with a well-developed instinct for self-preservation. The warmth of affection he was beginning to feel for Lavinia Renshaw, after only two meetings with her, was too disconcerting for his peace of mind, and he knew it would be sheer folly to pursue an affair that was doomed from the start.

But intending to leave Venice shortly and knowing the ball would be his last opportunity of seeing her, Maxim's resistance had wavered and he had found himself drawn to the ball as if he were a puppet and she were pulling the strings. He was attracted to her by the sincerity in her gaze, sensing that her charm and personality was unlike any other woman he had known. She had a distinctive beauty of which she seemed totally unaware, and a natural femininity which remained unflawed by self-interest. But Maxim's instinct told him that he must be wary, otherwise he would find himself drawn deeper into something over which he would have no control.

'I have been watching you for quite some time,' said Maxim, 'and think, perhaps, that you should have come to the ball as Columbine.'

'Columbine! But she was—'

'A flirt,' he told her softly on a teasing note, his eyes twinkling down into hers through the eye holes in his mask.

Lavinia cocked her head sideways, looking up at him. 'Are you not afraid that I might be affronted on being compared to such a character?'

'No. Typical of Columbine's character—who flirted outrageously with Harlequin, by the way—you show supreme intelligence and charm in the presence of such madness and sheer stupidity which surrounds you tonight.'

'Do I?' Lavinia laughed, entering into the spirit of his light banter. 'Nevertheless, if you have, as you say, been watching me for some time—and I have to say that I am disappointed that I am so easily recognisable despite the trouble I have taken to disguise my identity—it cannot have escaped your notice that Robert, the man I am to marry, is dressed as Harlequin.'

'I have noticed—and I would recognise you anywhere,' he murmured, looking down at her upturned face, 'despite the wig you are wearing—which makes you look adorable. Besides, I only had to look for the mask to know who was behind it. I have also observed that you do not flirt with your betrothed as one would expect a woman to flirt with the man she is to marry.'

'But surely to flirt means to show romantic interest without having serious intentions. Believe me, Mr Purnell, Robert is not the sort of person who would appreciate anyone flirting with him.'

Before Lavinia knew what was happening, Maxim had deftly danced her through some long net drapes on to a balcony, drawing her away from the light and standing close beside her near the balustrade. Warning bells began ringing inside her head, telling her of the impropriety of being on the balcony alone with this man Robert deemed unsuitable because of his unsavoury vocation, but she felt far too happy to object and refused to listen to them.

Appreciating the feel of the cool air on her face, Lavinia watched as Maxim removed his mask so that she could see his face, feeling her heart do a somersault when his handsome features were revealed to her. He boldly stared his appreciation until Lavinia had the distinct feeling that his imagination went further than the thin material of her gown. She stood quite still when he reached out and traced her mask with his fingers.

'I'm happy to see you did not return the mask to the shop.'

'Did you think I would?'

'It did occur to me. But the risk was well worth taking.'

'I did not tell Robert. I—I know I should have—but he would have been angry, knowing I had received a gift from a man other than himself.'

'Then it is time Robert began to appreciate the woman he is to marry and started paying her attention and showering her with expensive and exotic gifts,' Maxim accused, his unfathomable eyes locked onto hers.

Having taken the time to observe Robert Feltham, a man he recognised, having seen him on occasion in London although they had never been introduced, Maxim found it difficult to understand why someone as young and lovely as Lavinia could consider marriage to a man who had no sense of humour and was old enough to be her father. Feltham was also a man who had nothing to recommend him in either character or manner when dealing with others.

Maxim's attack on Robert caused a hot, embarrassed flush to mantle Lavinia's cheeks. 'He—he does buy me things,' she said, making a feeble attempt to defend the man she was to marry, a man she held in the highest regard and of whom she was extremely fond. 'But he has worked too hard to attain his wealth and the position he holds in society to squander his money on anything he considers frivolous and unnecessary. I know the mask I am wearing must have cost you dearly—and it has not escaped my notice that it has acquired an added sparkle from when I tried it on in the shop.'

'You deserve only the very best, Lavinia. I assure you that the jewels are not fake.'

'No. I didn't think they were. Which is why, when the evening is over, I should return it to you at your address. It—it's beautiful, but far too valuable. You really shouldn't have given me such a present,' she said helplessly, recalling his huge loss at the ridotto the evening before. 'I'm sure you can't afford it.'

Maxim's dark brows snapped together above angry eyes and his jaw tensed. Clearly it was the wrong thing to say and she felt she had offended him. After all, it wasn't for her to say what he could and could not afford.

'I think that's for me to worry about,' he said tersely.

Embarrassed and ashamed for speaking with un-characteristic bluntness, she drew a fortifying breath. 'I'm sorry. I imagine you are going to tell me I was rude to say that.'

'You were. I am not a pauper, and if I give anyone a gift I expect them to accept it gracefully and not raise ridiculous objections. You do want to keep it? You do like it, don't you?'

'You know I do,' she said quietly.

Maxim sighed, placing his hands on her shoulders and looking down at her seriously. 'Then what's the problem? Lavinia—I would be mortally offended if you were to return it to me. It is a gift—from me to you. Accept it as such. When I see how beautiful it looks on you it was worth every penny—and I will know that every time you look at it you will think of me.'

'Yes—I will—and thank you,' she whispered. 'I shall keep it always.'

When he dropped his hands she turned and looked down into the small, high-walled garden below, dis-cernable from the light shining from the many win-dows of the palace. A pale crescent moon hung in a cloudless sky that was littered by myriad stars. A wisteria vine had escaped its prison garden and trailed out of control over the rusticated walls, and budding jasmine and honeysuckle gave off a heady, intoxicating scent which rose up to where they stood on the balcony.

Lavinia asked herself why she suddenly felt nervous being alone with Maxim, and to her consternation found the answer. It was because he encroached too closely upon her, and because she was afraid he would come closer still.

They stood in silence for a moment, and she knew he was as aware as she was of the combustible nature of their relationship. It was disturbing, an awareness that was uncomfortable. This was only the third time they had met and already Maxim had established himself in her mind, and she was troubled by her own susceptibility. She had thought herself immune to any man, but Maxim Purnell had infected her with a fever of his presence.

'What are you thinking?' Maxim asked after a moment.

'I was thinking how lovely both the night, and the scent coming from the flowers in the garden below are,' she answered truthfully.

'And are you enjoying the ball?'

'Immensely,' she laughed. 'I've never in my life experienced anything like it. It's all so unreal—like living a fantasy.'

'Venetians are illusionists and fantasists, entwining the past, the present, and the imagined—which is the concept of the Carnival. Artifice and manipulation are all part of their heritage, and they thrive on it.' He paused, looking at her appraisingly as she gazed into the garden below. 'Have you any idea how lovely you look tonight?' he murmured.

There was a soft, caressing note in his voice which should have caused Lavinia to take flight, but instead she merely looked at him inquiringly and smiled.

'If I do then it is more to do with the peacock's plumage I wear and the spell the Masquerade has cast on me than anything else. Believe me, I am exactly the same woman you plucked from the lagoon.'

He laughed, his strong white teeth flashing in the dim light, and Lavinia realised that when he did that he seemed much younger than his twenty-eight or twenty-nine years.

'I cannot argue with that—although as I recall, there was more to see of you when I plucked you out of the water,' he replied, his voice threaded with intimacy.

A warm flush crept beneath Lavinia's mask and through her veins when she remembered how he had been forced to tear her dress before placing his hands on her bare flesh. 'I think you recall too much,' she chided gently, smiling up at him obliquely.

'And I promise not to embarrass you by referring to it again. Tell me, is this your first visit to Venice?'

'Yes.'

'And what impression has it made on you?'

'Nothing I have heard or read about it equals the magnificence and wonderful reality.'

'I agree. People come from all over the world to see Venice—to dress up in Carnival clothes, to wear masks, to gamble...to fall in love,' Maxim murmured, his gaze dropping to her lips, wanting to crush her in his arms, to lose himself in her sweetness.

'With Venice?' she asked, watching his gaze drop to her lips, feeling her senses mounting to dizzying heights.

Maxim smiled, studying her closely, seeing her eyes shimmering behind the mask. 'If not with Venice, then with themselves—or each other.'

Lavinia lowered her eyes, the physical content of the last few moments playing havoc with her emotions. 'W-when I first arrived I was disturbed and overawed by its sheer beauty.'

'You make it sound like a love affair,' he murmured.

Lavinia looked at him inquiringly and felt her eyes held by his. A tingle ran down her spine. There was something in their depths, something in the way he was looking at her which seemed to carry a message—if only she could understand it.

'Do I?'

'Yes.'

She flushed, never having experienced the sort of love affair he spoke of. 'Yes—I—I suppose it must.'

'You do not look like a young lady in the full flush of love.'

'Nevertheless, Robert—Mr Feltham and I are to marry as soon as we return to England.'

Maxim gave her a lengthy perusal before saying, 'Do you love him?'

Lavinia stared at him, momentarily at a loss to know what to say, for to tell him she loved Robert would not be true—at least, not in the way Mr Purnell would interpret the word love. But then, that kind of love she could not envisage, and since her meeting with this man, she doubted if what she had once felt for Thomas Dorsy could have come anywhere close.

'Robert is a good man—a man of honour and well respected within the circles in which he moves.'

'I am sure he is. But that was not what I asked you.'

Lavinia sighed, lowering her gaze. 'No. I know that. But I prefer to keep my feelings where my betrothed is concerned to myself,' she said quietly.

'And you care enough about him to marry him?'

'Yes, I do.'

'Then what are you doing out here with me?'

Lavinia stared at him, at a loss to know how to react or what to say in answer to his pointed question. 'I—I don't know,' she replied desperately, noticing how warm and sensual his gaze had turned, how relaxed he was.

'Have you—a woman betrothed to another man—not considered the impropriety of being out here alone with me?' Maxim asked calmly, his eyes beginning to glint with amusement.

'No—as a matter of fact, I haven't,' she answered nervously.

'I'm pleased to learn that, like myself, you do not allow convention to dictate your every move,' he murmured, raising his hand and gently touching the side of her jaw with the backs of his fingers.

'But I do,' she replied, feeling her flesh burn beneath his touch, realising that a gambling man must find the rules of social etiquette, which so governed her life, extremely tiresome. 'I come from a conventional family, Mr Purnell, who believe in all the important things such as honour and integrity, doing the right thing and behaving in a proper manner.'

He arched a sleek black brow quizzically. 'And truth?'

'But of course. There has to be truth.'

'Then why didn't you tell your betrothed of our encounter yesterday—and that I sent you the mask?' he persisted.

Lavinia stared at him, aware of how close he was to her. She could feel her body beginning to tremble, and the infuriating thing was that he was perfectly well aware of the effect he was having on her as he sought to tie her in knots about her dealings with Robert.

'How do you know I haven't told Robert about our encounter?'

'Because if you had you would have returned the mask.' A lazy grin swept over his handsome face, and the force of that white smile did treacherous things to Lavinia's heart rate. 'Admit it, Lavinia. Admit that you are here with me because you want to be. Because you find yourself irresistibly drawn to me—as I am to you. Is that not so?'

Lavinia looked at him, despite her desire not to, not for the first time finding herself at a loss to understand him. 'No—of course not. You—you make me feel uneasy when you speak to me like this—and look at me the way you are doing now. There is nothing between us.'

'Isn't there?'

'No—and I have given you no reason to suppose there is.'

'There I must contradict you. You didn't return the mask. The mere fact that you kept it told me how you feel.'

'Please do not speak to me like this,' Lavinia implored helplessly. 'I don't understand you. I don't understand what it is you want.'

Lavinia was too innocent and naïve not to let her emotions show on her face, and for a long moment Maxim's gaze held hers with penetrating intensity. The clear blue eyes were as enigmatic as they were silently challenging, and unexpectedly Lavinia felt an answering thrill of excitement. The darkening in Maxim's eyes warned her he was aware of that brief response.

'I think you do, Lavinia,' he murmured.

For a moment Lavinia was thrown into such a panic she could not think coherently. He was standing so very close that she suddenly wanted to escape, to return to the others. And yet, at the same time, she could not move, and she allowed Maxim to draw her against his chest, her eyes wide open as he bent his head and placed his mouth over her own, plucking the breath from between her parted lips, his mouth warm and searching.

They both felt the sudden excitement of physical contact. Lavinia had never been kissed in her life, and she could not have imagined how pleasurable it could be. Too innocent and naïve to know how to hide her feelings, she followed his lead and instinctively yielded her mouth to his, and the moment

Maxim felt her response his arms tightened around her, circling and possessive, desire, primitive and potent, pouring through his veins.

Holding her hips pressed to his, he could feel the slender body beneath the column of white silk tremble against his as waves of pleasure shot through her. Raising his hand, he caressed the nape of her neck, his lips leaving hers and tracing a line down the column of her throat, his breath warm on her flesh, before finding her mouth once more and tasting the wine-flavoured softness of her lips.

To Lavinia, absolutely seduced by his kiss, what he was doing to her was like being wrapped in a cocoon of dangerous, pleasurable sensuality where she had no control over anything. Not even herself. She shivered with the primitive sensations jarring through her entire body, feeling herself pressed to the hard muscles of his chest.

When Maxim at last pulled his mouth from hers he drew a long, shuddering breath, meeting her gaze and seeing that her eyes were naked and defenceless. His tanned features were hard with desire, and, aware that someone could appear at any moment, he knew that he must keep their passion under control.

Lavinia trembled in the aftermath of his kiss, unable to believe what had happened and that she desperately wanted him to repeat the kiss that had stunned her senses with its wild sweetness. Maxim was still holding her gaze, and she looked with longing at his lips.

'Don't look at me like that unless you want me to kiss you again, Lavinia,' he murmured huskily, his eyes dark with passion.

With her heart beating hard against her ribs, slowly she raised her eyes to his and, leaning forward, again boldly touched his mouth with her own, feeling her breath sucked from her body as, unable to resist what she so innocently offered, he clamped his mouth on to hers once more, causing the blood to pound in her head and her senses to reel as her mind retreated down an unknown, forbidden path, plunging her into an oblivion that was dark and exquisitely sensual.

Drawing a shattered breath, and out of sheer self-preservation, an eternity later Maxim raised his head, astounded by the passion that had erupted between them, astounded that this woman had the ability to make him lose his mind so completely.

'Don't, Lavinia,' he murmured when she swayed against him. 'We have to stop this. Someone may come on to the balcony at any moment and then where would we be?'

Lavinia's senses were drugged as she stared at him bemused, her eyes large and luminous. As reality began to return and she came back to full awareness— of her surroundings, with the sound of music and laughter returning to her ears, she was shocked by the explosion of passion between them, shocked by what she had done. What had happened surpassed anything she had ever known, but Maxim was right. It must stop. She stepped back.

Making a sound that was a cry of mingled shock and fright, Lavinia was scarlet faced beneath her mask, wide eyed and trembling like a jelly. 'This—this is madness.'

'You voice my thoughts exactly.'

'It—it should not have happened. I—I must go. Robert will be looking for me. Oh, dear,' she whispered in sudden panic, 'what have I done? If—if we return separately, no one will know we have been out here together.'

Maxim stopped her, putting his hand on her arm as she was about to pass, seeing that her lovely eyes behind the mask were apprehensive and deceptively innocent. 'Wait,' he said gently. 'Calm yourself first. Don't let him see you like this.'

'Like what?'

'With your eyes aglow with passion and your lips trembling.' He smiled down at her, touching her cheek gently.

'He—he will think I have been dancing.'

'If dancing makes you look like this, then you should dance more often.'

'With most of my face hidden behind the mask he will be deceived.'

'Disguises are meant to deceive, Lavinia.' He frowned. 'You are not angry with me, are you?'

'I am not angry,' she replied quietly, meeting his penetrating gaze. 'Only afraid of what might happen as a consequence of this night.'

Maxim put out a hand and took a step towards her.

'No,' she cried with a hint of anger. 'Do you enjoy inducing feelings in me that can come to nothing?' She thrust his hand away and whirled from him violently. 'I must go,' and then she was gone, her white dress seeming to melt as she went through the curtains.

Maxim let out a deep breath and stood for a moment looking after her, then he turned his back and stared in moody contemplation at the garden below. He became lost in a deep reverie which was broken by the sounds from the ballroom beyond, and when he finally left the balcony some minutes after Lavinia, he had reminded himself harshly that he was technically involved with another woman who had borne his child

Lucy, whose very existence demanded his absolute and undivided attention. The child deserved better from him than this stupid preoccupation he had suddenly acquired for Lavinia Renshaw, a woman he hadn't known existed until a few days ago, a woman who was bent on marrying another man, a man Maxim would calmly and unhesitatingly like to tell to go to hell.

With her equilibrium shattered Lavinia slipped back into the ballroom, feeling like an adulterous wife returning to her husband and extremely conspicuous after what she had done. Moving through the crowd she tried to calm herself, ashamed of the weakness she had just displayed to Maxim Purnell. It was ridiculous, she told herself. This was only their third time of meeting and he had already gone much further than she should have allowed.

No decent, upstanding woman would have done what she had just done, she thought with bitter self-revulsion. No, indeed. Any moral, respectable, God-fearing twenty-year-old would not have gone out on to a balcony alone with a man, allowed him to kiss her like that and, worse, enjoyed the experience. She was horrified and afraid of the feelings unfolding inside her.

Eventually she located Robert and found herself looking at him in a way she never had before. The ugly truth of it was that she wasn't attracted to him—she never had been and never would be. Instead, she was attracted to Maxim Purnell, who had fascinated her from the moment she had opened her eyes to his after he had pulled her from the lagoon.

Robert was standing with the Eveshams and Julia and Daisy, who was flushed and breathless from dancing. Lavinia was immensely relieved that no one seemed to notice she had been missing. With her heart still racing, she glanced towards the balcony, just in time to see a tall figure dressed in black and wearing a white bauta mask emerge and become lost in the crowd.

After that the ball lost its glitter for Lavinia, and the rest of the night passed in some kind of haze. Before she knew it it was over. With dawn peeping on the horizon, amid what seemed to be a flotilla of boats all leaving the palace, they were ferried back to the Scalini house.

From the moment Lavinia had left Maxim on the balcony at the palace she had been living on a razor's edge. It was time for calm reflection; standing on the

balcony of her room on the upper floor of the splendid old house, she lifted her face to feel the early
morning Adriatic breeze cool her burning cheeks.
Gazing out over the rooftops of Venice towards the
Lido Channel, she could see the sun rising like molten gold on the horizon, bringing with it the cry of
sea birds.

The night's events and what she had done swept
over her in a wave of horror. At the mere thought of
how she had almost thrown herself at Maxim Purnell,
her fingers trembled and she was forced to draw a
deep, uneven breath. It was as if the magic of the
masquerade had cast a spell on her and made her
behave totally out of character, for she would never
have behaved in such a bold manner in Gloucestershire.

It was obvious that she had not been thinking
clearly. Coming to Venice was a fantastic adventure,
plunging her into a world so very different from the
one she knew, and what had happened at the ball was
beyond anything she could have imagined before—
but it could not continue like that. She could not go
on living in a world of dreams and letting her emotions get in the way of her common sense.

A sudden noise coming from the room next to
hers—Julia's room—dragged her from her melan-
choly thoughts. Glancing curiously towards the balcony only a short distance from her own, she strained
her ears, certain she had heard voices followed by
the sound of grunting and moaning. The French window which opened on to the balcony was open, for

she could see the fine net curtain billowing out as it was caught and tugged by the gentle breeze.

Lavinia thought she could hear low voices, but then she was unsure. It sounded more like a groan. The unusual noises made her think that perhaps Julia was ill and that she might be in pain and needing help. Draping a robe over her nightdress, she left her room and padded towards her sister's, finding the door had been left off the catch. Listening carefully, she heard Julia's muffled laughter and a man's voice, who seemed to be urging her in subdued tones to be quiet.

Curiosity and a sudden need to know the identity of the man her sister was entertaining at this hour, when Lavinia thought everyone in the house but herself would be sleeping off the exertions and excesses of the ball, made her move closer to the door, knowing instinctively who she would find there. She dreaded having her suspicions confirmed, but she had to know.

Her stomach was trembling as she soundlessly pushed the door open and stepped inside, and for a moment she was transfixed with horror. The room was large and in the centre was an ornate bed draped with blue silk, but what she noticed right away was Robert and Julia standing beside the rumpled bed.

Chapter Four

Robert had his back to Lavinia and the sight of his nakedness, of his almost skeletal body and bare buttocks, held her riveted. Her footsteps had been muffled by the thick blue carpet, so neither of them had heard her enter. She watched as Robert's arms wrapped themselves around Julia, who wore a bright red and yellow silk robe which gaped open at the front to expose her large, pendulous breasts.

Rigid with horror, Lavinia stared at the appalling spectacle of Robert kissing Julia with such violent passion—the kind of passion she had thought him incapable of feeling—that she quickly realised that the groans she had heard were of pleasure, not pain. Watching in mesmeric silence, she saw Robert almost devour Julia's lips, before bending his head and placing his mouth over the hard nipple moving tantalisingly before him. Julia, a willing supplicant, laughed deeply in her throat. Winding her braceleted arms round her lover's neck and closing her eyes, she threw back her head to stress the curve of her heavy breasts. Unbeknown to Lavinia, she had already tasted the pleasure of ardent love.

Lavinia's mind reeled as she sought some explanation that might excuse their conduct, telling herself that things were not always what they appeared to be, but there wasn't one. She felt physically sick with the force of the pain that attacked her. How could they? How could Robert, with his pettishness, his temper, his insufferable arrogance all directed at her, behave so disgustingly?

Feeling a rush of bitterness, she clenched her hands so tightly that her nails bit into her palms. Experiencing the full impact of Robert's treachery, anger leaped in her and she had a longing to hurl herself across the room and batter them both. Drawing a deep, silent breath, she shrank back in the doorway, wanting to get out of that room and never have to look upon either of their faces again. Managing to force her shaking limbs to move, she left the room as silently as she had come, and all she could see in her mind's eye was the love scene she had just witnessed.

Entering her room, she closed the door. Tears came into her eyes and she had to swallow against the constriction in her throat as fear for her future fought with her rage. She had been so stupid. How dare they do this to her? she accused silently with sweeping scorn, believing what her eyes had seen. There could be no excuse. They were both guilty of betrayal. Engulfed by tears of anger and misery, by her own ineptitude and her inability to control her own life, she flung herself on to the bed, sobbing wretchedly. Never before had she lost control of herself as she did then. Her normally quiet serenity and innate composure had been shattered.

When she could cry no more she went on to the balcony, feeling utterly drained and exhausted. But, she thought with calm reflection and with bitter self-reproach, how could she attack either Robert or Julia on a moral level when she was guilty of the same? Had she not betrayed Robert in her thoughts and by kissing Maxim Purnell at the ball?

Desperately needing to sort things out, she went over the events of the night; no matter how hard she tried, she could not get past the incontrovertible fact that everything was changed. Coming to grips with Robert's treachery, she faced the knowledge that the future they had planned together was over. She could not marry Robert now. But what could she do? Her natural honesty and pride urged her to a confrontation and a final settling of accounts with him, but she couldn't. Not yet.

However, Julia forced her hand when she came to her room shortly afterwards, still dressed in her garishly coloured robe, which was wrapped around her voluptuous body. It was as if she wanted to flaunt what had happened earlier between herself and Robert in the face of his betrothed.

Lavinia's face was ravaged with weeping, but otherwise it was expressionless. She looked at Julia hard. 'What are you doing here?' she asked coldly, her mind torn between disgust and sheer astonishment at Julia's effrontery.

Julia moved to stand before her. Suspecting that the movement she had seen in the doorway of her room when she had been entertaining Robert had been Lavinia, she had come to gloat. Her face was transfigured with the joy of flinging the searing truth in the face of her pretty little sister at last.

'Why so hostile?' Julia asked, her penetrating eyes studying Lavinia in detail. 'Dear me, Lavinia. You do look quite dreadful. What's the matter? Too much champagne at the ball?'

Lavinia glared at her, no longer fearful of a woman she now knew hated her. The virulence of that hatred washed over her. 'I know what is going on between you and Robert, Julia. Don't insult me by denying it. I went to your room earlier and saw the two of you together.'

Julia saw the mask replaced by an expression of contempt.

'I have no intention of denying anything. I have no reason to,' she retorted flippantly.

'Was that the first time he has been to your room?'

'No.' Julia laughed. 'Of course not. Our affair began shortly before your father died—when I was in London,' she boasted shamelessly, uncaring how much the knowledge of it would hurt her sister. 'Good Lord, Lavinia. What do you expect from a man of Robert's years? Would you have him live the life of a eunuch?'

If Lavinia had known what a eunuch was she might have replied, but she hadn't the remotest idea, and she wasn't going to show her ignorance by asking.

'He would have married me,' Julia continued, 'but I have no money—and to Robert money is an important and necessary commodity. You know Robert's type. They marry only for prestige and money—and look elsewhere for sexual fulfilment.'

'I am beginning to realise that.' Lavinia's lip curled scornfully, the contemptuous way Julia spoke increasing her anger.

'That was when he became aware of your legacy. It was just what he wanted. So don't be concerned,' she jeered. 'I might be the one he wants in his bed, but you are the one he will marry—a quiet little virgin bride with an even greater attraction of thirty thousand pounds, rather than an impoverished widow—thanks to your father.'

'My father left you generously provided for—which is more than your husband did and more than you deserve,' retorted Lavinia scathingly, recalling the time when her father had been seriously ill and Julia had taken herself off to London to enjoy herself, callously leaving others to care for him.

'You were no blood relation to my father, which is why he left the bulk of his estate to Edgar and myself. After our mother died and knowing how ill he was, you hoped he wouldn't live long, didn't you, Julia—confident there would be something in his will for you when he died. How disappointed you must have been when you discovered how little he had left you—how little he cared for you.'

With her hands on her hips Julia glared at her. 'I was. But I was always miserable when I was around him. And now you have found out about Robert and me, it is something you will have to learn to live with.'

Lavinia stared at her, as if her ears were deceiving her. That Julia thought that she would still marry Robert after this would be laughable if it were not so serious or so sordid. Robert didn't love her, she knew that, but she had hoped he felt some fondness for her. But she now saw the cynical calculation and the cold-blooded way in which both he and Julia had insultingly played upon her innocence.

'No. I will never accept it. It is not possible.'

Julia was surprised and her eyes became wary. 'You mean you will not marry Robert?'

'Never.'

Momentarily silenced, Julia could see that Lavinia's face was ghost white, the turquoise eyes which she had always envied as hard as ice and as cold, and she knew that she meant it. Suddenly she could feel her own world beginning to crumble and that it was not to her advantage to have given Lavinia an insight into how things were between herself and Robert.

She had always believed the substance of Lavinia's make-up to be nothing stronger than milk and water, and that she was meek, malleable and submissive to the will of others. Suddenly finding herself confronted with Lavinia's blazing contempt, Julia was beginning to realise she was made of sterner stuff. If Lavinia did not marry Robert, he would certainly not marry her, and would look elsewhere for some other gullible woman to marry with a fortune. And then where would she be?

'I think we should discuss this with Robert,' Julia said.

'I have no intention of confronting him with this. Not yet, anyway. I am too disgusted. Marry him yourself, Julia. After all, you are more his age than I,' she retorted scathingly.

Julia's features became ugly. 'Don't you think I would marry him if he asked me? But he won't. He never will.'

'Then you'll just have to go on being his mistress,' Lavinia taunted, the cold mask she had worn when Julia had entered her room settling back into place. Her dismissive words were of confident contempt.

'I am aware that when Robert finds out about this he is going to be extremely angry, but the situation is of his making—and yours. Understand this here and now, Julia. I will never marry Robert, and neither will I return to live at Welbourne House with you in it—which, unfortunately, is still your right. What matters to me now is what I do with my life. I will shape it to my own design without any interference from you or Robert. Now please leave my room. I have nothing further to say.'

Beside herself with rage, Julia left the room, leaving Lavinia staring at the closed door long after it had shut with a final click.

Deep in thought, Lavinia considered her situation and what she must do for the best. That was when she thought of Maxim Purnell. In her present terrible plight, he was the only person who could help her. But would he want to?

Would he marry her?

He might, she thought with a cool calculation born out of desperation—for thirty thousand pounds. If, as

Robert had told her, he had lost such a large sum of
money at a ridotto, then he might be tempted to
marry her if he knew so much wealth would come
his way.

Within half an hour of Julia leaving her room, and
feeling as though she had been born anew as a result
of some extremely painful form of gestation, Lavinia
calmly slipped out of the house and into the quiet
streets without anyone seeing her.

On reaching his apartment after the ball, Maxim
picked up some letters of business correspondence
awaiting his attention. Perkins, his valet, who also
doubled as his secretary, had brought them to his
attention before he had left for the ball, but he'd put
them aside, feeling that they could wait. Now he
flicked through them, observing from the many different addresses scrawled across them that they had
been following him around Europe for the past two
months. He browsed through them absently until he
came to one missive on which he recognised the
handwriting.

It was from Alice.

After hurrying through the narrow streets to the
house where Maxim was staying, Lavinia was admitted by a servant and shown to his apartment on
the upper floor of the house. Tentatively she went
towards the rather forbidding-looking door. As she
stood before it, a wave of doubt swept over her, causing her to hesitate, to question what she was doing,

but then she took a deep breath and squared her narrow shoulders, reminding herself that in her weakened and helpless state he was the only person who could help her.

Taking the bit between her teeth and vibrant with hope, she knocked on the door, waiting for what seemed to be an age. Eventually she heard a sound from within and the door was thrown open.

'What is it?' came an irate voice which Lavinia recognised immediately and almost sent her scurrying back down the stairs in fright. 'I told you I did not want to be—' Maxim stopped when he saw Lavinia standing there. Their eyes met and locked for a moment, Maxim's opening wider and wider, experiencing astonishment and incredulity, before brusquely recollecting himself. 'You! What the devil...?'

Apart from a towel wrapped around his narrow waist he was stark naked, bringing a soft gasp to Lavinia's lips and causing her cheeks to flush scarlet. Shocked to the depths of her virginal innocence, she was unable to take her eyes off his strong, muscular body, so eternally savage, proud and golden—and not one bit as puny as Robert's, which had been exposed to her earlier. Her carefully sheltered upbringing had not prepared her for the sight of a near-naked man of Maxim Purnell's splendid physique.

'I—I—forgive me. I had to see you—but I can see you do not look too happy.' Nothing had prepared her for the cold reception she received.

'Please,' he said brusquely, stepping aside to let her pass. 'Come in.'

At a glance Lavinia was struck by the spaciousness and splendour of the lavish apartment. The shutters had been opened to allow the bright morning sunlight to pour through, highlighting the gilt-stuccoed ceiling and the rich elegance of the furniture. Fragile porcelain figurines reposed on polished surfaces and marble stands, along with an impressive range of expensive Venetian blown-glass objects—all the different kinds of glass which Venetian craftsmen had been producing for centuries and for which Venice was famous. They told Lavinia that this apartment must belong to someone who was extremely rich, and who must be a very good friend of Maxim's to allow him to stay here.

Maxim closed the door behind her.

Pulling herself together, she looked at him and said, 'I had to see you. It is fortunate that I remembered where you live.'

'Is it? Why? What do you want to say to me that is so important? You must have excellent reasons for pursuing me here.'

Maxim was unconcerned that she had arrived when he was about to take his bath, and that he'd only had time to wrap a towel round his waist before answering the door, fully expecting it to be his valet. Picking up a robe from the back of a chair, he thrust his arms through the sleeves and secured it with a belt round the middle, before whipping away the towel from underneath.

Nervously Lavinia stared at him in silence, acutely and embarrassingly aware that he was completely naked beneath the thin robe that rippled on his athletic body when he moved. He was mocking her, making her mission appear trivial, making her wish she hadn't come. His eyes were cold, his face rigid, all emotion withheld by an iron control. What had happened between her leaving him on the balcony at the palace and now? Did he regret what had happened between them? With a painful effort she tried to suppress her disappointment. If she wanted to accomplish what she had set out to achieve, then she must cast off her pride and humble herself.

'You have taken a scandalous chance—risked compromising your reputation—by coming here,' Maxim said harshly, regarding her without anger but with a terrifying firmness and a hard gleam in his eyes.

'Yes—I know.'

Lavinia swallowed nervously. This was too much. How could she begin to tell him the reason that had brought her to his apartment to see him when he looked at her like that? So much had happened that she was overwhelmed with emotions.

'Well?' Maxim asked, his voice frank and unemotional as he tried not to let his mind dwell on this beautiful girl with a face like an angel and her large turquoise eyes shining with innocence. It struck him how very feminine she was, with the gold treasure of her hair, drawn from her face by a narrow band of blue ribbon, tumbling down her back like a silken curtain. Wearing a dress of summer blue, the skirt full with a tight waist, Lavinia was unlike anyone he had ever seen. The neckline was modest, the sleeves ending at her elbows with a delicate froth of white lace caressing her lower arms.

In silent, helpless protest Lavinia averted her eyes from Maxim's sternly handsome face as they glazed over with tears. How could he be tender and passionate one minute, and then cold and hard and unreasonable the next? Agonisingly aware of her mistake in coming here, she realised she must go. It was imperative that she got out of that room and away from his presence. With great difficulty she swallowed hard, keeping her head lowered so he would not see her tears.

'Forgive me,' she whispered. 'I can see my presence irks you. I should not have troubled you. If you don't mind I would like to leave.'

Abruptly she crossed the carpet to the door and he followed with all the stealth of a panther. When she was about to open it his hand pressed firmly on the wood, preventing her from doing so.

'No,' he said on a gentler note, looking at her downcast face, seeing for the first time how distressed she was, how tired and tense. Something stirred in the region of his heart. 'You came to say something. You must tell me what it is before you leave. Come. Tell me the purpose of your visit.'

Lavinia shook her head. 'No. I can't. I made a mistake.'

'You can't say that until I know what it is.' On a sigh he placed his hands on her shoulders and turned her round to face him. 'Lavinia, look at me.'

Unwillingly she met his eyes, and he could see the pain moving in their glorious, liquid depths. He also recognised desperation when he saw it, and for some unknown reason Lavinia Renshaw was extremely desperate about something.

'What is it?'

'I came to ask if you would marry me,' she told him at last.

Maxim was silent, looking at her hard, incredulously, as though she had suddenly changed before his eyes. Lavinia was making an offer, he realised, with quiet courage and no games. His expression became grim, and he could almost hear the funeral drum-roll of his heart.

'No.'

The word was uttered without anger, but was none the less cold and final.

Very quietly Lavinia turned her face away and her heart sank. Had he exploded with fury and injured vanity she would have understood it better than this deadly quietness which frightened her. With despair she saw the end of all her hopes of persuading him to marry her.

'This is plain speaking,' he said.

'Necessity drives me to it.'

'Rather that than to know you came here out of inclination.'

'I am not inclined to do anything out of inclination.'

'I am glad to hear it.'

'And you refuse?'

'Precisely. I'm not in the market for a wife. I don't know what has prompted you to come here and ask

me this, and I am flattered. What man wouldn't be—
to be propositioned by a beautiful woman?'

'It was presumptuous of me, I know.'

'Yes, it was,' he answered, moving away from her
and standing by a round table in a haughty pose, very
stiff and upright, with a suggestion of arrogance
which came naturally enough to him. His eyes remained fixed on her face without the trace of a smile
to soften their steely expression.

'Oh, please,' she whispered, unconsciously moving towards him, profoundly embarrassed, unchecked
tears beginning to run freely down her face. Until that
moment she wouldn't have believed she could feel
more humiliated than she already did. She wished the
ground would open up and swallow her. 'You have
no idea how difficult this is for me. Please don't
mock me.'

'I'm not. I realise something traumatic must have
occurred to make you come here and ask me to marry
you. At least tell me what it is.'

Lavinia swallowed hard, wiping away the tears
with the back of her hand in a childlike gesture that
had Maxim delving into the pocket of his robe for a
handkerchief and handing it to her, trying not to let
her anguish and the dampness clinging to her sooty
lashes and tear-bright eyes weaken him.

'Robert has deceived me. He has betrayed me with
my sister.'

Maxim nodded. Everything was becoming clear to
him now. 'I see,' he said coldly. 'And what does that
make you? Isn't it hypocritical of you to react like a
hurt and angry child whose favourite toy is broken,

when you are guilty of the same?' he reminded her cruelly.

His remark was like a slap in the face, but she had to concede it was true. 'Yes, I know,' she answered wretchedly, her tears having ceased.

'After all, I do not remember you trying to fight me off,' he said pointedly, trying to thrust away the poignant memory of how she had melted in his arms lest it weakened his resolve to have anything further to do with her. 'You let your ardour run away with you then. How do you know it wasn't the same for Robert and your sister? Anyway, how do you know they are having an affair? And if they are, why isn't he marrying her instead of you?'

'Because Julia is my half-sister, on my mother's side, and quite penniless. Robert will not marry any woman who does not bring with her a generous dowry. I—I caught them together in her room. It—it was dreadful. I cannot marry Robert after this, and I cannot live at Welbourne House—my home in Gloucestershire—with my sister either. I have nowhere else to go and I don't know what to do.'

'So you thought you would come here, hoping I would provide you with the solution to your dilemma? Am I right?' Maxim demanded.

'Yes,' she admitted. She could almost feel the effort he was exerting to keep his anger under control.

Maxim's eyes glittered with a fire that burned her raw when he looked at her, and his voice was deadly calm when he spoke. 'When and if I decide to marry, I prefer to do the asking myself.'

'I—I thought that after—'

'What?' he jeered, ignoring the way the colour drained out of her soft cheeks as he continued with deliberate brutality. 'That because we kissed—because we are attracted to each other—I might be swayed?'

'Yes.'

Maxim's eyes narrowed and his jaw clamped with grinding resolution as he stood looking down at her, trying to ignore the mute appeal in those large, luminescent eyes, seeking refuge in his anger. 'Then I'm sorry. Life isn't like that. I have kissed many women I have been attracted to, but that doesn't mean to say that I wanted to marry any of them.'

Lavinia was conscious of a sudden surge of anger, realising just how stupid and naïve she had been in turning to this arrogant and unfeeling man for help. How dare he treat what had happened between them so casually, as if the kiss was insignificant and meant nothing at all. She was ashamed that she had been such a willing participant. But perhaps this was nothing out of the ordinary and he was used to kissing ladies all over the place. And perhaps ladies accepted his kisses in their stride. After all, she thought bitterly, how would she know? Gripping her hands tightly by her sides, she regarded him coldly.

'I do not have your experience, Mr Purnell. Apart from yourself, no other man has kissed me,' she told him with simple honesty, giving Maxim further insight into just how truly innocent she was.

'Nevertheless, you were misguided to think I would marry you. You must understand that I can't marry you.'

She gasped as a sudden thought occurred to her. 'You—you are married? Is that why?'

'No.'

His dark face was inscrutable, but Lavinia saw something flicker behind his eyes. 'Then you are in love with someone else?'

'No. But it makes no difference. I will not marry you.'

Mortified and humiliated, Lavinia nevertheless managed to lift her chin a notch and look at him directly. 'Not even for thirty thousand pounds?'

Maxim's entire face instantly became hard, shuttered and aloof. His brows snapped together with brittle anger and a feral gleam appeared in his narrowed eyes as they locked on hers with angry disgust. 'Now you do insult me,' he said, his voice so controlled that Lavinia felt an icy chill sweep down her spine. 'I cannot be bought, either. And what makes you think you are worth thirty thousand pounds?'

Lavinia gasped, her humiliation complete. 'Now it is you who insult me,' she flared, a fresh surge of anger rising up inside her like flames licking round a dry log, furious with herself for being stupid enough to think he might help her.

'If you have so much money then what you do should not be a problem. You can live where you choose or buy yourself another husband—which shouldn't be too difficult. You have other assets to your credit besides thirty thousand pounds,' he ground out with suave brutality, his insolent, contemptuous gaze raking over her.

Maxim's jibe, savage and taunting, flicked over Lavinia like a whiplash. Stung to anger by his harsh words, hot colour flooded her cheeks and her soft lips tightened as she exerted every ounce of her control to keep her temper and her emotions in check. 'I can't. The money is a legacy left to me by my father. It will not be made available to me until I am twenty-five—unless I marry.'

'I see. Then if you don't find some other fool to marry, it would seem you have a long wait ahead of you.'

'Are you telling me you are a fool, Mr Purnell?'

'To have become involved with you I must be. Don't you think you're taking a huge risk asking me to marry you—knowing nothing about me? Tell me. What exactly do you know?'

'Very little. I know you are a gambler—that you gamble with large sums of money—'

'And sometimes lose,' he told her.

'Yes, I know that.'

'No doubt Robert told you,' Maxim drawled sarcastically, with heavy emphasis on Robert's name and without taking his cold and merciless eyes off her. 'Did he, by any chance, tell you that I lost a large amount of money at a ridotto the other evening?'

'Yes.'

'Which gave you reason to suspect I might be in dire need of some more?'

'Yes.'

'And yet, knowing this, you are prepared to risk your thirty thousand pounds? How do you know I won't marry you and stake the whole lot on one game of cards.'

'I don't. I can't say that I approve of gambling on cards—'

'There are many other forms of gambling besides cards,' he cut in coldly, giving her a look that was a hundred times more deadly than his anger had been a moment before. 'And isn't what you are proposing a gamble? You took a chance that what happened between us at the ball might have put me into such a state of passion that I would fall at your feet.'

'I did not,' Lavinia burst out, blinded with wrath and humiliation, her anger in full spate—an anger she hadn't realised she was capable of. She was beginning to realise that all was lost, and yet now she was glad he had refused her, glad she had been saved from marrying this cold and unfeeling man, this stranger. The mere thought of tying herself to him for the rest of her life was fearful.

'I realise that I have gambled and lost and that there is nothing left for me to say other than I am sorry I asked you,' she continued furiously. 'I have no experience, you see. I may seem stupid to you, but when you kissed me I had no idea I was nothing more than an amusing diversion. Forgive me. I should not have come here—I realise that now. You have made it quite clear. I will trouble you no further. Good day to you, Mr Purnell.'

Lavinia turned abruptly and moved towards the door, holding her head high as she tried to preserve what little there was left of her pride. Maxim Purnell did not deserve that she should abase herself for him.

When Lavinia turned from him Maxim cursed silently beneath his breath. He wanted to tell her to stay, to draw her into his arms and kiss her as he had done at the ball; if he had not received Alice's letter reminding him that he had been away too long and that he had a duty towards his child, he might have yielded to Lavinia's request, might have let her persuade him, and enjoyed doing so. But his absolute responsibility was to Lucy and he couldn't change that, but when he looked at Lavinia his conscience was torn one way, his feelings another.

'Wait,' Maxim said, reaching out and taking hold of her arm.

Lavinia turned, surprised by the expression in his eyes. It had a yearning quality, nostalgic almost, as if he was crushed by some scarcely discernible problem, but she was too angry to be moved by it. Her eyes frosted over. 'Kindly take your hand off my arm,' she seethed. 'Don't touch me.'

Maxim dropped his hand. A cynical smile twisted one corner of his mouth and his blue eyes remained unwarmed. 'What do you mean to do now?'

'That is none of your business,' she replied coldly.

'Then my advice is that you forgive Robert his dalliance with your sister and marry him. Better the devil you know.'

Lavinia turned her head and glared at him. 'I don't want your advice. I don't know what I'll do. But I'll find some way out,' she said fiercely. 'I will find a way out of this without you or Robert.' She took a step forward but hesitated, looking back at him. 'I find myself beginning to regret your prompt action in jumping in to rescue me after I fell into the lagoon. All things considered, it would have been best if you had left me where I was,' she said viciously, and meant it.

Lavinia left him then. I hate him, she seethed silently, repeating the words over and over all the way back to the Scalini house, hoping the fury and the passion would convince her that all those other emotions didn't exist. Her heart twisted agonisingly in her breast, telling her she could not possibly survive the humiliation of Maxim's brutal rejection. But her mind told her coldly that she would.

Left alone with a raw ache inside him, the vexing tide of anger which had consumed Maxim began to subside. His mind was locked in furious combat with the desire to go after Lavinia and the urge to forget her, but he knew the latter was impossible. Perhaps it was because she was as unlike Alice as it was possible to be. Everything about her threw him off balance. Lavinia's mere presence resurrected emotions he thought had died when he had seen Alice for what she was.

Her proposition pounded inside his head, combining with the torment of his own harsh rejection. He saw her as she had been when he had pulled her from the lagoon, and how lovely she had been at the ball, filled with innocent, unselfish passion when he had drawn her into his arms and kissed her. He realised just how devastated she must have been when she had discovered that Robert was having an affair with her sister, understanding the inexplicable anguish she must have been through, and how she had humbled herself by coming to him—to ask him to marry her. And like a heartless idiot he had shunned, scorned and humiliated her, which she had not deserved and for which he despised and reproached himself with a virulence that was unbearable.

Lavinia had stirred his desire as no other woman had succeeded in doing for a long time, so, unable to leave things like this between them, after he had bathed and dressed he walked to the Scalini house.

Chapter Five

When the maid came to tell Lavinia that Mr Purnell was waiting in the salon to speak to her, her first reaction was to refuse to see him, but, realising it would cause considerable speculation in the household if it became known she had turned him away without receiving him, she smoothed her hair and her skirts and went down to the salon.

With his hands clasped behind his back, Maxim stood looking down at the canal. Despite her firm resolve to remain calm and unmoved by him, Lavinia felt her heart give a sudden leap. He turned on hearing her enter, and she saw his face change when his eyes met hers across the room.

Lavinia stood for a moment in the doorway as if she had no wish to be alone with him. And then, with her head held high, she closed the door and calmly moved to stand in the centre of the room, finding it impossible to greet him with any degree of casualness after the harsh words they had exchanged just a short while ago.

'I don't know what you hope to achieve by coming here, Mr Purnell,' she said frostily. 'I think everything has been said between us.'

'Has it?' he asked, his voice echoing in the large white and gold salon.

'Yes. And I must thank you for being so frank with me.'

'I had to come. We can't leave things like this between us.'

Without emotion, Lavinia stood perfectly still as Maxim came closer. There was an aura of calm authority about him. His expression was now blank and impervious, and he looked unbearably handsome. The sight of his chiselled features and bold blue eyes never failed to stir her heart.

Maxim stood gazing down at her, looking deep into her eyes, observing with sorrow that the pink bloom he had adored so much had gone from her cheeks, and that there were faint purple smudges beneath her eyes, which told him that she'd had very little sleep, if any, since returning from the ball. The lovely face was as white as alabaster, and her eyes glittered through tear-damp lashes.

What was it that attracted him to her? he asked himself. Her sincerity? Her gentleness and purity, of both body and mind? Was it her smile, her touch, that set the blood pounding in his veins like an inexperienced youth? Ever since his feelings for Alice had died he had thought himself immune to such weaknesses as love and passion—and yet Lavinia affected him deeply.

Maxim was seized by a passionate longing to protect and revere this lovely young woman who had
crept into his heart. He ached to treat her as she
should be treated, to tread the hesitant steps of court-
ship and woo her as she deserved, but it was no good
dreaming of what might be. He saw that she was
looking at him frankly, openly, and with a dispassion
so chilling that he was intensely moved by it, and yet
he sensed that beneath it all was a heartbreaking de-
jection.

'You've been crying,' he said quietly.

'My state of health need not concern you.'

'But it does. I feel that I am responsible.'

'Please don't flatter yourself.'

'I don't. It was not my intention to cause you pain,
and I could not leave Venice without putting things
right between us. I owe you an apology. It was wrong
of me to speak to you so harshly. I apologise for my
boorish behaviour. I said things to you of which I am
deeply ashamed.'

'Ashamed, Mr Purnell!' Lavinia exclaimed with a
hint of sarcasm. She had been sorely wounded and
was determined not to make this easy for him. 'I am
certain there is nothing for you to be ashamed of.
And as for apologies—don't you think it's a little late
to withdraw anything you said to me?'

'Nevertheless I do apologise—and I shall not be
happy until you tell me I am forgiven.' He smiled
crookedly at her, willing her to respond, but there
was no answering spark in her eyes. 'When I returned
to the apartment after the ball, I received a letter from
someone who never fails to rouse my temper—and

your proposal was the final straw. I quite understand
how hurt you must have been when you discovered
what was going on between your betrothed and your
sister.'

'I doubt it,' she replied coldly.

'Believe me, I do,' he murmured, his words full
of meaning and his expression suddenly so sombre
that Lavinia thought that maybe he did, but she
would never know the truth of it.

'It—it was wrong of me to approach you,' she said
tersely. 'It was extremely stupid of me. I see that
now.'

'Why did you come to me?'

'I thought I made that clear. I confess that at the
time I knew of no one else who could help me. You
were my one and only hope—and I deceived myself
most shamefully into believing you would want me.
I now realise my mistake and how foolish I was. I
did not realise that when I ran from Robert I might
be about to unite myself with another as unworthy as
he,' she said scathingly, unfairly, carried away by her
own anger, and by an almost physical need to convince Maxim Purnell that she didn't want him. 'But
it need not concern you, Mr Purnell. I shall return to
England and consider my situation there.'

'And in the meantime?'

'In the meantime nothing is changed. I will not
marry Robert, a man who can see no further than my
legacy and has no feelings for me. I will not barter
myself for security or money. It is degrading—which
is something you have taught me,' Lavinia said with
deriding cynicism, a proud light shining in her eyes

as they held his. 'There has to be more to marriage than that.'

Maxim raised an eyebrow inquiringly, the corner of his mouth twisting wryly. 'Such as love?'

'I can't answer that—never having known the kind of love you speak of. I strongly suspect that love is a contradiction of emotions which should be given freely and has nothing to do with marriage.'

'And desire? Passion?' he asked, regarding her closely, his gaze narrow and assessing.

'At least desire and passion are honest emotions.'

'And all consuming,' said Maxim.

'And I would say that there speaks a man of experience,' she said coldly. 'But I would think those kind of emotions are not as consuming as love. I would also say that when passions are spent they are easily appeased and forgotten,' she remarked drily, referring to the brief passion that had been ignited between them at the ball, a passion they both knew would have flared into something more and run out of control had it not been checked. 'I strongly regret what happened between us last night. Believe me, Mr Purnell, I am not the kind of woman to go around kissing just anyone.'

Maxim's firm lips twisted in a morose smile, while inwardly admiring her perception even in a state of shock. 'I hope not. But a face behind a mask can be deceptive—and you were so beautiful at the ball— so very beautiful,' he said, his expression softening, his gaze lingering on her lips, remembering what it had felt like to kiss them.

Lavinia gave a hard, contemptuous laugh, stiff with pride and anger, the humiliation and the hurt she had suffered at his hands never far away. 'And the opportunity was beautiful, was it not? The Carnival atmosphere of the ball—the revelry—the excitement. Just like the passion that flared between us it was enchanting while it lasted—but with the dawn I realised that the magic was just an illusion.'

'It needn't be.'

'Yes, it does. But I have much to thank you for. You see,' she said, her eyes shooting turquoise sparks of anger and not wavering from his, 'from now on, if I ever find myself in a similar situation, I shall be too distrustful, too much on my guard against men's wiles, to allow myself to be deceived by charm, soft words and a handsome face. So now, Mr Purnell, you can leave, knowing that you have at least achieved something. You can leave Venice and forget you ever met a stupid woman who quite shamelessly threw herself at your head.'

Halted abruptly in the midst of this unpremeditated outburst of feeling, Maxim wanted to shake her. He knew she was playing a part, that behind the hard expression and glib words, the real woman, the warm and passionate Lavinia, was still to be found. His ill-considered treatment of her earlier when he had vented his fury on her had driven the tantalising creature he had kissed at the ball to the bottom of the lagoon, and replaced her with this angry young woman who was being extremely careful at keeping him at arm's length.

Unable to prevent himself, Maxim reached out to touch her, taking her arm and pulling her towards him.

'That I can never do,' he said, drawn by the depths of the bewitching turquoise eyes looking into his and by the softness of her quivering lips. Forgetful of where he was and mastered by a passion almost beyond his control, he took her face between his hands, his clear blue eyes penetrating as they probed hers. Desire was in his own, and something more, something so profound that it held Lavinia spellbound.

'You little fool. I came after you because I was deeply touched by your distress and couldn't help myself,' he said fiercely. 'I don't want to hurt you. I care about you. I do care what happens to you. Deeply.'

Like a magnet Maxim's eyes were drawn to her mouth, and he became lost in the exciting beauty of her.

'Please, Maxim—don't,' she whispered, recognising the desire in the smouldering depths of his eyes. 'This is not a game.'

'Pity. It's just getting interesting.'

Before Lavinia could guess what he meant to do she was caught in his arms, and with her head reeling she found herself imprisoned against him. After all that had been said between them she could not let this happen. She struggled furiously when he bent his dark head and his lips took possession of hers, yet, despite her frenzy to escape, there was little she could do.

Maxim kissed her with such accomplished persuasion that gradually she melted in his arms, finding his mouth so warm after the chill she had endured. Maxim had awakened her to love at the ball, but she had been denied its fulfilment—not that she knew what fulfilment was, only being aware that she wanted him to go on kissing her, to feel his hands on her body, as she had seen Robert do to Julia, and observed the pleasure they gave and received from each other. She offered Maxim her lips, responding and yielding to his kiss where she should only have received.

A whole range of uncontrollable feelings were induced in her by his kiss, and her eyes fluttered closed when she felt a stir of immense pleasure sigh through her tired body. All she was conscious of was Maxim's mouth on her own, kissing her with commanding strength and passion, becoming aware of his hand stealing up the back of her neck beneath her hair, imprisoning her head. He deprived her of thought, leaving only feelings, and they filled her with such a sense of languorous pleasure that she seemed to be floating.

There was a sound behind them but they paid little heed, but then Maxim tensed and wrenched himself away from her, breathing heavily. Dazedly Lavinia looked up at him in surprise, but he wasn't looking at her. His eyes were directed at the door. Turning her head she looked round, and to her horror there stood Mrs Lambert, white-faced and in a state of shock, and Julia, her eyes blazing fiercely. Beside her was Robert, his expression one of absolute horror, his cold, malevolent eyes fixed on both herself and Maxim. The Eveshams were also there, with Sophia looking on with vicious amusement on her plain face.

With guilt-stricken shock Lavinia gasped, startled, her face flushed, her eyes glowing and her lips soft and moist from Maxim's kiss. Quickly she took hold of herself. At any other time the situation would have been one of extreme delicacy and she would have been swamped with shame at being caught in such a compromising situation that would be sure to ruin her reputation, but the scene she had witnessed earlier between Robert and Julia had been far more shocking than what Robert now witnessed between herself and Maxim. The explosion of anger and hatred that shot through her when she met the eyes of her betrothed was almost beyond bearing. Robert had betrayed her, degraded her and for that he would pay.

Sir John and Lady Evesham melted into the hallway, taking a reluctant Sophia with them, realising it was best to leave Robert to deal with the unenviable task before him.

Robert was visibly trembling with rage, and when he spoke there was a deathly sickness in every note. 'What is the meaning of this? We cannot deny what our eyes have seen. Sir,' he hissed, glowering at Maxim, 'have the decency to take your hands off Miss Renshaw. She is my betrothed.'

Robert's angry statement told Lavinia that Julia hadn't told him about the scene between them earlier when she had come to her room.

'How dare you compromise her!' Robert exclaimed, beside himself with fury, casting a severe,

critical eye over Lavinia. 'Your disgraceful conduct
and the impropriety of such wanton behaviour dis-
gusts me, Lavinia. Don't you dare insult my intelligence by telling me that this is not how it looks.'

Lavinia took a deep breath, feeling Maxim's arm
tighten about her protectively.'

'The situation is exactly how it looks,' Maxim said
coldly, favouring Robert with a long, withering look.

'Robert,' said Lavinia, aware of Mrs Lambert's absolute astonishment and that Julia, who hadn't an in-
kling who this ravishingly handsome man was she
had found kissing her sister, was glowering from her
to Maxim as if she wanted to throttle them both, 'I
don't believe you've been introduced. This is Mr
Maxim Purnell. Mr Purnell, Mr Robert Feltham.'

'I don't think there is any need for introductions,'
seethed Robert, flexing and unflexing his hands by
his sides in vexation.

'No,' said Maxim, eyeing Robert with cynical contempt. 'There isn't.'

'Lavinia, go to your room,' Robert ordered. 'I'll
speak to you alone when this overbearing scoundrel
has had the decency to leave the house.'

'I think not,' Maxim said, his voice like steel and
a murderous expression on his face. His mouth was
tight, his eyes flashing dangerously, his icy anger far
more intimidating than any show of hot rage. 'I regret
to inform you, Feltham, that Miss Renshaw is no
longer betrothed to you,' Maxim told him coldly.

Two high spots of colour appeared on Robert's
thin cheekbones, the rest of his face was chalk white.
He glared at Lavinia. 'What's this?'

Calmly Lavinia went to stand in front of him, her eyes on a level with his. If he expected her to cringe and cower then he was going to be disappointed. She gazed at him coldly, showing not the least fear. 'What Mr Purnell has told you is the truth, Robert. I have taken it upon myself to end our betrothal. I am not going to marry you.' Her eyes slid to Julia, finding it hard to believe that this woman, who was looking at her with so much hatred, was her sister. 'I thought Julia would have informed you of this.'

'Informed me? Be so good as to explain what you are talking about.'

'I thought she would have told you about my going to her room earlier and finding the two of you together. I saw you, Robert.'

Robert looked dumbfounded. 'Saw me? What did you see?'

Lavinia's smile was one of absolute contempt. 'Do you really want me to tell you that in front of Mrs Lambert, Robert? Very well. I saw you with Julia,' she accused him angrily, thrusting her face closer to his, thinking she must have been out of her mind ever to have considered marrying such an obnoxious man. 'I saw you kiss her, caress her—as lovers do. I heard her sighs and groans—and your own, Robert. Would you like me to go on?'

Lavinia's disclosure brought a gasp of shock and outrage from Mrs Lambert. 'No,' she cried, looking from Robert to Julia in absolute horror and disbelief. 'Julia! What Lavinia is saying cannot be true. Tell me it isn't.'

Julia looked at her aunt, showing no shame for what she had done, and she certainly wasn't about to deny it. 'I can't, Aunt. It is true.'

'Oh—you wicked, wicked girl.'

Absolutely enraged, the strength of Robert's temper could be vicious when roused. Lavinia's exposure wounded his vanity, and the anger and hatred burning from his eyes when he rounded on her made Lavinia think he was actually going to murder her right there.

'You sneaking little slut. So, you saw me with Julia, did you? And was what you were doing with him any different?' he hissed, pointing a quivering finger at Maxim. 'You women are all the same. You look so pure, so innocent, but underneath you're nothing but a pack of bitches on heat—which is how you should be treated.'

With fury blazing from his eyes he raised his hand to strike her, but Maxim stepped forward, grasping Robert's arm in mid-air in a vice-like grip, his expression savage as he halted the physical threat to Lavinia.

'If you value your life, I wouldn't do that if I were you,' he warned, the words delivered in a cold, murderous voice, his eyes like dagger thrusts boring into Robert's. 'If you lay one finger on her I'll break your neck.'

Rubbing his arm when Maxim released it, Robert seemed to freeze, his mind registering the physical threat in his voice, his small eyes searching his granite features. Maxim Purnell was a man who seemed to operate control at all times, a man who brooked no argument from anyone, and his look forced Robert to step back.

'You can't threaten me,' he said, remaining defiant, not quite recognising the depth of Maxim's fury, but Lavinia saw the taut rage emanating from every line of his powerful frame, causing a trickle of ice-cold fear to run down her spine as she had her first insight into the violent forces he kept leashed inside him.

'No?' Maxim inquired, with a sardonic lift to one dark brow and a dangerous edge to his voice. 'I meant every word I said. If you so much as touch her I will kill you—which is something I would not regret. Perhaps I should tell you that Miss Renshaw is now betrothed to me. I came here to ask her to be my wife and she has consented. Is that not so, Lavinia?' he said, his voice so soft and tender that it would have fooled anyone into believing that he loved her, but it did not fool Lavinia.

The memory of his rejection was still too fresh and raw in her mind. He looked at her, smiling into her stunned face, willing her to speak the words he wanted her to speak, and she complied, unable to do anything else when he looked at her like that.

'Yes,' she acknowledged quietly, holding his gaze. 'Yes, I have.'

'But you can't,' wailed Julia petulantly, coming to life at last when she saw her own world beginning to crumble about her ears. 'Lavinia is my sister and not yet twenty-one. She cannot marry anyone without my say-so.'

Lavinia turned on her, speaking with contempt. 'Because you could never hold a rightful place at Welbourne, you have always been resentful of Edgar and me, showing both of us nothing but contempt all your life—so spare me your sisterly concern now, Julia,' Lavinia scorned, speaking with a deadly calm. 'Besides, I shall be twenty-one very soon. What you and Robert have done—what you intended going on doing even when he married me—I find disgusting and deplorable. I can only thank God that I found out before it was too late.'

'Nevertheless I know my rights,' hissed Robert, desperation not far away as he saw Lavinia's legacy slipping away from him. 'You are betrothed to me and I don't intend letting you get out of it so easily. I can sue for breach of promise.'

'Then do so by all means,' said Maxim, not two feet away from him, looming over him, smiling an absolutely chilling smile, his clear blue eyes gleaming with a deadly purpose. 'But I would strongly advise you not to make an enemy of me, Feltham. If you do I will crucify you. I'm a powerful man, with powerful friends, and I'll happily destroy you if you so much as bring a breath of scandal to Lavinia's name. She is under my protection now, not yours. I would advise you to remember that she is to remain in this house until I leave Venice. She will accompany me, of course—as my wife. I shall arrange for a special licence for the ceremony to take place right away.'

Robert fixed his cold eyes on Lavinia, purposeful and menacing. 'You naïve little fool,' he hissed acidly. 'You have no notion of what you are letting yourself in for, have you, tying yourself to a disinherited, impoverished gambler? Go ahead. But don't say I didn't warn you. The legacy your father left you won't last beyond his first game of cards.'

With these parting words, his face distorted and ugly almost beyond recognition, Robert saw something so terrible in Maxim's metallic eyes that he abruptly left the room without further discussion. Julia followed him, leaving Mrs Lambert in some distress, finding it difficult to know what to say.

'I am so very sorry, Lavinia, dear,' she said softly, her expression pained. 'I had no idea that anything of this nature was going on. Julia and Mr Feltham! Oh, dear. It's all come as such a shock.'

'It's all right, Mrs Lambert,' said Lavinia gently. 'Try not to worry about it. Perhaps it's happened for the best. Robert and I were never suited—and I can't for the life of me imagine why I thought we were.'

'But—but you? You and Mr Purnell,' she said, looking from one to the other, remembering how he had so gallantly come to Lavinia's rescue when she had fallen into the lagoon. 'You are not even acquainted. Don't you think you ought to get to know each other a little better before committing yourselves to something as serious as marriage?'

'There's no time,' said Maxim gravely, beginning to wonder what he had committed himself to by announcing to everyone that he and Lavinia were to be married.

'Very well,' said Mrs Lambert, turning to go. 'Just as soon as Valentina and Leonardo are awake, I shall inform them of everything that has occurred—and in the light of such disgraceful conduct from Robert and Julia, carrying on like that in their house, I cannot blame them if they insist on them leaving and finding somewhere else to stay. Oh, dear—and Daisy must be told. But she never did trust Robert,' she said, shaking her head at the whole sorry business and going out of the room in a flurry of skirts.

Left alone with Lavinia, Maxim knew he was in trouble and cursed himself for a fool. Everything was ruined, he thought bitterly. Everything he had hoped to accomplish where Lucy was concerned had been dashed because he couldn't keep his hands off Lavinia Renshaw—but he recalled that when he had kissed her, he had not been thinking of either Lucy or Alice.

Lavinia had the power to drive Alice from his mind, but thoughts of his daughter gave him sharp pangs of conscience and he felt guilty of betrayal. When Alice discovered he had married someone else, she would try removing Lucy from him as far as possible. He hadn't meant for any of this to happen, and he could see no way of extricating himself with honour. Too late, he knew he shouldn't have come. The danger had been too great. He should have stayed away and tried to forget he had ever met the lovely young woman he had plucked from the lagoon, but he had been unable to prevent himself going after her, being drawn to her like metal filings to a magnet. What had happened was the fruit of his own folly and there was no escape.

In the cool, calculating manner which he adopted whenever he was dealing with a business transaction, he realised he would have to draw up fresh plans which would prove satisfactory to Lavinia; whatever was decided, he felt a deep sense of responsibility towards her. Her problems were pretty desperate, that was obvious, and she had no defences against the world as he knew it. It was important that she was protected from men like Robert Feltham, and her reputation must be preserved. However, he was unprepared when she turned on him angrily.

'Now see what has happened because you couldn't keep your hands to yourself,' she cried accusingly, her voice trembling with fury. 'How dare you force yourself on me like that?'

'Why?' asked Maxim smoothly, gazing down at her and noting the telltale flush on her cheeks and the soft confusion in her deep blue gaze. 'Because you can't help the way you feel every time I do? You melt in my arms as though you belong there.'

'But I don't. We both know that,' she told him, mentally struggling for some way out of a situation which seemed doomed to end in further pain and humiliation for her whatever happened. Silently she stood looking at Maxim. The tension she had been under since she had taken it into her head to go to his apartment had sapped her strength and she began to tremble. With a sigh he moved behind her, putting his hands on her shoulders and gently massaging her neck.

'Stand still,' he commanded softly when she was about to protest. 'You'll find this soothing.'

Obediently Lavinia did as she was told, trying not to think of his cool fingers on the back of her neck as he gently worked at the knotted muscles that were making her head ache.

'Are you all right?' he asked, feeling her begin to relax. 'I can feel you trembling.'

She nodded, swallowing hard. 'Yes. But if you had kept your hands to yourself none of this would have happened,' she said softly, falling silent as he continued to massage her neck, and she knew he was thinking of those few passionate moments prior to Robert entering the room. 'It was very noble of you to tell them you came here to ask me to marry you,' she said on a calmer note, 'but you don't have to hold fast to what you promised. You shouldn't have said it.'

'I know I shouldn't. But the fact remains that I did.'

'And do you mean to keep your word?'

'Yes,' he said. 'Yes, I do. Besides, seeing that I was the one who kissed you, I felt duty bound to save your reputation. After being caught red-handed with you in my arms, I had no choice but to rescue you from the scandal that would be sure to ensue and follow you to England.'

'I didn't ask you to.'

'I know.'

'You are not obliged to marry me, and I certainly don't expect you to. You can reconsider,' Lavinia said, closing her eyes with a sense of ease and well-being, feeling the tension beginning to melt from her body as his firm fingers continued massaging her neck.

'I won't. But listening to you now, I am beginning to think you are trying to dissuade me,' he said softly, his mouth so close to her ear that Lavinia could feel his warm breath on her cheek. 'Have you forgotten so soon that it was you who asked me to marry you? Don't tell me that you've changed your mind.'

'I don't know. What prompted you to say it?'

'Because I couldn't bear hearing the pompous jackass speak to you like that—bullying you in that appalling manner.' He stopped massaging her neck and turned her round, looking down at her steadily. 'And like all bullies he stepped back when confronted with a superior strength.' Maxim smiled crookedly. 'But I meant what I said. I will marry you, Lavinia. You obviously need looking after by someone. But I have to attach a condition—which we must discuss first.' His voice had an ominous ring to it.

Perplexed, Lavinia looked up at him, suddenly wary. 'A condition? What do you mean?'

'We will discuss it, but not now—not here.' Maxim noticed how tired and weary she looked, how pale, and that she was struggling to keep her eyes open. 'When did you last go to bed, Lavinia?'

She shook her head. Sick and weak, she looked at him. 'So much has happened that I can hardly remember. It was the night before the ball, I think.'

'I thought as much. I order you to go to bed and get some rest. Afterwards you must return to my apartment and dine with me. We will talk then. But this time you must not come alone. I am sure Signora

Scalini can spare a maid to accompany you. Do you understand, Lavinia?' he asked when he saw her eyelids begin to droop.

She nodded, looking up at him in defeat, too tired to argue at that moment. The glow of the sun coming in through the open shutters lit up her magnificent eyes, and Maxim succumbed to the impulse which was tormenting him. He kissed her long and passionately, before letting her go.

After Daisy had been told every detail about what had happened and finally left, Lavinia was at last able to think about Maxim, about his character and the way he looked. There was a certain insolence in the way he moved and in the way in which he lifted his proud, dark head. Vigour emanated from him with a vibrancy which set his eyes alight, and softened what might otherwise have been too much darkness in a face that was forbidding in its strong masculinity. Beneath his calm sophistication was a man with many diverse and complex shades to his nature which most men lacked. Hidden deep inside was an innate amusement, watchful, mocking, and a keen perception of his own infallibility.

There was also the fact that he was a gambler. At any other time she would have said that to consider a man with this failing for a husband was absolute madness but, like the gambler *he* was, this was one time she would have to take a chance, even if she risked losing everything.

Chapter Six

Thrown into a turmoil of agitation about returning to Maxim's apartment, Lavinia dressed with care in an oyster satin gown, her only adornment being a single strand of pearls around her throat. The purple and gold of the evening sky was sinking into the lagoon when she arrived at his apartment by boat. She was accompanied by one of the maids, who Maxim immediately sent back to the Scalini residence with the message that he would see Miss Renshaw home himself.

Lavinia gave him a scandalised look, at which he smiled that devastatingly lazy smile of his.

'I think it is permissible for two people who are betrothed to spend a little time alone together.'

Maxim had dressed for dinner in snug-fitting grey trousers and dark green coat, with a grey silk waistcoat and white silk shirt. His black hair gleamed and fell casually over his forehead, giving him a youthful look, and his clear blue eyes set off the deep tan of his skin.

Taking Lavinia's hand, he escorted her inside the apartment, thinking how poised she was, and that her beauty was breathtaking as she moved serenely beside him. This young woman who had captured his senses was lovely—so pure, so virginal—and he was certain that what he saw was a mirror image of what was within. He was achingly aware of how difficult it would be telling her what he had decided.

The candleglow enhanced the beautiful furniture and brought out the rich hues in the Venetian glass objects and the paintings on the walls, creating a warm, intimate atmosphere.

'Do you feel better now you have rested?' he asked.

'Yes. I didn't realise how tired I was.'

'I hope you're hungry. Perkins has been slaving away in the kitchen all afternoon.'

Lavinia gave him a querying look. 'Perkins?'

'My butler, secretary and cook.' He laughed. 'Perhaps I should call him my general factotum. But whatever he is, he has become indispensable to me. He knows all my idiosyncrasies and is sensitive to my every mood.'

Lavinia was surprised to learn he had a butler, having thought him to be in Venice alone. But somehow it seemed appropriate that he had someone to look after his needs. She couldn't imagine Maxim Purnell washing and ironing his own shirts and polishing his own boots.

Maxim seated her at the circular table over which was draped an exquisite cloth of snow-white Burano lace. It had been laid to perfection with silver and crystal, which sparkled in the light. He poured a light, sparkling wine into long flutes and Perkins—a serious-looking man of middle years—appeared with the food. It was delicious and cooked to perfection, and Maxim proved to be the perfect host.

'This is a lovely apartment,' Lavinia commented. 'Have you been in Venice long?'

'No. A few days, no more. I've been travelling Europe myself for the past two months, and I am now on my way back to England.'

'And has your visit to Europe been for business or pleasure?' Lavinia queried, keen to know a little more about the background of this perplexing man. 'I would have thought you were past the age when gentlemen came abroad on the Grand Tour to expand their knowledge.'

'Unfortunately that is so. My reason for coming was mainly business—but it has not been without its pleasurable moments,' he murmured, his eyes coming to rest meaningfully on her face. 'Especially in Venice.' He smiled when he saw a soft flush mantle her cheeks and she lowered her eyes to her plate.

Lavinia sensed that his candid mood did not extend to discussing more about himself. His evasive tone told her that.

'The apartment belongs to a friend of mine who is in Rome just now. Whenever I come to Venice—which is not all that often—I stay with him and his wife.'

Over the meal neither of them mentioned the marriage proposal, the talk being mainly about Venice and the other cities Lavinia had visited in Italy, and during the conversation Maxim asked her about her home in Gloucestershire, quietly observing how her eyes clouded and that she seemed to withdraw into herself. He was curious.

'Did you have a happy childhood?'

She sighed, wistful. 'When I look back I suppose some would say it was somewhat neglected—despite belonging to a wealthy family. My father was a land-owner and a successful businessman,' she explained.

'How was your childhood neglected? In what way?' he probed gently.

'Oh—I was well taken care of, fed, clothed, and educated,' she told him hesitantly.

'You went away to school?'

'Oh, no. Nothing like that. Edgar, my brother, was sent away. He's seventeen now and finishing his education at Oxford. I had a governess.'

'And what was she like? No,' he said, smiling with humour, 'wait. Let me guess. Let me give you my impression of what I imagine a governess to look like. I imagine her to be at least a hundred—terrifying to look at, who rarely speaks of anything other than the rudiments of education and stands over her pupils like some grisly prophet of doom while they work at their lessons.'

'Good gracious.' Lavinia laughed, her laughter sounding like the purest water on glass to Maxim—cool and crystal clear. 'I could not imagine a worse fate than being taught by a governess like that. Miss Leigh was strict but she was not terrifying. She was at Welbourne House for eight years, and was rather elderly—at least that's how she always seemed to me—but she was certainly not a hundred.'

'I was jesting,' Maxim murmured, his eyes twinkling mischievously, strangely unwilling to let her stop talking about her past.

'I know that,' Lavinia smiled in response. 'I remember her as being a strict disciplinarian and an extremely clever woman. Everything she did was carefully thought out and controlled. She was also a robust woman, who was never ill and hated weakness in others. But she was kind to me and a good teacher. She taught me all I know. I have much to be grateful for where she is concerned.'

'And your mother? She is dead, I take it. What was she like?'

A profound sadness clouded Lavinia's eyes, which did not go unnoticed by Maxim, and his curiosity about her childhood deepened.

'I—I never spent much time with my mother—in fact, I can only remember her absent-minded smile whenever she came to the nursery, or on the rare occasions when I was taken downstairs and her eyes would alight on me. Oh, she—she was never unkind, but she was absolutely devoted to my father and focused all her attention on making him happy.'

'But he was not her first husband.'

'No. My mother married my father and came to live at Welbourne House after the death of her first husband—Mrs Lambert's brother. When I came along I think I got in the way of things. I always felt remote from both my parents. Most of my childhood was spent upstairs in the nursery. I can't remember my father ever touching me—although I suppose he must have when I was little. Both my parents were vague figures on the perimeter of my life,' she told him quietly.

'You must have been very lonely.'

'Yes—I was,' she confessed, meeting his gaze. It was one of pure absorption, urging her to confide her innermost secrets, which she found strange, for she had never told anyone how unhappy she had been as a child, not even Daisy. 'My life was as cloistered as a nun's and sometimes I felt as if I were suffocating. It was my parents' indifference towards me that hurt the most.

'When Edgar came along, his arrival drew their interest because they now had a son and heir.' Lavinia looked down at her hands to hide the pain she always felt when she recalled her parents' joy when Edgar had been born. 'They adored Edgar— everyone did,' she whispered quietly, remembering that there had never been any love left over for her. 'They worshipped him. He became the centre of their lives.'

'Are you close to your brother?'

'Yes—very. I wasn't jealous of him or anything like that.'

Maxim nodded, understanding her pain. 'And Julia? Forgive me but I could not help noticing the enmity between the two of you when I saw you together earlier.'

They exchanged a smile. 'You are very perceptive,' said Lavinia, 'but then it wasn't too difficult, was it? Julia and I have never been close—not like sisters should be. She always felt that she never belonged at Welbourne, you see, and always resented

Edgar and me. When we were children her behaviour towards both of us was extremely harsh. Fortunately, she spent most of her time with her aunt, Mrs Lambert, in London, until she married.'

'And her husband?'

'He was killed in a riding accident. Unfortunately for Julia, he left her without a penny and a mountain of debts—most of them settled by my father, who never had much time for her. But he promised my mother before she died that he would always take care of Julia and, despite the way he felt about her, he was not a man to go back on his word. After that she came to live at Welbourne House—and there she will remain until she finds herself another husband.'

'Which is the reason why you will not go back to live there,' Maxim stated quietly.

'Yes. After what she has done, nothing will induce me to reside under the same roof as her again.'

'That I can understand. And Daisy?'

'I regret that Daisy and I didn't meet until we decided to come on this trip to Europe. She's a lovely, warm person. It would be difficult for anyone not to like her.'

'It seems to me that you have had a somewhat lonely childhood at Welbourne House. Were there no other children?'

'No. When Edgar went away to school, it was left to the servants to entertain me. They were kind in their own way, but they were too set in the way of the house to understand an adolescent girl. Looking back, I can see that Cook was my saviour.'

'Oh?' Maxim smiled. 'And what memories do you have of Cook? Happy ones, I hope.'

'Yes. I'm sure I must have got under her feet, but she never sent me away when I visited her while she worked. My happiest memories are of sitting in the rocking chair in the kitchen beside the huge open range, where she used to do all the cooking for the household, and she would tell me stories of her youth. She was married to a sailor who used to sail all over the world, and she would tell me such wonderful and colourful stories of the foreign places he visited—stories which, looking back, I am sure she added extra spice to, embroidering them to make them sound more interesting and exciting to a little girl eager to listen.'

'She must have been a wonderful person.'

'Yes, she was,' she murmured, slanting him a soft smile. 'I remember going to bed at night and lying awake, reliving those stories and imagining myself being transported to all those exotic places she had told me about.'

Maxim listened silently, thinking what a strange and lonely child she must have been, and how she must have yearned for children of her own age.

'So, with the absence of parental interest, and no companion other than an ageing governess and the cook, I can well see what you mean by a neglected childhood.'

'Yes,' Lavinia said gravely, meeting his gaze. 'I suppose it could be described as one of the most unloving and miserable a child could have. But when one is living it, it is not apparent. It is only when it is over that it becomes clear. If I am blessed with children of my own, I shall make quite certain that they do not suffer as I did.'

Maxim listened to her with sympathetic understanding. He himself had been raised in a household with so much love and laughter that he could not imagine being a responsibility grudgingly accepted.

'And has there been no romance in your life, Lavinia?' he asked with the hint of a smile, his eyes fixed warmly on her own. 'No young squire to sweep you off your feet? Discounting the obnoxious Mr Feltham, of course.'

She flushed softly beneath his probing gaze, thinking of Thomas Dorsy and how bright and handsome he'd looked in his uniform when he'd waved her farewell to go to India with his regiment. 'Yes—I admit there was someone—once,' she confessed.

'Tell me about him?'

'Oh, there's nothing to tell really,' she said, her voice soft with memory. 'His name was Thomas Dorsy.'

'From Welbourne?'

'Yes. His father was an old and intimate friend of my family. He was also an eminent lawyer in Welbourne. He wanted Thomas to follow in his footsteps—but Thomas had ambitions of his own.'

'And was he handsome?'

'Very—and he had the merriest, warmest laugh, and the bluest eyes and fairest hair this side of heaven. To my romantic, seventeen-year-old imagination he was Apollo and Lancelot all rolled into one—a thousand times more wonderful than all the knights of King Arthur's round table. No legendary hero could compare.'

Maxim was surprised to find himself resenting and thinking jealously of the young man Lavinia had known before. 'He sounds like the answer to every maiden's prayer. And what happened to this prince among men?'

The question seemed to discomfit her. As if stalling for time she looked straight ahead, fighting a sudden mistiness in her eyes. She waited a moment before answering, and when she did her voice was low, almost a whisper. 'He was a soldier. He—he was killed in some skirmish or other in India.'

'I see. And would you have married him if he hadn't been killed?' asked Maxim quietly, knowing she hadn't loved this young soldier—having told him herself when she had come seeking him out at his apartment earlier that she had never been in love.

'Yes, I think so. There was an understanding between us that we would become engaged when he returned to England.'

'India is a long way away. It could have been years before he returned. What if you had met someone else in the meantime?'

'I don't think so. Thomas expected to be away for less than three years, and I was just seventeen when he went away. His parents grieved terribly over his loss. He was their only child, you see. It was shortly after that when I met and became betrothed to Robert.'

At that moment Perkins—a dark and pensive man of few words—came in to take away the dinner things. Maxim stood up, walking round the table and taking Lavinia's hand.

'The night is warm so come and sit on the balcony for a while—not too long, though. The mosquitoes tend to be keen close to the canals. They hang like a net curtain on the waterfront. Have you been bitten?'

'No. Although I've fared better than Daisy. She seems to be susceptible to bites and stings from every insect imaginable,' she told him, realising that he had smoothly gleaned from her an exact picture of her life, right up to the moment she had been flung into the canal, and yet his own life still remained a mystery to her.

Settling herself in a chair across from him, she breathed deeply. The air was heavily perfumed with the heady smell of lemon-scented magnolias trailing over the balustrade, and hyacinths filling the terracotta pots on the balcony. A sleepy, almost dreamlike atmosphere prevailed over Venice both day and night, as though life lived beyond the weathered walls was somehow set apart.

Using her fan to waft away the tiny insects which came to annoy her she relaxed, content to gaze out over the little canal and up into the star-strewn sky, to listen to the music floating on the air from the many cafes in the squares, and conscious of Maxim's watchful gaze—alert, waiting, and more than ever before she was aware of him as an attractive man as she studied his handsome profile, and how effortlessly he could turn her bones to water.

At length Lavinia broke the silence between them, broaching the subject uppermost in both their minds.

'Before you left me this morning, you said there were conditions to be discussed. What did you mean by that?' she asked, looking across at him. Having removed his coat and neck cloth, his white shirt was partly open to reveal the strong muscles of his throat. A wave of sleek raven hair slanted across his forehead, and his eyes, darkened in the dim light, were full of decision. Propping his ankle on the opposite knee he fixed her with a studied gaze.

'It seems to me that your options are limited, and that a husband is the only possible solution to your problems,' he pointed out, sounding terribly businesslike, Lavinia thought. 'Do you agree?'

'Yes.'

'The way I see it you are desperate to break away from the people you know, and you cannot do that unless you have money, and to acquire your legacy before you are twenty-five you must marry.'

'That is correct—but it sounds rather mercenary when you put it so bluntly. However, the money will naturally be my dowry—and I do realise that a marriage based on such unfortunate and shaky foundations as ours is going to take some working at.'

'That's just it, Lavinia,' Maxim said, looking at her directly, not a muscle of his handsome, authoritative face showing any expression. 'It isn't going to work.'

She looked at him in puzzlement. 'But—I don't understand.'

'You will after I have explained. You will be considerably relieved when I tell you that I do not want your money.'

Lavinia was becoming more bewildered by the second. 'What are you saying?'

'That I will marry you and then—for reasons of my own—petition to have the marriage declared void when we return to England.'

Thrown off her balance, Lavinia stared at him uncomprehendingly. 'Oh—but—I—I don't understand.'

'I'm sorry. I'm not being very subtle, am I? It has to be this way.'

'But—on what grounds?'

'Non-consummation. What else?' Noting that she looked quite bewildered Maxim looked at her quizzically, his brows drawing together in an inquiring frown. 'You do know what that means, don't you, Lavinia?'

She flushed, looking down at her hands in her lap to hide her confusion. 'Yes. Yes—of—of course I do,' she uttered hesitantly, not entirely sure that she did, but so embarrassed that nothing would have induced her to admit it. Her sexual innocence and lack of knowledge regarding the male species had her puzzled. 'But—but why?' she asked, suddenly aware of all the magic disappearing from the night. This wasn't how she had thought it would be—what she'd expected—how she'd wanted it to be. Any romantic plans she'd had were being demolished by him.

'I can't tell you. But that is how it has to be,' Maxim said, having decided not to tell her about Alice or Lucy, knowing she would refuse to go through with the ceremony if he did.

The biggest problem would be telling Alice because, once Julia and the Eveshams returned to England, the scandal about him being caught in a compromising situation with Lavinia and then making her his wife would be bandied about in every assembly room and drawing room in London. It was inevitable that Alice would hear of it from Sophia Evesham, the two of them being friends, and he could imagine her fury. But once she learned he was to seek an annulment, he had no doubt that she would be mollified.

Maxim had every confidence that it wouldn't be too difficult securing a decree of nullity. It could only be obtained by an Act of Parliament and could take up to three years. The cost of a private Act and the related proceedings would be expensive, but not impossible to secure—if it was proved that he and Lavinia had lived apart and that she was as pure as she was now. He would have to make sure that he kept his hands to himself, which would be no simple matter, for she had absorbed his attention completely from the moment he had plucked her from the lagoon.

A tension had sprung up between them and Lavinia rose quickly, standing close to the balustrade and looking down into the dark water of the canal, turning her face away from Maxim's probing eyes in an attempt to hide her feelings, which were pinned to her face for him to see. But she could feel his eyes watching her, his blue gaze seeing and interpreting with great skill.

Trying desperately to hide her shock, disappointment and dismay, Lavinia was oblivious to the boats
going up and down with their passengers. There was
no room in her vision or her heart but this one vast
disappointment. A host of conflicting emotions were
tearing round inside her head, and all of a sudden
nothing made any sense. With a painful effort she
fought to dominate her hurt and disappointment and
accept this blow that fate had dealt her, aware of
Maxim's eyes scrutinising her from where he sat. The
silence between them grew uncomfortable, despite
the noise of the city, and she felt as if she was waking
to a nightmare from a happy dream. How stupid she
must seem to him, how naïve and gullible.

Stiffened by pride, her only feelings being of anger
and hurt pride, her voice was quiet and taut when she
spoke. 'Tell me, Maxim. For what reason did you
say you would marry me?'

She turned and looked at him, and Maxim peered
at her, frowning. Her lovely eyes held a feverish glitter, and he saw that her expression had hardened and
that her slight smile was full of irony.

'I am not so foolish as to think you have fallen
head over heels in love with me—and I am grateful
that you made no false declarations as such,' she said
icily, a cold hand clutching at her heart.

'No, I have no intention of doing so.'

'At least you are honest.'

'I told you that I feel responsible for the way
things have turned out for you. In the eyes of everyone you will be painted a scarlet woman—a shame-

less wanton, with no moral standards. You have broken all the rules that govern respectable society.'

'And Robert?'

'Robert's affair with Julia will not be made public, so you will be the one vilified and shunned, not Robert. I recognised the Eveshams when they arrived to witness our rather intimate embrace, and I know that Sophia is renowned for her spite. On returning to London she will make quite sure that your humiliation is complete. So be content when I say that I am willing to marry you. Let that be enough.'

With eyes blazing Lavinia moved towards where he still sat. There was a nonchalance in the way he looked up at her, which fed her anger. 'What? And be grateful? How dare you pity me!' she cried, her voice shaking with fury, feeling that her humiliation was truly complete.

Maxim rose, her reaction to his terms of marriage and the look on her face wrenching his heart.

Lavinia turned from him and strode quickly across the room, hot, angry tears welling up in her eyes. 'I would like to go now. I'll find my own way back.'

'Lavinia, wait,' he ordered, striding after her. Taking her arm, he spun her round.

She wrenched it from his grasp and glared at him. 'Get off my arm—you—you arrogant, insensitive brute. Let me go.'

'I will not let you leave until you have heard me out,' he said, his hands locking on her shoulders. In the glowing light his face was suddenly grim, his dark eyebrows drawn together in a straight line. 'You're going to listen to me if I have to force you to listen. Stand still, damn you,' he said when she struggled to free herself from his grasp.

She flared up. 'Why?' she cried, her colour high, her eyes ablaze. 'Why should I listen to you? This is madness. All of it. I haven't known you a week and already you are turning my life upside down. I don't even know who you are—and I don't think I want to any more. I find your conditions humiliating and insulting, and I have no wish to hear more. At heart you are no better than Robert and I want nothing from you. Nothing—do you hear?'

'Devil take it, Lavinia,' Maxim shouted in angry frustration. 'All I have done is ask you to marry me— out of concern, not pity.'

'I am quite capable of leading my own life without you. I'll find someone else to marry me,' she announced recklessly. 'For keeps. It shouldn't be too difficult.'

'I don't believe you,' he said flatly. 'Who will you find at such short notice? Another pompous little rat like Robert, who can see no further than your legacy? Oh, yes,' he sneered, 'there will be plenty of men like that ready to jump into his shoes.'

'And why should you care? I am not yours and never shall be.'

'All right—I admit it. I curse the day I became involved with you—but, like it or not, I am involved and I want to help you.'

'I want no favours from you,' she flamed, meeting his gaze squarely, astounding him by the violence of her outburst. 'You—you vile clod,' she lambasted him uncharacteristically, not given to flinging abuse at people and unable to think of a more appropriate word just then.

Maxim arched a sleek black brow, one corner of his finely chiselled mouth quirking into something that looked suspiciously like a grin to Lavinia. '*Clod!* Come now, Lavinia. That's damned unflattering to say to a man who will very likely be staking a great deal to get you out of a fix.'

Lavinia's expression remained wary and antagonistic, and it was then that Maxim saw the pain behind the anger and defiance in her lovely eyes.

'There you go again,' she said scathingly. 'Do you have to gamble on everything?'

'You stubborn little fool,' he murmured, sensing a softening in her attitude. 'I may be a gambler, but I am also a businessman—and I happen to be extremely good at both.'

'And I bet you are acquainted with all the gaming halls in Europe,' she accused with angry derision.

Despite the intended insult in her words, Maxim grinned, feeling extremely tolerant, thinking how lovely she looked with her colour up and her eyes sparking fire. 'Intimately,' he agreed.

'But I thought you lost a lot of money at a ridotto the other night,' she asked, her eyes full of uncertainty.

'What? Enough to make you suspect that I might have put myself in Queer Street and readily jump at the chance to seize your legacy by marrying you?' He grinned. 'No. Although it was enough for it to be noticed and talked about. I don't normally lose such large amounts, but the ridotto was the night after I met you. For some reason which was not obvious to me at the time, I couldn't concentrate. My fingers were all thumbs and I made mistakes.'

Despite her anger, Lavinia was secretly flattered to learn that he had been thinking of her, and yet at the same time appalled that he had lost a large sum of money. 'I hope you are not blaming me for your misfortune at the tables.'

'I wouldn't dream of it,' he laughed. 'Now, what do you say? Will you marry me—and be willing to let me petition for a decree of nullity when we return to England and you have obtained your thirty thousand pounds? Will you allow me to help you?'

'I still don't know why you should put yourself out for me in this way. I am nothing to you.'

Maxim wanted to shake the stubbornness out of her. 'I am doing this because I happen to care about you, damn it—and because I care what happens to you. I am willingly offering you a solution to your problems.' And creating more for myself, he cursed silently because, if she agreed, it would be interesting to see how long he could remain detached from the marriage.

'Have you the remotest idea how humiliated I shall feel when my husband has our marriage declared void? And what will happen to me then?'

'You will have your thirty thousand pounds to begin a whole new life.'

Lavinia sighed, folding her arms across her chest and thoughtfully moving away from him. The truth of what was happening struck her with awesome finality. She had been shamed and humiliated by

Robert beyond endurance and beyond decency, and now here she was, faced with an annulment to her marriage to Maxim before it had even taken place. The very idea revolted her. It was immoral. Her mind revolved in a maddening spiral as she struggled to come to terms with it, because she could see no other option open to her.

'Well?' asked Maxim after several patient moments of watching her pace up and down, waiting for her response, her lovely face set in lines of indecision.

Lavinia stopped pacing and looked across at him, meeting his gaze squarely. He spoke in a businesslike manner, his voice and his expression unemotional, his heart a chilling quagmire of considered assessment, and she was sickened to think that ever since that first moment when he had plucked her from the lagoon and she had opened her eyes and gazed into his, he had seemed to be the incarnation of every romantic hero throughout history, with a disturbing ability to reduce her to the state of a quivering jelly.

Here she was, considering uniting herself with the most handsome man in Christendom, and yet she had never felt more lonely and despairing in her life. The arguments against marrying him rolled back and forth like an endless flooding tide. He pitied her like he would a whipped cur, and he would play his role as saviour heartily, but he did not want her for his wife. Having been the one to seek him out and ask him to marry her she had little to be proud of, and it goaded her to think that if she accepted his offer she must rely on him for his support.

As dearly as she wished to hurl an angry refusal in his face, she restrained herself, hardening her mind. She was about to embark on a meaningless alliance with a man whom she believed was sincere in wanting to help her, but in the end he would want rid of her. And yet he was offering her freedom. Yes, she thought, at least she would have that, and then she could take charge of her own life. Fate had dealt her a cruel blow, but she need not be the victim of circumstance.

She looked at him steadily, her face showing no trace of emotion as, with her head high, her pride and self-respect all that she had left, she answered him.

'Yes. Very well,' she said stiffly. 'I will accept the marriage as only a temporary affair—a marriage in name only—to be annulled as soon as my father's lawyer has released my legacy. I have nothing to lose and much to gain. Misfortune placed me at the mercy of Robert, and I have little liking for the bargain between us—but it is clear that my future lies in financial independence sooner rather than later.' After all, she thought cynically, where had honesty and fidelity got her in the past? 'However, I would like to make a pact. I have conditions of my own.'

Maxim arched an eyebrow inquiringly. 'Which are?'

'That you make no attempt to kiss me again. You will not touch me. You will keep your distance. Is that understood?'

'Perfectly. I was going to suggest it myself.'

In this, as in everything else, Maxim was firmly committed to accomplishing his goal, and he was determined to avoid any further confrontation with her. It would only complicate matters, and he didn't need any further complications. But despite his words and his determination not to allow her to venture too close, he could not resist one last urge to tease. He lowered his eyes and moved to where she stood close to the open balcony, an infuriating amusement dancing in their depths when he paused in front of her.

'But don't tell me you didn't enjoy my kisses,' he said softly, tormenting her senses, his eyes settling on her softly parted lips, 'because I won't believe you.'

Lavinia averted her eyes at the flippant way he referred to something which to her had meant so much. He obviously found it amusing, but she wasn't laughing. She would like to tell him that it didn't mean anything to her either, but she would be lying, and with his infuriating ability of seeming to know exactly what she was thinking, he would know it too.

'Why did you kiss me if you were not serious?'

He shrugged. 'It's a normal physiological reaction in the male species when confronted by a beautiful woman. And I am a keen appreciator in the beauty of women,' he said softly.

Lavinia turned away as heat coursed through her. With her newly acquired knowledge she believed him. The amusement in his blue eyes to something that was so serious to her was unbearable.

'But I cannot deny that I am strongly attracted to you, Lavinia,' he went on, his voice having taken on a note of gravity. Coming to stand behind her, he placed his hands on her shoulders and turned her to face him, looking deep into her eyes. 'In that I am sincere—and if it were at all possible I would not be speaking of petitioning for a decree of nullity.'

A slight, cynical smile touched her lips.

'Why do you smile?'

'I was thinking that for the time we will be together before we are free will be like a masquerade—only without the magic. Rather like a Carnival of Love which turns into a tragedy once the mask is removed.'

'I'm sorry, Lavinia. That's how it has to be. But it need not be a disaster. After a brief encounter—sometimes at first sight—which is what happened between us, the attraction—passion or desire, call it what you like—is as real and as potent as an attraction that develops over a long period of time. I do not like these conditions I have imposed on you, but there are important matters in England that forbid me to enter into a serious and lasting relationship with you—unless, of course, circumstances change and we find ourselves drawn together and mutually agree not to part.'

That was something Lavinia refused to let herself hope for. Swallowing hard against a lump that had risen in her throat she nodded, wondering what could be so important that he was being forced to put a brake on their emotions like this. 'Please don't torment me with words, Maxim,' she begged. 'This is difficult enough for me to handle.'

'I won't,' he promised, his voice filled with finality. 'Of course, if these conditions are not agreeable to you you can still draw back,' he told her. 'What I am offering you is a way out of your predicament.'

'I know. I am grateful—and I am moved by your concern for my well being and future happiness. But you must admit that the circumstances are unusual.'

'I do admit it. Do you object?'

Lavinia shook her head. 'No. All I ask is that you explain it a little more.'

'What do you want to know?'

'How will you secure a decree of nullity to our marriage?'

'Through the Ecclesiastical Courts. They have the power to release parties from the marriage bond on grounds of non-consummation or if the parties are too closely related by blood. Divorce of a valid marriage has to be obtained by a private Act of Parliament, which must be preceded by a separation in the Ecclesiastical Courts. It will be tedious and extremely costly, but I shall take care of that,' he said, aware that the procedure was so expensive that only the wealthy could avail themselves of it. 'It could also take the best part of three years—but I shall see that you get your thirty thousand pounds long before that so you can begin a new life.'

'And you are willing to do that—for me?'

Maxim looked at her, a grim smile touching his mouth. 'Yes. If I had exercised any decency, any restraint over my ardour, I would not have shamed you and made a spectacle of you in front of your relatives and friends.'

'What will my life be like when I am married to you—until I am free, that is? Shall I live with you—in your house?'

'You may live precisely where you choose to live—but not with me. You will be perfectly free. Knowing your circumstances, might I suggest that you go and live with my aunt at Thornhill Farm in Kent until you decide what to do. It's where I was brought up and I think you will like it there. However, I shall ask you to keep the fact that you are my wife to yourself. Apart from Aunt Ursula—who has always been like a mother to me and has a right to know what is happening beneath her roof—for the time being no one else must know.

'It could complicate matters for me,' he said, for he didn't want Alice finding out about his marriage to Lavinia at the risk of incurring her fury, knowing that she was more than capable of denying him access to Lucy. It was inevitable that she would find out some time—when Lavinia's sister and Sophia Evesham bandied it about London on their return—but it would suit him if she found out later rather than sooner. 'Do you understand?'

'Yes. Thank you.'

'Is there anything else you want to ask me?'

She shook her head. 'No. I—I think I would like to leave now.'

'Of course. I will escort you back in the boat.'

'No,' she answered, her voice sounding sharper than she intended. 'If you don't mind—I would rather you didn't.'

Maxim nodded, understanding. 'Very well. As you wish. I will ask Perkins to accompany you instead.'

'Thank you, but I can go back by myself.'

'No. I insist.'

Returning to the Scalini residence, to her surprise, Lavinia found that she was at peace with herself now that her decision had been made to enter into this strange marriage with Maxim Purnell. She felt glad that she had agreed to it. In fact she thought, with cold logic, that it would have been madness to have rejected a match which guaranteed her the chance to live her own life as she chose to live it, while leaving her fully her own mistress. All things considered, things hadn't turned out badly after all.

The scent of wisteria with cascades of delicate mauve blossom was heavy on the night air. Shadows and poles and slowly sinking steps punctuated the sepulchral stillness on the empty canal as the boat drew close to her destination and, apart from the gentle lap of the slick, black water against the walls on either side of them, Lavinia was struck by the silence. The canal was enclosed and dark. Above, there was only the sky, with its disquieting shadows, beyond which lay the dawn. She bent her head backwards and glanced up at the Scalini residence, to see Robert looking down at her from the balcony of his room, which caused a shiver to pass down her spine.

Lavinia and Maxim were married in a quiet ceremony at a little church buried within the heart of

Castello. The only people present were the Scalinis, Mrs Lambert and Daisy, and Tom Player.

Tom looked on in puzzlement. Maxim had explained to him the reasons why he was marrying Lavinia Renshaw but considering he had been contemplating marrying Alice when they had last spoken—after he had paid his uncle a visit on his return to England to reconcile matters between them—it all sounded a bit of a muddle and rather strange to him. Tom had grave misgivings about the whole affair, and he didn't think Maxim would find it as simple as he thought, annulling his marriage to this lovely young woman who came out of the church on his arm as his wife. To his mind she was everything Alice wasn't, and when he saw the glances Maxim cast her way, he very much thought that he was already halfway to being in love with her.

After being severely chastised by Mrs Lambert, Robert could not be persuaded to do the honourable thing and marry Julia. Intending to return to England, he left Venice the day before Lavinia's marriage to Maxim. Mrs Lambert and Daisy were to remain for a further two weeks in Venice, and Lavinia was deeply sorry to say farewell to both. However, she promised to call on them when they returned to their home in London just as soon as it could be arranged.

Angered by the whole affair and humiliated by Robert's treachery, Julia was to remain in Venice with them. On coming back to England, she would return to live at Welbourne House. Unfortunately, her aunt declined to offer her a home with her and Daisy in London, and she had nowhere else to go. Her aunt also thought that living in close proximity to Robert in Gloucestershire might bring him to his senses, and that in the end he would do the honourable thing and marry her.

It was hard for Lavinia to leave Venice, and as the coach rolled on towards the Alps, with a feeling of nostalgia she vowed she would return to the splendid city, a city wedded to the sea and sitting sedately like a grande dame in her golden crown, with her jewel box wide open to the sun. Like a visiting lover she would return.

Chapter Seven

After a long and tedious journey through Europe Maxim and Lavinia arrived at Thornhill Farm, a rambling old farmhouse on the outskirts of the village of Rotherfield in Kent.

When the coach stopped before the front door, Maxim looked at Lavinia, knowing how nervous she was about meeting his large family. 'Try and relax,' he said softly. 'Though you may find living at Thornhill different from your own life in Gloucestershire, remember that these are hard-working, exceptional people. Since the death of my own parents, Aunt Ursula and her family have given me invaluable care and assistance to achieve my goal in life. I am extremely fond of them all, and savour their love and their friendship. You'll like them, I promise you.'

Lavinia smiled at him nervously. When she stepped from the temporary haven of the coach, she would be stepping into a new world, and she would feel very much a foreigner in it. Seeing her hesitation, Maxim got out and put up a hand to help her down.

'If you are ready, Lavinia.'

She nodded, lifted her resolve, and took a firm hold of her courage and his hand.

A tall, handsome woman in a plain black dress came out of the house to meet them, smiling broadly, and behind her Lavinia saw what she could only describe as a sea of beaming faces of adults and children alike. Maxim was immediately enfolded. It was clear to her that they had all been waiting for his arrival, and the manner in which all the children squealed with delight and threw themselves at him in a flurry of arms and legs, told her that they worshipped him.

Never having seen people greet each other with so much joyous abandonment, the happy scene brought tears to Lavinia's eyes. She blinked them aside when Maxim took the tall woman's arm and drew her towards where she stood beside the coach.

Ursula Metcalf had been a widow for five years. Maxim's mother had been her sister. She had four children, two boys and two girls, all of them grown up and married, and all had provided her with grandchildren, eight all told.

'Aunt Ursula, this is Lavinia. I told you all about her in my letter,' said Maxim, looking at his aunt pointedly.

Ursula met his gaze and nodded, understanding that he wanted no one other than herself to know about his marriage to this lovely young woman, and why. 'Welcome to Thornhill, Lavinia,' she said with a gracious smile, looking down into the wide, innocent eyes. 'I do hope your stay will be a happy one. Did you have a pleasant journey?'

'Yes—thank you,' Lavinia replied, finding it difficult hiding her nervousness.

'And has Maxim told you anything about us?'

'A little,' she answered, glancing at Maxim with wide-eyed uncertainty.

Ursula laughed chidingly. 'Is that all? Well—I can see we must remedy that. Come and meet some of the family,' she said, putting a gentle arm around the younger woman's waist and drawing her forward.

'Some?' gasped Lavinia, unable to believe there could be more.

'Yes,' laughed Ursula. 'My sons, Ben and Will, are mending the fences in the far pasture. It will soon be dark so they'll be along shortly. And whenever it's time to eat they always arrive on time,' she smiled pointedly. 'We have a meal ready for you. I am sure you must be famished after your long journey from Dover.'

Lavinia was introduced to children and adults alike, trying to make a mental note of all their names, which, being so many, was no easy matter. Ella and Marion, Ursula's daughters, were married to Paul and Michael respectively, and both were dark and extremely pretty. Margaret, a small woman with auburn hair and an open, warm and friendly face, was Ben's wife, and Stella, who she suspected was the quietest of them all, was Will's wife. Ben, the eldest, lived at Thornhill with his family, and the others lived in their respective cottages close to the farm.

All the children eyed Lavinia with a great deal of interest, and with all the curiosity a stranger produced—especially when the stranger appeared on the arm of Uncle Maxim, who quietly thought her poise and loveliness was breathtaking as she moved amongst them.

The atmosphere inside the house was warm and welcoming, and if anyone was curious about Lavinia's relationship with Maxim, they made no comment and accepted the situation for what it was. They also accepted her, fussing and wanting to please, and Lavinia knew it was not out of conventional politeness, but because this was as they were. When Ben and Will appeared, two well-built young men, the thickness of their girths telling Lavinia that they were overfond of indulging their appetites, they all became seated at the huge table groaning with food in the parlour, where tonight the whole family was assembled for the evening meal in honour of Maxim's presence.

As the meal progressed with much gaiety, Lavinia was entertained throughout in a manner she had not thought possible, and in this relaxed and congenial atmosphere she soon began to feel her nervousness evaporating like the steam from the kettle simmering away on the huge open range. She sat among the family, quiet and shy but at ease, comfortable— studying each and every one of them, and meeting Maxim's unwavering eye every now and then when he looked to see how she was coping with it all.

Ursula, who presided graciously over this happy gathering with a good deal of pride, observed these exchanges and took particular note of how Maxim's features would soften each time they caught his wife's glance, and she smiled quietly to herself. One of her many attributes was intuition, and her intuition told her that her nephew's preoccupation with Lavinia in Venice, and his gallant attempt to befriend her, would lead him along a route he had not bargained on. Maxim thought he would be able to put her out of his life as effortlessly as he seemed to negotiate his many business deals, but Ursula knew it would not be that simple.

After the meal when the families began drifting off to their own homes close by, Maxim settled his gaze on Lavinia.

'I'm afraid that I must be on my way, too.'

Lavinia's eyes flew to his, her heart plunging despairingly. 'You're not staying?'

'No.'

'Maxim has his own house, Lavinia,' Ursula explained, and the sharp, secretive look she cast her nephew did not go unnoticed by Lavinia, but she was too dismayed to read anything into it just then.

'Oh! I—I didn't know. I—I thought—'

'What? That he lived here at the farm? No, my dear. Maxim hasn't lived here for years—although he still looks on Thornhill as his home, don't you, Maxim?'

'You know I do, Aunt,' he confirmed, his eyes shifting with a glowing fondness to the older woman, before bringing them back to Lavinia. 'Walk with me to the carriage, will you, Lavinia?'

Silently she walked beside him out into the night, blinded to her unfamiliar surroundings by the acute disappointment that swamped her, conscious only of the fact that he was to leave her. Perkins was already inside the carriage, waiting with his usual calm aplomb. Maxim paused, his face poised over his wife's, mysterious in the shadows.

'Have you far to go?' Lavinia asked, searching his eyes above her own. They had been together for so long that she was already feeling the wrench of their parting.

They stared at each other in a struggle that racked them both.

'No. I live nearby.' He read the consternation and recognised the worry in her eyes. 'You will be all right here, Lavinia. Ursula will see to that,' he said, soothing her fears as much as he was able.

'Yes—yes, I know.' He seemed the embodiment of unquestioning authority as he stood there, and she wanted to tell him she would miss him, that she thought she was falling in love with him, but that wasn't part of their arrangement—and she clung to the arrangement made between them as a shield.

But deep inside her things beyond her control were combining to make her feel helplessly drawn to him, like his kisses in Venice, which had made her body vibrate to his touch. But she didn't fool herself into believing it had been anything deeper than pure, common, indiscriminate lust that had prompted those kisses, and that to a man as handsome and virile as Maxim, she must be one of the most uninteresting, unattractive women he'd bothered with in his entire life.

Lavinia had married him knowing all that it entailed and that he was never going to make any undying declarations of love to her, and she knew not

to ask him for more than he could give. When she
had her legacy she would quietly disappear from his
life, while trying to keep as much of her heart intact
as she possibly could.

Deftly, Maxim took her slender fingers within his
and lightly brushed a kiss on them, genuinely reluctant to be leaving her, which would have surprised,
delighted, and given Lavinia reason to hope had she
known this. Releasing her hand, he climbed up into
the carriage, and Lavinia watched it disappear down
the dark narrow lane until it was out of sight, though
she could still hear the rattling of the wheels passing
over the uneven road. All of a sudden she was
swamped with desolation, but then she felt an arm
placed gently about her waist and turned to find
Ursula beside her, smiling down at her with understanding.

'Maxim will soon be back. He'll more than likely
ride over some time during the next week or so.'

'Why does he not live here with you any more?'
Lavinia asked, her curiosity about Maxim and his
mysterious lifestyle beginning to get the better of her.

'Because he likes to be completely independent—
but not too independent,' Ursula chuckled softly,
'otherwise he would not have chosen to live within
easy reach of Thornhill.'

'And his mother was your sister?'

'She was. We were very close. She died two years
after her husband—a man she adored. Her death was
a terrible thing to me—and to Maxim. Simply terrible
it was.'

'And was Maxim their only child? He's never mentioned any brothers and sisters to me.'

'Yes he was—and it soon became evident to everyone that he was an exceptionally gifted child, with the amazing ability to learn quickly. He had a thirst for knowledge that left my own children standing—which was why he was sent away to receive the education he deserved. But as you have seen for yourself tonight, Lavinia,' Ursula said, smiling down at her in the dim orange glow shining through the open doorway, 'he did not lack for company as he was growing up. Now—come along inside. I imagine you're tired after your journey. I'll show you to your room.'

Lavinia allowed herself to be taken back inside and up to the room which had been prepared for her, and as she snuggled in bed beneath the feather quilt, she gave a great deal of thought to Maxim and his warm and wonderful family, finding herself looking forward to her first day in this new and strange environment.

Two days later Maxim presented himself at the Winstanley residence in London, where, since his departure for Europe, Alice had resided with Lucy and her stepmother. Caroline Winstanley was an extremely wealthy woman whom Alice's father, George Winstanley, had married two years before his death. Maxim was only slightly acquainted with her, but well enough to know that she had little liking for her stepdaughter.

Being the only one at home, she received him in the drawing room.

'Alice is not at home at present, Mr Purnell,' she told him, seeming pleased to see him.

'I'm sorry. I thought I'd surprise her,' Maxim replied, meeting the direct and intelligent brown eyes of Caroline Winstanley, a small, slim and still-pretty woman, with dark hair peppered with grey and calm features.

'I am expecting her back soon, so if you would like to wait I will order some refreshment.'

'Thank you. Whilst I am waiting perhaps I might see my daughter.'

'I know how eager you must be to see Lucy after so long an absence, but do you mind if I talk to you first? There are certain matters I would like to discuss with you.'

Maxim would have preferred to see his daughter, but his sense of unease and sharp instinct told him that Mrs Winstanley had something on her mind that troubled her. He settled himself in a chair, calmly waiting for her to speak, knowing before she opened her mouth that it concerned Alice.

'You've recently returned from the Continent, I believe,' she said by way of conversation as the maid fussed around with a tray of refreshment.

'Yes. I've been in both France and Italy. With the growing unrest and open insurrection seeming more than likely to be transformed into revolution in France, with a great deal of my money invested over there, I felt compelled to put my affairs in order.'

'I agree that it's all extremely worrying. All the time we get news of disturbances in the French provinces. I do believe the peasants have a grievance and that their want of bread is quite desperate. I can well imagine how the nobles and clergy are all dreading the ideas of liberty which are afloat,' Mrs Winstanley said, handing Maxim a cup of tea and looking with irritable impatience at the maid hovering by the table. 'Thank you, Jenny. That will be all for now.'

When the maid had closed the door behind her, Mrs Winstanley lost no time in coming to the point, her eyes fixed on Maxim's expressionless face. 'I'm glad Alice isn't here because I wanted to speak to you privately. It does concern you, after all.'

Her faint intonation of warning set Maxim on edge. He became guarded.

'What is it? Would I be correct in thinking that it concerns Alice.'

'Yes,' she replied, confirming his suspicion. 'I do not like raising indelicate matters—and I'm sure you will think I'm speaking out of turn—but I cannot be quiet on this subject.'

'Mrs Winstanley,' said Maxim, placing his cup on the table in front of him and leaning forward, resting his arms on his knees. 'I don't think there is anything you can tell me about Alice that I don't already know.'

'Perhaps not. It's just that if you have come here to agree to her terms and heal the breach with your uncle—in which event Alice will agree to marry you—I do hope you know what you're doing.'

Maxim smiled grimly. 'So do I.'

'Ever since she became aware that you are the Earl of Brinkcliff's heir, she has become obsessed with the idea of the title. To rise from simple origins to become her Ladyship, Countess of Brinkcliff—to be envied and admired and to enjoy all the power and privilege that goes with the title—is the summit of her ambition.'

'I know that,' Maxim replied, hiding his thoughts behind a coolly polite façade.

'And yet you will still agree to do as she asks— no, demands—even though it goes against your own judgement?'

Maxim frowned, his expression grave as he considered her question. There was a time when he had been in Italy, when he had seriously contemplated returning to England and becoming reconciled with his uncle and marrying Alice, to try and salvage something out of their relationship for Lucy's sake. The trouble was, he had never expected his decision to be beset by anything as powerful and consuming as Lavinia Renshaw. For the first time in his life he was at the mercy of his emotions, when reason and intelligence were powerless.

'Ever since Alice learned she was to bear my child she's been determined to penalise me because I refused to give in to her every whim—to seek a reconciliation with my uncle. I do realise that if it is the only way I can have Lucy with me, then eventually I must seriously consider her demands—unless I decide to seek legal custody in the courts, which is something I shrink from doing.'

'And if not, then you will make Alice your wife—knowing what she is like? No,' Mrs Winstanley said when he was about to interrupt. 'Please, hear me out while there's time. You know her character—and, much as I hate to admit it, the truth is that she is her father's child,' she said with bitterness. 'Unfortunately I was misled by my late husband before our marriage. I learned very quickly that he cared less for me than he did for my money. Had he lived, I have no doubt that he would have fleeced me of every penny.'

Having known George Winstanley, who had been a small shipping merchant of moderate means, a man of dissolute character who had sought his pleasures in brothels and gambling dens—which was where he met his end in a brawl after being accused of cheating at cards—Maxim knew that what she said was the truth.

'As you—and no doubt the whole of London—will remember,' she continued, 'he came to a bad end—and badness will come out—which is obvious when one looks at his daughter. I can only pray that Lucy has not inherited her mother's bad blood.'

Maxim winced, his eyes turning to blue ice, but he remained still and silent as he let her continue.

'Oh, Alice is beautiful, yes—but her behaviour is quite shocking. There are depths which I am only now beginning to perceive. You probably think I should not be speaking like this about my husband's only child, but I feel I must. I know her mother tried raising her as best she could but, being an only child, she was much favoured by her father, who overruled her mother's discipline. Alice is ambitious and greedy—and the most immoral young woman I know.'

Maxim listened to her quietly. He knew she was telling the truth, but still he waited, knowing there was more to come. Mrs Winstanley would not have gone to all this trouble if it was merely to refresh his memory as to Alice's character.

'Immoral? Kindly explain to me what you mean by that?' Maxim glanced towards the door, thinking he heard a footstep out in the hall, but he thought no more about it as Mrs Winstanley went on.

'She is not normal. Alice brings degradation and destruction to all who come under her spell.'

'That's harsh speaking, Mrs Winstanley.'

'And not without foundation, I do assure you, Mr Purnell. It is my belief that she was born wanton—dangerous, even—and she seems to go out of her way to shock people.'

'Then why do you remain in the same house as Alice?'

Perched straight backed on her chair, Mrs Winstanley gave him a direct, meaningful look. 'You have a daughter living in this house, Mr Purnell.'

Maxim's face tightened. 'What are you saying? That Lucy is not cared for?'

'That is precisely what I am saying. Alice spends all her time shamelessly gallivanting about London on the arm of an assortment of men with disgraceful reputations. Often she does not come home until the next day and frequently brings one of them with her. Her present, most ardent, admirer is Sir Francis Newbold—another is Claude Lauriston, the Comte de Chemille, who is presently in London. They are both dissolute gamesters, and quite infatuated with her. But it is the French comte who, I might add, is almost twice her age, and has proposed marriage to her. Are you acquainted with him?'

'I am, although he cannot be counted among my friends.'

'He intends returning very soon to his château in Normandy if things remain as they are over there. The implications of this could prove disastrous to yourself if you do not agree to Alice's terms.'

Mrs Winstanley searched Maxim's features, expecting a reaction, but there was nothing, except for a muscle that began to twitch in his jaw at the mention of the Comte de Chemille.

Inside Maxim seethed. The mere thought of Alice's name in connection with this man—a blackguard, wild and with the reputation of a sewer rat— sent his temper soaring, but not out of any feeling or concern for Alice. She could associate with whomsoever she damned well pleased, just as long as she kept them away from Lucy. However, Maxim had reason to be alarmed. In her determination to marry well, Alice might decide to accept the Frenchman's offer of marriage if he did not marry her himself.

'I take it you have no liking for the Comte de Chemille either, Mr Purnell.'

'None. Strip away his fine title and you are left with nothing. It is because of his indolent, arrogant breed, their determination to cling on to the old, oppressive feudal regime and their refusal to engage in trade, that France is crumbling. The Comte de Chemille is unconcerned that privilege has become a burden, that people starve because they cannot afford to pay the soaring food prices, that the taxes are intolerable.'

'Which, by all accounts, is why they are rebelling and refusing to pay the taxes—even going so far as to attack their lords' châteaux, and in many cases setting fire to them.'

'That is happening. In the wake of the peasants' refusal to pay dues, like many other aristocrats, Claude Lauriston may be returning to his château to reassert his authority. One obvious means would be to starve his villagers into submission by cutting down unripe corn—which, by all accounts, promises to be abundant this year after two failed harvests.' He smiled slightly. 'I'm sorry. These are matters I normally discuss with my business managers, not ladies whose houses I visit. Tell me about my daughter. How is she?'

'She is well enough—if somewhat withdrawn and quiet. She is not an outgoing child at the best of times, and is developing a somewhat nervous disposition.'

'And is Alice not concerned about this?'

'Alice is not concerned about anything other than her own needs, Mr Purnell. She has little to do with her daughter,' Mrs Winstanley told him bluntly. 'Lucy is often sent to stay with her sister in Surrey because she doesn't want to be troubled with her. Miss Sharp—the nurse she employs to look after her—has sole charge and the responsibility that goes with it. Alice tolerates Lucy—so long as she gives her no trouble.'

'And Miss Sharp? What is she like?'

'Middle-aged—and terribly strict. I do the best I can, Mr Purnell, but Alice resents my interference in what she frequently reminds me is the nursemaid's domain. I may be her stepmother—who, I might add, pays for most of her extravagances since her father left her with very little money—and while I am aware that I occupy a position of some influence, where Alice's favour is concerned it is nothing but a fragile flame.'

Maxim's mind acknowledged what Mrs Winstanley was telling him, and for some reason Lavinia's face intruded into his memory. He recalled her telling him of her own upbringing, of how she had been a responsibility grudgingly accepted by her parents— neglected and unloved, spending years in virtual solitary confinement while attention had been lavished on her younger brother. Maxim had seen for himself the forlorn look in those wonderful eyes of hers, and had been moved and saddened by it. There was no way on God's earth that he would allow the same thing to happen to his daughter.

'My advice to you, Mr Purnell, is to obtain custody of Lucy through the courts. It will mean accusing Alice of being an unfit mother, but it will be worth it if it will remove the child from her influence. You must forgive me if I mention your uncle in this instance—it is not my wish to interfere or to offend you, you understand—but perhaps if the two of you were to become reconciled, your position as the next

Earl of Brinkcliff would become much stronger and carry more influence with the courts.

'You must realise that if you don't agree to marry Alice, there is every possibility that she will marry the Comte de Chemille and take Lucy with her to live in France. In which case, access will be difficult for you—and if revolution does break out, the consequences could be dire.'

Maxim tensed, having already thought of this himself. He nodded thoughtfully. 'Yes. I do realise that, Mrs Winstanley, and I must thank you. I appreciate you telling me this.'

At that moment they both looked towards the door when it opened. Alice stood there, poised and as beautiful as Maxim remembered, but there was a hard, feral glitter in her green eyes when they came to settle on her stepmother.

'Thank you for entertaining Maxim for me, Caroline. But, as you can see, I am home now, so please leave us,' she said, dismissing her stepmother as she would a servant.

Without haste Caroline stood up and looked at Maxim, who had also risen and towered over her. 'Goodbye, Mr Purnell,' she smiled. 'It's been nice to talk to you.'

Maxim nodded, his face grim as he watched her go out, leaving him alone with Alice. His eyes became riveted on her, and she almost cringed before him—almost, but not quite.

'This is an unexpected pleasure, Maxim. Your trip to Europe was satisfactory, I trust? I see you so rarely these days,' she complained petulantly.

Maxim raised a dark eyebrow. 'I wasn't aware that you wished my company. However, you do not look surprised to see me, Alice,' he said, suddenly remembering the furtive footsteps he had heard out in the hall earlier. 'You have several faults, but I did not realise that listening at doors was one of them.'

Alice did not deny that she had overheard some of what her stepmother had been discussing with him—although not the last part when Caroline had told Maxim to become reconciled with his uncle, in the hope that, as the future Earl of Brinkcliff, his position to obtain custody of Lucy through the courts would increase his chances considerably. Knowing this, Alice's vicious, scheming mind would wield an indiscriminate blade.

Alice sighed somewhat wearily as she sauntered purposefully towards him, a petulant droop to her bottom lip. 'I do hope you're not going to believe what she says, are you? I'm not nearly so wicked as she wants you to think. Caroline has detested me since the day she married my father. Sometimes I really do wish she would take up with someone else and leave.'

'And what would you do without her money to finance your extravagant lifestyle, Alice? Your father left you little enough to live on for you to enjoy yourself in the manner to which you have become accustomed.'

'Now you are being unkind,' she pouted, lowering her eyes and running a finger slowly up his chest. There was a hardness to his voice which made her uneasy.

Having dressed with care earlier to go for a carriage ride through St James's Park with Sir Francis, with her lavender silk dress cut revealingly low and her full breasts swelling invitingly over the top, knowing just how lovely and irresistible she looked, Alice stood close beside him. Maxim's appreciation of beautiful women had once assured her success, but now she had a distinct feeling that it was not going to prove as easy as she expected.

Maxim admired her beauty; indeed, what sighted man would not. She had skin as white as alabaster, hair as black as midnight and a figure to rival Venus. The soft blend of her sultry perfume enveloped them both in an invisible cloud, and when she gazed at him, her lips parted in that self-assured smile of invitation he remembered well, a smile which at one time would have sent his senses spiralling and the blood pumping rapidly through his veins.

Alice was all temptation and he had denied his body such pleasures for many months, but he made no move to touch her. She made Lavinia seem like an angel. He saw a hard gleam in the depths of her slanting eyes, a gleam that belied the soft feminine allure. It wasn't attraction he saw, but a cold-hearted calculation that turned his blood to ice.

'If you listen to Caroline's malicious lies it will ruin everything. I heard what she was saying about Sir Francis, Maxim—and I must tell you that he means absolutely nothing to me. He merely keeps me amused. However, Claude Lauriston, the Comte de Chemille, is quite another matter...' she preened

'…and it is true that he is besotted with me and has proposed marriage.'

'And you have become well acquainted with the Comte?'

'But of course. After all, a woman needs an escort.' Alice's eyes narrowed and glittered. 'Do you see him as a threat?'

Maxim's face tightened with distaste. 'No. More of an inconvenience.'

'Maxim,' she reproached, pretending offence by his harsh tone, 'you have to trust me. It's important that you do. Please don't think I'm the sort of person Caroline accuses me of being. Of course I have gentlemen friends—and I flirt a little bit. I admit it. But now you are back I shall devote all my time to you. What are your intentions?'

'You mean, are they strictly honourable?' he returned imperturbably. 'I haven't come back with my tail between my legs, if that's what you were hoping.'

'No,' she said icily. 'I can see that. Perhaps you would like Lucy and I to return to live with you at your house in Grosvenor Street?'

'No, Alice. Lucy, yes. Not you. I've had three years to consider my intentions where you are concerned, but that is in the past. My prime concern now is Lucy. She is my present and my future. That I have not lost sight of,' he assured her.

'And you have made up your mind that I have no place in your future?'

'Yes,' he answered calmly, knowing his answer would not have been so firmly spoken had his life not become enmeshed with Lavinia's. He wondered how Alice would react if she knew he was already beginning to look forward to a future that included the woman he had married, knowing Lavinia would be as surprised as he was by the revelation.

However, he wasn't ready to reveal his marriage to Alice unless he had to. The Lamberts and Julia intended extending their time in Italy for a further two or three weeks, and the Eveshams were not expected back in England for at least another month, so he was confident that their secret was safe for the time being.

Alice's eyes glittered like shards of glass. 'And if you think I'm going to let you take Lucy and cast me off like a soiled bedsheet, then think again, Maxim. You will leave me with no choice but to marry Claude.' She tossed her head haughtily. 'I have a fancy for him, anyway.'

Maxim's look was bordering on contempt. 'Come now, Alice. This is me you're talking to—the man who knows you too well. I don't believe you have a fancy for anything or anyone except furthering your ambition.'

Sensing that she was in danger of sliding further down the ladder, Alice tried to soften her features. 'You are the one I am bent on marrying, Maxim—the father of my child.' She pressed herself against him and threw back her head to give him the full benefit of her beauty, a calculating expression in her eyes and a sly smile curving her lips. 'Come now—you do still want your daughter, don't you?'

'Damn you, Alice,' he said fiercely. 'You know I wouldn't be here if it weren't for Lucy.'

'I don't believe you. You do care for me—and I can't help thinking of you. I care for you more than you realise.'

'If you cared for me you wouldn't give a damn about a title.'

'But if we marry you must see it's important. It cannot be ignored.'

'You ask too much. You must realise by now that I will not be pushed, cajoled or manoeuvred into any-thing by you or anyone else. From the moment you made yourself available to me you have worked to this end. How galling it must be for you, when I refuse to succumb to your demands as you expected I would,' he said coldly.

'Yes, it is, but it isn't too late,' she persisted. 'The first step to respectability would be for you to marry me.'

'No,' he said, and there was a cold finality in his voice that struck Alice hard. She winced, seeing cru-elty in his merciless stare. 'I will not be manipulated or gulled into marriage. The truth is that you would be a pitiful excuse for a wife and I want none of it. You no longer interest me. You're spoiled, demand-ing and irrational. If I were to marry you our lives together would be a mess—my own a nightmare.'

Undeterred, Alice tilted her head back a little fur-ther, her body touching his. 'Kiss me, Maxim,' she murmured in an attempt to weaken him.

With a glower of contempt he shoved her aside. 'Stop it, Alice. You've already used every feminine ploy in existence on me, but it won't work,' he growled, making a deliberate attempt to alienate her by moving away.

'You had no objections before Lucy was born, as I recall.'

'You were undeniably appealing—to me,' Maxim pronounced, his gaze mocking, 'and how many others? You, Alice, are promiscuous and a slut.'

Alice's eyes narrowed viciously. Deep inside she was simmering with rage that he dared to cast her off like a common whore—and that he firmly refused to be drawn on the subject of his title. Ambition burned in her. During the last few years many noblemen had propositioned her to become their mistress, but only the French comte had offered her marriage.

Claude was no longer a young man and certainly nowhere near as handsome as Maxim. Nor could his wealth come anywhere close. Money was important to her, but more importantly she wanted position—and Maxim could give her both. His stubborn determination to remain alienated from his uncle added to her frustration. She had broached the subject many times, confident that he would weaken one day, but this time she sensed there was a change in him. She could feel her position in his life slipping away and she didn't like it. She recalled the day when she had given birth to his daughter and how she had cursed because she had not given Maxim a son. If she had, her power over him would have been considerably greater.

'And I suppose you're going to accuse me of being an unfit mother after listening to Caroline's spiteful outpourings.'

'You're an unnatural mother. A cat would be a better mother than you. Whatever differences there are between us, Alice, I will not permit you to destroy Lucy's happiness. Good Lord, do you think I'm going to stand by and watch her being influenced by you—to grow up and associate with the kind of riff-raff a decent woman would not be seen dead with? I'll do whatever it takes to secure her future. I want the best for her, which is why I think she will be better off living at Rotherfield with me.'

Alice clenched her fists by her sides and glared at Maxim hard. 'No. Never. Lucy is my daughter. She stays here with me.'

Maxim looked at her, his stance menacing. 'Spare me your concern, Alice. You've no love for Lucy. Ever since she was born you've scarce looked at the child. You've resented her since birth because she wasn't the son you desired—which would have made your hold over me even greater. Nevertheless, I have a right to see my daughter and I would like her to come to Kent for a few days. I hope you have no objections to that?'

'Lucy!' she sneered. 'That girl is all you care about. If you want to play nursemaid then go ahead. I'll send her down to Rotherfield with the woman I employ to look after her.'

'Thank you. And now may I see her? After all, she is the reason why I came.'

At three years old Lucy was everything Maxim could have wished for in his daughter. He always treasured the time he spent with her. She was his child, his blood was in her veins, and she had her being because of him. She was an intelligent, raven-haired little bundle of high spirits, whose blue eyes sparkled with trust and light—at least they had, before he'd left England. Now, as he entered the nursery and saw her in a green linen and lace gown and starched cap perched on her glossy curls, playing quietly by herself with some wooden bricks, the heart-breaking void in her wide eyes wrenched his heart.

He coolly acknowledged the nursemaid, who was sewing at a table close to the window. She rose when he entered and bobbed a little curtsey. 'It's all right, Miss Sharp. Attend to your duties. I'm here to see Lucy. Lucy?'

On hearing his voice Lucy's head jerked up, her eyes seeking his. His own glistening with emotion, after placing a long beribboned box on the table in the centre of the room he immediately swept the little girl up into his arms.

'Papa!' she gasped, as she was caught up in an emotion-ridden embrace.

'Hello, princess,' he murmured, his lips pressed against her soft cheek. 'I hoped you'd be downstairs to welcome me.'

'Mama doesn't like it when I go downstairs,' she said quietly. 'I have to learn to be good and not to make noise.'

Anger flowed hot through Maxim's veins, which he contained with effort.

'Have you come to take me home?'

'Not yet, princess. Not today. Papa has things to do. But in a day or so you're coming to my house in Kent to stay for a while. Would you like that?'

'Ooh, yes. Will Mama come too?'

'No. Just you and Miss Sharp. I want you all to myself. Now, give me a kiss, and, if it's a really nice kiss, maybe I'll find a present for you.'

Lucy immediately obliged. Flinging her arms about his neck, she kissed his cheek resoundingly.

'Let's see what we have here,' said Maxim, sitting at the table and cradling her on his knee. 'I've brought you a very special present all the way from Venice.'

'Venice? Is that a long way away?'

'Very,' he laughed. 'It's a beautiful town in Italy, full of enchanting palaces and built in the water. One day I'll take you there and show you.' Holding her lovingly, he helped her little fingers untie the ribbon and pull the lid away.

'Oh, Papa,' she gasped, her eyes big and round with delight when she saw the exquisite china doll lying on a bed of white satin. It had glossy blond curls and was dressed in a gown of silver and white lace, and came complete with petticoats and more gowns, and all the paraphernalia necessary to complete the wardrobe of a lady of quality. 'She's beautiful.'

'I think so too. What will you call her?'

This was an important decision for Lucy to make. She thought hard for a moment, and then said decisively, 'Angel—because that's what she looks like.'

'I think Angel is a very nice name, Lucy,' Maxim agreed, clasping her in a hug.

Maxim's return journey to Rotherfield Hall was spent in indecision, but by the time the carriage passed through the tall iron gates, he knew he would not, could not, form any kind of union with Alice. A vision of Lavinia's glowing eyes and entrancing smile drifted into his mind— his wife in the eyes of man and God. He knew now that he was not prepared to let her go and determined to use every method of persuasion to make her stay. He smiled, already looking forward to it.

Chapter Eight

At Thornhill Lavinia wrote a lengthy, tactful letter to her brother at Welbourne House, explaining all about her decision not to marry Robert, and—making no mention of Julia—that their parting had been mutual. When she went on to tell Edgar about her marriage to Maxim, she was too embarrassed to write that her husband intended ending their union as soon as possible, so she left it out. Knowing Edgar, despite his youth he would be outraged on finding his sister being treated so abominably, and would appear at Thornhill and demand to know the reason why.

Lavinia settled down and enjoyed the life on the farm. She loved the close companionship of the other women, and found the children scampering about all over the place on their sturdy little legs adorable. She would play their simple games and, when one or another of them plopped themselves into her lap when they were worn out, read them stories, of which she had a multitude. Wide-eyed they would listen, enraptured. Their happy, smiling faces and spontaneous laughter often made her want to cry. Had she ever

173

looked like that? she wondered poignantly. She didn't think so.

The way of life at Thornhill was delightful, and she knew that when the time came for her to leave it would tear her apart. But she couldn't stay. She would have to face it eventually. But never had she felt so close to so many people—to a family; it made her realise how much she had missed as a child, and why Maxim, aware that her childhood had been starved of affection, had brought her here.

Lavinia had been at the farm for four weeks when she wandered into one of the small hay barns to look at the litter of six puppies Bess, the black and white collie dog, had given birth to three weeks before. Having found their legs, the puppies were tumbling about all over the place. Sitting contentedly in the hay she watched them, delighting in their antics. Counting only five, she frowned and began looking around for the one that was missing, having gone further afield to explore.

Hearing a soft mewling coming from beneath the hay she scraped it away from the wall. Seeing a hole in the stonework she knew immediately that the puppy had somehow found its way through and couldn't get out. With Bess looking on with a good deal of interest as she kept sniffing and whining at the small opening in at attempt to entice the puppy out herself, she drew the dog aside and put her hand inside, tentatively feeling around. Her fingers came into contact with all manner of debris, but she was unable to locate the small furry bundle.

Lying on her stomach to enable her hand to reach further into the hole, she breathed a sigh of relief when she felt it, but the little monster didn't seem to want to be caught and wriggled itself free. In exasperation she pulled her arm out, considering asking one of the men for assistance. Raising her head, a sudden gasp escaped her lips when she saw Maxim standing in the doorway silhouetted against the light behind him. With his arms folded over his chest and his shoulder propped casually against the door jamb, he was watching her with a lazy smile.

The anger caused by his visit to Alice was gone, gently alleviated by his journey to Thornhill and, to a greater extent, by his desire to see Lavinia, and the amusement he felt as he watched her lying on her belly in the hay trying to wrestle the puppy out of the hole in the wall. His lips quirked in a half-smile as he watched her trying to get hold of it, speaking softly as she tried to coax it out.

At first he had been sorely tempted to go and help her, but it would have deprived him of the pleasure of watching her from his vantage point by the door. Until that moment he had never thought so much pleasure could be derived in simply watching a woman who was oblivious to being watched.

'Maxim!' she gasped, aware of how she must look to him. She had been so engrossed in what she was doing that she hadn't heard him come in.

Maxim's gaze was long and sure, and Lavinia found herself unable to move as she feasted her eyes on his handsome face, thinking how casual he looked dressed in a loose white shirt tucked into cream-coloured breeches that hugged his narrow hips, and disappeared into brown leather riding boots. For the past month he had occupied all her waking moments and she had longed for the time when he would come to Thornhill, having hoped he would have done so before now.

Swallowing uneasily, she was disturbed by his sudden presence and the scorching heat of his perusal in the quiet stable smelling of warm hay. He was lithe, powerful of hard sinew and rippling muscle, his shining black hair falling in an unruly casual sweep across his forehead. The atmosphere was sultry, and tiny insects and dust spiralled in the thin shaft of light shining in through the small window festooned with cobwebs.

'Ursula told me I might find you here,' he murmured, moving towards her. He felt a sharp stab of discomfort as he admired the way she looked in the shimmering light lying in the hay. Her body spoke invitation with every graceful movement, and he allowed his eyes to wander in a drowsy inspection, savouring every facet of her beauty, unable to drag his gaze from the vision of her loveliness so temptingly displayed. Dressed in a simple pale blue gown, her hair spread loose about her shoulders with bits of hay sticking to the luxuriant golden tresses, he realised with a startling awareness how much he had missed her these past four weeks—and how much he wanted her.

'I—I didn't hear you come in,' Lavinia said, her face flushed from her exertions and her embarrassment at him finding her lying in such complete disarray. She was quite put out that he had been silently watching her and had made no effort to alert her to his presence. 'You should have made your presence known to me.'

'What! And deprive myself of the pleasure of watching you?' he murmured.

Reddening profusely beneath his deepening grin, Lavinia averted her gaze, considering it best to ignore his comment. 'One of the puppies has disappeared into this hole. I can feel it but it stubbornly refuses to come out.'

'Here, let me have a go.'

Sitting beside her in the hay and half-lying, he thrust his arm inside the hole, his expression one of studied concentration while he groped around. Suddenly he smiled and withdrew his arm, a wriggling pup covered in dust in his hand. After giving it a brief rub down and making quite sure it was unharmed, Maxim returned it to the others in the warm nest Bess had made for them in the hay, where she proceeded to lick it vigorously.

Kneeling and peering into the nest, her cheeks adorably pink, Lavinia reached out and gently stroked the velvety coats of the puppies huddling round their mother.

'Are you enjoying your time at Thornhill?' Maxim asked.

Lavinia turned her head and looked at him, tucking her hair behind her ear in a casual gesture that made Maxim's pulses leap. 'Yes—very much,' she answered, again focusing her attention on the pups, whilst remaining acutely aware of her husband's continued gaze where he sat close beside her in the hay.

'I thought you would,' he murmured.

After a moment Lavinia glanced up at him and caught him watching her. 'Maxim.'

'Yes.'

'Why are you staring at me?'

'Because I can't help it.' Lavinia smiled then, the first genuine, unrestrained smile she'd given him since entering the barn, and it had a radiance that made his heart quicken. 'And because you have a beautiful smile,' he said quietly, gently tracing the curve of her cheek with a stalk of hay. Driven to the brink of distraction, every nerve in his body was aware of her sensuality.

'Have you come to tell me we are to go to London to visit my father's lawyer, concerning my legacy?'

'If that is what you want—but when you hear what I have to say, you might agree with me that it is no longer necessary.'

'Oh! It all sounds very mysterious. What are you saying?' she asked curiously.

Maxim grinned, a wicked glint in his eyes. 'All in good time,' he murmured, raising his hand to touch her tumbled hair. He spoke softly, but there was something in his eyes, a softness, a glowing, that made Lavinia's heart beat wildly. Glancing at him from beneath her long, curling, sooty lashes, her smile stayed on him, and he basked in its warmth. 'What are you thinking?'

Lavinia sighed, hugging her knees and looking at him softly. 'I was thinking that life is so very strange.

Everything can be so straightforward every day and all the people you know can be so predictable—and then, in the time it takes to blink an eye, everything can change.'

'You mean like tumbling into the Venetian lagoon,' he teased gently.

'Yes. Do you regret being on board the ship that day when I was thrown from the boat?' she asked him.

The serious look in her eyes, which were soft and limpid like two dark blue pansies, was Maxim's undoing. They were pulling him inexorably into their depths, and he wanted nothing more than to wrap himself in her sweetness. From the moment he had first laid eyes on her, all the days of self-denial, of wanting her, that he had lived through in frustration, had tested his restraint far beyond any limit. Surrendering to the call of his blood, he moved with unconscious thought and answered her question with his mouth, pulling her down into the hay and sliding his fingers into her wealth of hair.

'Maxim—please don't,' Lavinia begged, making a feeble attempt to push him away. 'No one's ever—'

'Hush, my love,' he breathed, his lips against her mouth, his eyes dark and sombre with passion. 'I know—I know,' and he placed his lips on hers, unable to tear himself away.

At that moment Maxim didn't care about their agreement or the consequences. His only desire was to hold her, to kiss her, to make her his wife in the true sense and to hell with the consequences, and the way she was responding, with such tender sighs, pressing herself closer, kissing him with a confidence and total lack of shyness that would have astounded her had she stopped to think, he knew she would take no persuading to forget their agreement either.

Lavinia moaned with pleasure when Maxim sucked the sweet breath from her mouth, telling himself to go slowly, to be content with whatever she was willing to permit, but desire so primitive and potent poured through him when he felt the length of her body moulded to the hardened contours of his own that he found it virtually impossible. Slowly her hand travelled upwards, over his shoulder to the nape of his neck, her slender fingers slipping through his hair. Maxim's mouth slid in a line from her lips to the soft flesh of her throat, venturing further to more tantalising ground.

With her head thrown back and the hay rustling softly beneath them, Lavinia gasped as his kisses progressed with a feathery lightness, but she was unprepared for the salvo he was about deliver to her senses when his hand slipped inside her bodice and drew her breast out, his mouth covering her nipple and beginning to explore with a feverish hunger. His bold tongue tormented and teased, and he was delighted when he felt the soft pink bud harden.

With a silent moan Lavinia was shocked at the things he was doing to her, but she was powerless to stop him. Her skin began to glow and tingle as his lips continued their sweet torture. They were moist, warm and gentle, kissing her brow, her cheeks, her lips, exploring boldly, and she felt her nipples begin to throb and swell and long threads of warmth begin to radiate from them. New sensations and heat went staggering through her as Maxim continued his assault, and it was all done with an intensity and absorption that had her trembling.

The fire that had been building inside her exploded into flames. Beneath his caress her body, her breasts, were beginning to throb with a sweet pulsating ache as she continued to permit, to welcome and enjoy, the invasion of his tongue as it flicked over her exposed flesh, and when his mouth found her mouth once more, she parted her lips to receive his kiss. What he was doing to her was unlike anything she had ever known. It was like floating on a cloud of dangerous and terrifying sensuality, where she had no control over anything.

A desperate need became a torment inside Maxim, and he knew he had to stop now before he went too far. Deeply touched by the exquisite sweetness of her surrender, he dragged his lips off hers, his mouth hovering above hers, bruised and moist after their kiss. He stared at her dewy skin, at her eyes turned dark with passion, with a hunger that almost made the notion of forgetting their agreement and making love to her there and then in the hay seem too inviting to resist.

Lavinia looked so very sultry and seductive, lying there beneath his gaze, breathtakingly alluring, her lips curved in a sublime smile. Half-lowering his eyelids, his gaze passed over her with deliberate slowness, devouring every detail of her, pausing at length on her lips.

'Dear Lord! You are too damned beautiful to be true,' Maxim whispered, his lips nuzzling her ear, his voice thick with passion. 'It's torture for me just to look at you. You, my dear wife, are a brazen wench. I have been seriously deceived. I thought you as innocent as a new-born lamb. I knew as soon as I looked at you that you were something special. Just how special I am now beginning to realise.'

Lavinia's soft perfume mingled with the warm-smelling hay, sending his senses reeling. Once again his lips found her throat, and the force of passion building inside him threatened to crumble the wall of his restraint. Taking her hand and gently placing his lips on her moist palm, he sighed before looking at her, his eyes smouldering.

'I have missed you.'

'Have you? I'm glad to hear it.'

'You do realise that this wasn't part of our agreement, don't you?'

'Yes,' she breathed, her huge dark-lashed eyes lustrous and warm.

Lavinia's skin had blushed to the colour of a soft pink rose—a flower well worth cultivating, Maxim thought as a leisurely smile lifted the corner of his mouth. 'I find seducing you extremely pleasurable. Despite our agreement, my dear wife, I find I cannot treat you with the impartiality I should.'

'Do you mean you regret our arrangement?'

'No. I will say that I have decided to take our marriage a stage further—that I have a far better arrangement in mind,' he said, his mouth returning to savour her lips. After an eternity he raised his head on a sigh. 'No matter what I said when I agreed to our marriage, my sweet, it does not change the fact that I want you.'

Much bemused, Lavinia looked at him, welcoming this change in him, but surprised and unable to understand it.

Maxim noticed her puzzlement and again placed his lips in the warm, soft hollow of her throat where a pulse throbbed just beneath her flesh. His hollow laugh held a trace of mockery. 'You see, I have become quite entangled in my desire for you, Lavinia. You have captured my attention like no other woman has in a long time.'

Lavinia leaned on her elbow, looking down at him. 'I am surprised.'

'Oh?'

Her eyes twinkled mischievously. 'I would not have taken you for a love-smitten swain.'

'Neither would I,' he chuckled, pulling her back down into the hay.

'Maxim,' she gasped. Sensing he was about to become carried away again she placed her hand on his shoulder and forced him back a little, despite his resistance. She looked at him in desperate appeal for him to stop kissing her so that she could make sense of all this. 'I don't understand what you are saying— what it means.'

He sighed. 'Are you so casual about the way you look—the way you are—that you are not aware of the effect it has on me? I am no saint, Lavinia. The very sight of you, the feel of you in my arms, knowing you are my wife, wrenches at my insides, twisting

them so painfully that my whole body aches for release. My passion for you is hard-driven. I crave to
have you as my wife—in my bed.'

Gnawing on her bottom lip, she gazed up at him.
'Are you telling me that you no longer want to end
our marriage?'

'Do you?' he murmured, the warm light of desire
in his eyes as he lowered his head, his kisses playing
tantalisingly upon her lips.

'Please don't be evasive, Maxim.'

Lavinia sighed when he continued to kiss her. He
was being quite impossible.

Hearing the plea in her voice, Maxim raised his
head and smiled down at her. 'All right. I will tell
you that lying here with you in my arms, feeling how
willingly you respond to my attentions, makes me
unwilling to release you. I know I am bound by our
agreement made at the beginning, but it will be hard
for me to break the vows we made to each other and
before God.'

'I know,' Lavinia whispered. Having been brought
up in the church, this troubled her also. She had been
uneasy about the whole affair from the start.

'We gave our sacred vows to each other in
church—that we would remain man and wife until
death do us part. Even though our marriage has not
been consummated—and we did not intend for it to
be—are we not bound by our vows? I think those
vows, made before God, supersede any agreement we
made.'

Looking at him, Lavinia was bewildered by this
sudden change in their situation. However, she wel-

comed it wholeheartedly. Warmth began to seep along her veins as she began to realise what it would mean to her.

Maxim cocked an eyebrow. 'Do you want to remain married to me, Lavinia? Answer me truthfully.'

Meeting his engulfing blue gaze, she looked at him steadily, loving him. He hadn't made any undying declarations of love, but he had told her that he wanted to take their marriage a step further, that he no longer wanted an annulment, when they would both be free to continue with their lives separately. The years ahead had suddenly taken on a rosier hue.

'Yes. I think you know I do,' she answered, feeling that she had given him the answer he wanted.

'You're sure?'

'Yes. And are you sure?'

'I knew it the first time I held you in my arms. You have belonged to me since I pulled you out of the Venetian lagoon. You belonged to me then—my body knew it even if my eyes didn't see it. I want you and need you. I don't want to lose you, Lavinia. I cannot, will not, let you go. I want what every man wants from his wife—for her to give him comfort and ease throughout the days—and nights—of their lives together.' His eyes twinkled with a hint of humour. 'Oh—and not forgetting children. Do you like children, Lavinia?'

'I had no experience with them until I came to Thornhill—but now I do. Your cousins' children are adorable. And—I think they like me.'

'According to Ursula, they think you're an angel.'

'You have been discussing me with Ursula?'

Maxim drew away from her and sat up, releasing a long breath. 'Yes. I was interested to know how you are settling down at Thornhill. It is important to me that you enjoy your time here—especially if you are to remain in Rotherfield as my wife.'

Lavinia sighed, savouring the word. 'Wife!' she murmured. 'I don't feel like your wife.'

'You will, my love.' A smile played on his lips, curving gently. 'Very soon.'

'You certainly haven't treated me like your wife.'

'And you know why. But everything will be different now. It's time to forget the past. It's time for you to begin living—with me.'

'So—my lord and master is to take me to his home?'

'Yes. But not now. For the moment you must remain at Thornhill.'

Feeling a sharp pang of disappointment, Lavinia sat up. 'Doesn't it mean we can give up the charade and tell the world that we are man and wife?'

Maxim frowned, the expression on his face suddenly guarded. 'No. We can't. Not yet. I ask you to be patient a little longer.'

'You—you don't regret what has just happened, do you, Maxim,' Lavinia asked tentatively. 'What we have decided?'

'Regret? No. It's just that it is worrying when I know it can lead to serious consequences for those involved.'

Lavinia was puzzled. 'Those? Who?'

There was a torturous pause. Maxim was faced with the inescapable fact that when Alice learned of his marriage to Lavinia, her rage would be savage. He was afraid of the lengths she might go to exact her revenge, and strongly feared it would send her flying into the arms of her French comte. Her actions would be vicious in intent, monstrous in effect. But she would have to know. He would tell her himself at the first opportunity.

Lavinia was beginning to realise just how little she knew about this man she had married. She felt a stirring of resentment. 'Why, Maxim—does the idea of telling everyone I'm your wife not appeal to you?'

'It appeals to me very much. I'd like nothing better—but I can't. Not yet. Be patient, Lavinia. Be satisfied for now when I tell you that if the news that I have a wife is spilled too soon, it might prove disastrous to someone who is very dear to me.'

The sombre, bitter note in his voice penetrated Lavinia's mind, but she did not pursue the matter. No doubt as he drew her into his world these secrets would be revealed, as and when necessary, but until that time came she must be content.

Maxim peered into the nest. The six puppies were contentedly suckling Bess's teats. Smiling crookedly he looked round at Lavinia, his eyes warm and tender, his gravity of a moment before replaced by a gentle teasing. 'How does six appeal to you?'

'Six? Six what?'

'Children. See how proud and content Bess is with her litter.'

Lavinia flushed. 'And so will I be—just as long as it's one at a time.'

'On one condition,' he said.

'Oh?'

'That they all look just like you.'

'Willingly.' She smiled as he caught her up into his arms, causing her whole world to tilt once more.

When he was able to pull himself away from her Maxim stood up, casually brushing the hay from his breeches. Reaching down, he took Lavinia's hand and pulled her to her feet, yielding to the temptation again and wrapping her in his arms. His face was hard with passion, his eyes smouldering as once again his warm lips covered hers. Lavinia shivered with pleasure, her lips moving against his, unwittingly increasing his hunger. When he finally pulled his mouth from hers he drew a long, tortured breath, his gaze going past Lavinia to the door.

'We're going to have to stop,' he murmured. 'We have an audience.'

Slowly Lavinia's swirling senses began to return to the present. Turning and following the direction of Maxim's gaze, she saw the gaping faces of eight-year-old David and his five-year-old sister Mary, Margaret and Ben's children, standing in the doorway. Their eyes were as wide as saucers as they stared in wondrous awe at what they were doing, and before either Maxim or Lavinia could utter a word, they had turned and scampered off back to the house.

A lazy, seductive grin spread across Maxim's face. 'I think our secret is out.' Taking Lavinia's hand he drew her towards the door. 'Come along. We'd better follow them. I know Aunt Ursula will be delighted.'

Ursula was. Smiling knowingly, she looking from one to the other with approval as she smoothed down her pristine white apron.

Maxim laughed lightly. 'I can see David got here before us.'

'He did. And it's about time too,' she scolded gently. 'But I don't need a crystal ball to tell me what he saw happened. I suppose it's safe to assume the two of you have decided not to go your separate ways after all?'

'It looks like it,' Maxim replied, his arm sliding possessively around Lavinia's waist to draw her closer to his side. 'But I want it to go no further than the family for the time being. You understand that, don't you, Aunt?'

She nodded. Understanding why. 'You look happier than I've seen you, Lavinia,' she said softly, observing her pink cheeks and shining eyes.

'I confess I can't remember being so happy. Maxim has taken me by surprise,' she said, gazing up at him adoringly.

Ursula laughed. 'When Sir Galahad straps on his shining armour these things do happen. I wondered how long it would take you to realise you make an ideal couple.'

'You knew?' said Maxim.

'Women have a sixth sense about these things,' Ursula said, her eyes twinkling as she left them to go back to her work in the kitchen. 'Will you be staying for supper, Maxim?' she asked over her shoulder as she was leaving the room.

Maxim smiled slowly, his eyes settling on his wife. 'I will, Aunt—and perhaps breakfast.'

Chapter Nine

Later, when Maxim entered Lavinia's room, sensing her apprehension, he closed the door and slowly advanced towards her, his eyes never leaving hers. She waited passively, warily, for him to come to her, her heart pounding in her chest and feeling a strange fluttering in her stomach.

Looking down into her upturned face Maxim's fascinated gaze moved over her. Her shining wealth of golden hair tumbled about her shoulders, framing a face of heartbreaking beauty. Involuntarily, his gaze dropped to her mouth. It was a tantalising mouth, inviting. Seized by a passionate longing to protect, to treat with reverence his lovely young wife, he placed his hands on her shoulders, surprised when he felt the stiffness in her body and how it trembled beneath his touch.

'You're trembling,' he said softly.

'Yes, I know,' she admitted, her voice quivering nervously, his observation bringing colour to her cheeks. His touch was so light, and yet she could feel the strength in his hands. 'For the life of me I cannot think why.'

191

Maxim sighed and leisurely drew her into his arms. 'Neither can I,' he murmured, gazing down into her upturned face, the feel of her turning his blood to fire. 'Ever since we met I've been fighting against my need for you. You are so beautiful, Lavinia.'

Mesmerised by the silky smoothness of his voice, so filled with sensual promise, Lavinia melted against him. The warmth of his touch stole her breath, igniting a flame within her blood, and the intensity of his blue gaze held her transfixed. Its potency was intoxicating. Her senses became scattered, and she willingly let him wrap her in a crushing embrace and place his mouth over hers.

His kiss was just as exciting and devastating as ever, and she parted her lips to receive it. It was both fierce and tender, and unlike anything she had previously experienced. Curling his arm round her waist, his hand caressed her back, moulding her hips close. Lavinia was caught up in the stirring sensation his kiss always evoked, her arms sliding up his broad chest and fastening themselves round his neck.

Raising his head Maxim deftly removed her robe to reveal her white lawn nightgown. Instinct and the apprehension he saw in her liquid eyes made him hesitate about removing that as well. Lavinia didn't object when he lifted her up and carried her to the bed, but when he placed her on the sheets and stretched out alongside her, his long fingers beginning to pull her nightgown up over her knees, she jerked free.

'Maxim, please don't,' she begged.

Her obvious unease and confusion restored Maxim's sanity and made him relax his hold. Reaching to draw her back into his arms, she recoiled from his touch. He questioned her hesitation with a frown.

'Lavinia? What's the matter? It's not a human sacrifice I'm asking you to make.'

His words brought a flush to her cheeks and she averted her eyes. 'I—I know.'

Maxim reached out and took her chin, carefully turning her face around to look at him. 'Look at me.' Scarlet-faced, she raised her eyes. 'What is it? What do you think happens between a husband and wife when they go to bed together? Tell me.'

She looked at him, pain and bewilderment mirrored in her eyes. 'Forgive me, Maxim. I—I don't know what to do,' she confessed wretchedly. 'Or what you expect of me.'

At last Maxim knew what was wrong, the reason for her apprehension. He smiled, while mentally cursing her mother and her governess for not having told her what took place in a marriage bed. 'So that's it. For a start, Lavinia, I don't expect you to do anything. Didn't anyone ever tell you what happens between a husband and wife in bed?'

'No. You must think me very ignorant and stupid.'

'I don't. You are wonderful and sweet,' he said, looking across to where she lay, as if poised for flight. He sighed. 'Lavinia, come here and lay beside me. '

Slowly she did as she was told, lying in the crook of his arm. 'What are you going to do?'

'I'll show you.'

'Will it hurt?'

'Yes, but only the first time,' he murmured, planting a kiss on the top of her head. 'But believe me when I tell you that you are on the threshold of a great discovery. This delightful body of yours, my love, has some incredible surprises in store for you. I will only go as far as you want me to. You can tell me to stop any time you like,' he murmured leaning down and kissing her cheek, determined, despite his promise, that he would not stop until he had achieved what he intended. Nothing short of an earthquake was going to stop him making love to her now he'd started.

The soft seductiveness in his eyes and the velvety softness of his voice stilled Lavinia's panic and she tried to relax. Maxim bent his head and placed his mouth on hers, kissing her long and deep, having no intention of pulling back until he drew a response from her, even if he expired of unassuaged passion in the process. Somehow he was going to have to arouse her without becoming too aroused himself.

Slowly his hand travelled the length of her spine, moulding her hips and pressing her closer. Closing her eyes Lavinia shuddered against him. Fires were ignited inside her and Maxim drew a gasp of pleasure from her when his lips dragged themselves to her throat and down to her breasts straining beneath the thin fabric of her nightgown.

A moment later he rose and quickly removed his clothes. Lavinia gasped, fighting panic and drawing back at his maleness, from the sheer physical power of his body. He smiled at her reaction, stretching out once more alongside her, tenderly drawing her against his taut, tightly muscled body.

'Have you never seen a naked man, Lavinia?'

'No,' she answered.

'What do you think? Is it so bad?'

'No,' she whispered, looking into his eyes.

Maxim laughed softly. Lowering his head he kissed the soft flesh of her breast where her nightgown had parted, caressing the hard, rose pink nipple with his tongue. Slipping his hand down the length of her thigh, he slowly pulled her nightgown up and began to explore the soft, inviting contours of her body, so supple yet so firm. Hearing her gasp at the contact, he raised his head and looked at her. Her eyes fluttered open and he smiled, determined to be gentle. He would make her body sing with rapture before he was done.

But it was no easy matter ignoring the urgent heat and throbbing in his loins. Having no intention of relinquishing the territory he had gained, leaving his hand on her waist he claimed her lips once more, tasting her sweetness. There was a thoroughness to his kiss which ravaged Lavinia's senses—deepening and demanding, until a low moan of pleasure rose from her throat.

To Maxim's immense joy she arched against him, wrapping her arms around his neck and giving herself up to his caress. He gloried in her innocence, proud that no man had touched her like he was doing now, feeling a surge of tenderness for this lovely, unspoiled young woman who was his wife. Slipping her nightgown over her head almost without her noticing, at last the perfection of her body was laid bare for him to see.

Fighting back his rampaging desire, Maxim watched the reaction to his caress pass across her face as her body submitted willingly. His hands became more insistent and he gloried in her perfect beauty, placing a series of kisses over every inch of her exposed flesh, longing to bury himself in her but holding back.

Unconsciously Lavinia gasped in startled resistance when his hands and his lips became more daring and began exploring and caressing further. She hadn't realised how sensitive the small hollow in her throat, the flesh across her stomach and her breasts were until he kissed her, caressed her there. Effortlessly Maxim stopped her hand when, through a haze of desire, she saw her nakedness spread out before him and modestly tried to pull her nightgown over her, which drew a soft chuckle from him.

'It's too late for that, my love,' he whispered, renewing his wicked assault and kissing the taut skin of her stomach.

Lavinia's reaction was immediate and she gasped, the heat radiating from his body drugging her senses. His hands as they stroked her naked flesh were surprisingly gentle and hot against her skin. Maxim raised his head, and what Lavinia saw almost stole her breath away. Even if she intended fighting him, her physical resistance would be useless against his unswerving seduction. He would not release her until the vows they had made before God were securely tied in the physical, tender knot of passion.

In the soft candle glow his powerful body glowed bronze. His face was hard, his eyes dark with passion, and yet there was so much tenderness in their depths that Lavinia's heart ached. A startled moan of intense pleasure escaped her lips when his hot mouth enveloped her nipples as if he meant to devour them. Closing her eyes, she willingly gave herself up to the fierce stabs of pleasure shooting through her, wrapping her arms around him as though she couldn't bear to be parted, until she felt his hand travel down to the golden triangle between her thighs.

Maxim felt her resistance and raised his head. 'Lavinia, please,' he said huskily, his face taut with restraint. 'Trust me. Relax, my darling.'

Drawing a shuddering breath, she nodded, gasping when he continued his sweet torture, amazed by the sensual hunger that swept over her. Her skin felt incredibly sensitive and she felt hot all over, but this time it wasn't embarrassment. It was something else. Through a haze she looked into his face as he hovered above her, mutely inviting him to explore further. His fingers teased and toyed, and she yielded to the primitive, exquisite pleasure. Never had her body felt so many sensations all at once. It became a furnace, her limbs molten, and she clung to him, a pulsing, warm ache aroused deep within her, one that was unfamiliar and frightening, but she could not fight it.

Struggling not to break his control, Maxim could not believe Lavinia's ardour as she moved instinctively against him, and he realised with surprise and delight that his wife was a tantalising creature of intense passion and sensuality.

There was no fear left in Lavinia as she waited and longed for Maxim to take her, to do to her what she had dreaded. She didn't know what she wanted, but she was aching with unfulfilled need. Any resistance now fled as the voluptuous needs of her body soared and heat spread from her breasts to her loins. Her heart leapt and her breathing quickened with unbridled pleasure and combined terror when he covered her body with his own, drawing her hips beneath him.

Through the mist Lavinia saw the hunger, the tension, on Maxim's face, and for the first time she realised his own needs were as great, if not greater, than her own. Kissing her with urgent hunger, skilfully he built a desire in her so intense that she hardly noticed when he drove into her. Her body jerked and she gasped for breath, but the pain was short-lived. The magic didn't die and the pain turned to pleasure.

In the grip of a spiralling excitement Lavinia wrapped her arms around her husband when he seized her mouth in a plundering kiss. She returned it hungrily, expressing her love with all her heart and soul when they became one, straining to come closer, moving in unison. Her body began playing strange tricks on her as she was possessed by a delirium, a madness, which was warm and greater than anything she had ever imagined. It grew and grew, brimming over until she thought she was drowning in a sea of pleasure. Her body responded to Maxim as if she were another person—a wanton—and her senses soared until she thought she could endure no more. It ended in an explosion, and an oblivion of bliss claimed them both.

Utterly spent, Maxim rolled to one side, taking Lavinia with him. She lay with her head on his damp chest, the thick coils of her hair draped over them both. Limbs entwined, they lay together, neither of them moving or speaking until their hearts and breathing had slowed. Prey to a multitude of emotions, Lavinia sighed, aware of a sharp, sweet pleasure. Somewhere inside her a pulse still throbbed. She had not known it could be like this, and now she did Maxim would find her an eager, willing wife.

Maxim drew Lavinia's hair from her face and kissed her flushed cheek, feeling humbled by her beauty and her unselfish ardour. A surge of tenderness swept through him at her sweetness. She stirred in his arms and raised her face to his, her eyes like those of a wide-eyed kitten still dark with passion, her lips soft and vulnerable, her face one of pure tranquillity.

'How do you feel?' he asked, his voice gentle, his gaze so tender that Lavinia's heart contracted.

She sighed with contentment. 'Like your wife, and blissfully content,' she murmured, placing her lips gently on his chest.

'Did I hurt you?'

'I felt no pain, Maxim. Only pleasure.'

'And do you think you are going to enjoy performing your marital duties, my love? Are they as dreadful as you imagined they would be?'

Her lips quirked in a little smile. 'No. It was quite wonderful. Will it always be like that?'

'It will get even better—when I have taught you a thing or two.'

Her eyes widened. 'You mean there is more?'

'Much more,' he laughed, 'and I am convinced you will be an avid pupil. You leave me in no doubt about your inexperience, my love. Despite your wide knowledge of intellectual matters, your education in sexual matters is gravely lacking. Some things are impossible to simulate and the innocence of your body and mind is one of them. I am surprised your mother or your governess didn't instruct you as to what to expect.'

'My mother wouldn't have given it a thought, and I realise now that it was beyond my governess's comprehension that what she would consider to be an obscene act was necessary to ensure the continuity of the human race. No wonder I was watched before I went anywhere and everything I read was vetted first in case it corrupted my virgin mind.' Resting her chin on her husband's chest she gazed up at him. 'Tell me what I have to learn, Maxim.'

His hand came up to touch her tumbled hair, then he drew a caressing finger down the soft curve of her cheek. 'I shall have to teach you how to please me.'

'You mean I didn't?' she gasped, pretending offence.

He laughed deep in his chest. 'You did, you minx. But there's more. Much more.'

Wondering if he would like to show her, Lavinia moved her body provocatively against his, her lips parting in a heart-stealing smile. Even as she formed the thought Maxim read her mind, and he was acutely aware that his body was stirring once more with alarming intensity. Desire was there in his blue gaze, and something more. It was so profound that it almost stole Lavinia's breath.

'Don't you think you should try and get some sleep, my love?' he suggested huskily, secretly hoping she would say no.

She sighed. 'I'm not the least little bit sleepy, Maxim.'

Surrendering to the silent demand in his eyes, with her breasts brushing his naked flesh, Lavinia inched her way up to his mouth, lightly laying her lips on his. 'If I have so much to learn,' she breathed, 'when can I have my first lesson?'

In answer to her question Maxim rolled her on to her back and took control, his senses alive to every inch of her form languorously stretched beneath him. Their passion was all-consuming, bittersweet, ecstatic, ending in a pinnacle of pleasure.

Falling to sleep within the protective circle of her husband's arms, Lavinia had never felt so happy and content. With Maxim by her side she could not fail to continue to be so. She loved him. It was the truth, and she wanted to tell him that she loved him, but something held her back. It was important to her that she was loved equally in return, and Maxim had not told her he loved her. He had told her he wanted her and needed her. But that wasn't the same as love.

And besides, the annulment he had insisted on at the beginning of their marriage, and the casual manner in which he had told her it was no longer necessary, made her uneasy. Whatever it was that had made him enforce such harsh conditions must have been of a serious nature. Why had he changed his mind?

The following day Lavinia existed in a blissful state. Her happiness was full to overflowing. It was late afternoon and she had not seen Maxim since he had left her bed that morning. Sunlight spilled along the path on which she walked, so lost in thought that she didn't realise how far she had wandered from Thornhill. The day was warm and peaceful, and she could hear a stream tumbling along beside the path.

Tall trees cast their shadows across her way, and the leaves in a mosaic of glorious colours formed a canopy above. She sighed, content to be alone, to think of Maxim. Coming to the end of the path she paused, having reached a main thoroughfare. Wondering which way to go, she stood within the shelter of the trees pondering, seeing a carriage approaching. Looking straight ahead, her eyes focused on some tall wrought-iron gates, a huge weeping ash to one side of them. They opened on to a short, private drive which formed a circle in front of a magnificent three-storey house, built of golden yellow stone and enriched by splendid carving.

Unable to tear her eyes away she stared at it in admiration, for it was a house unlike any other she had ever seen. Its sheer size and grandeur told her that its owner was both powerful and wealthy. Lawns like velvet stretched beyond the gates, and she glimpsed a fountain spouting water high into the sky, before falling back to earth in a gentle, shimmering cascade. Flower beds and elaborately carved stone urns were brimming over with flowers, and a lake could be seen to the right of the house, with an island pavilion in the centre.

Drawn out of her reverie by the approaching carriage, curiously her gaze was drawn to its occupants. One of the women had striking features and shining black hair beneath a stylish, emerald green hat which matched her jacket. Two other women occupied the carriage. One she assumed would be the lady's maid, and the other rather elderly looking woman, dressed in plain black and holding a little girl on her knee, Lavinia thought would probably be the child's nursemaid.

Lavinia's presence was almost hidden from view by the thick foliage. She watched as the carriage swung in through the open gates, travelling halfway round the circular drive and halting at the bottom of a low, wide flight of stone steps. At that moment the great double doors of the house were opened by a footman from inside and a man emerged, going quickly down the steps to greet his guests.

Lavinia continued to watch in idle fascination. To her the perfectly groomed man was every inch an elegant, relaxed and poised gentleman, and evidently the owner of this majestic house. His dark blue jacket set off his broad shoulders, and his snowy white neckcloth emphasised his black hair and dark looks.

Suddenly Lavinia felt the pull of those looks, her eyes drawn to them like a magnet, feeling her body freeze when she recognised those chiselled features printed indelibly on her heart. Like a stone statue, unflinching, her eyes unblinking, she watched him open the door of the carriage and assist the woman in emerald green down the steps, feeling a stab of unbearable pain as the woman reached up and kissed his lips, smiling and looking incredibly beautiful.

Lavinia stared at the scene in ringing silence. Watching Maxim, her face lost what little colour it had. Unflinching, she saw him place an arm on the woman's waist, and Lavinia saw her look up at him and smile. Maxim bent his head to hear what she had to say, and what Lavinia took to be an affectionate gesture broke a hole in her emotional barricade.

Maxim moved towards the carriage, reaching inside and taking the child from the nursemaid. Over the distance that separated them, Lavinia saw his handsome face was full of laughter as the little girl flung her arms around his neck. With familiarity and affection Maxim held her in his arms and carried her up the steps. The woman's hand rested on his arm, and the group of people disappeared inside the house and from Lavinia's sight.

How long she stood there staring at the closed doors to that magnificent house she could never remember after that. It was the moment when her bright bubble of happiness had burst. Maxim's words when she had offered to return the mask to him at the ball hit her like a hammer blow—I am not a pauper, he had told her, and the words went on and on echoing through the tunnels of her mind. So, this was his. All of it. What an idiot, what a stupid, blind besotted fool she had been.

What he had done was underhand. He had deceived her. She should have known there was more to him than an amiable gambler. Oh, how dare he? she thought with a rush of unjust, angry pain.

Turning abruptly, she strode back down the path, unseeing. The sun which had shone so brightly had gone out of her day. Furiously she tried to face what she had seen. Before Maxim had come to Thornhill and asked her to be his wife in every sense, she would have had no reason or right to be angry because of their arrangement, but after last night everything was different. Rage, white hot and strong, coursed through her, bringing a suffering so excruciating as to be unsupportable.

How gullible she had been to let herself believe after his passionate kisses and soft words that he really did want her, for she now realised that his words had been hollow, his passion no different from the passion he might feel towards any woman he found himself in such confining intimacy with. Already she could feel the pain of her shattering loss.

Hurrying, stumbling back along the path which she had so recently walked with a happiness she could not conceive, now she saw nothing, heard nothing but the heavy pounding of her heart. Thankfully she managed to enter the house and go to her room without being seen, closing the door behind her and shutting her eyes tight, as though by shutting them she would shut out the reality of what she had just seen. But when she opened them again the sight was still there.

Who was the child she had seen—and the woman, beautiful, confident? Were they lovers? But Maxim had told her there was no one else in his life, and she had believed him. And that house! That magnificent, beautiful house. Some instinct, perception—whatever—told her that the house was his.

Maxim had deceived her cruelly, but what mattered to Lavinia more than his obvious wealth and opulent lifestyle, which went hand in glove when one owned a house such as she had seen, was the woman and how much she meant to him.

Rage enveloped her and she clenched her hands. Damn him. This was all his fault. This whole sorry mess. If he had stuck to their agreement and kept his hands to himself they could have gone their separate ways. There was nothing to ease the raw pain of the misery she felt. Wanting answers to her questions she went in search of Ursula. Better to face the worst and have it over with.

Ursula was alone in the kitchen, stirring something in a large iron pot on the stove that was giving off an appetising meaty aroma. Looking up, she smiled when Lavinia came in. 'Hello, Lavinia. Back from your walk, I see.'

'Ursula,' Lavinia said, going and standing in front of her, unable to contain herself a moment longer, 'please tell me who owns the big house I saw at the end of the path which takes you away from the village—the one that follows the stream.'

Ursula stood up straight and stared at her. The look on Lavinia's face gave her an uneasy feeling.

'It belongs to Maxim, doesn't it?' Lavinia went on when Ursula didn't answer, her eyes large, her expression calm, whilst inside she was screaming. 'Please tell me. I have to know.'

Ursula nodded, wiping her hands down her apron. 'Yes. The house you saw would be Rotherfield Hall. But come, let's go into the parlour where we are less likely to be interrupted.'

'I knew it,' flared Lavinia when they had closed the parlour door behind them. 'I saw him, Ursula. I saw Maxim. He has guests—a woman, an extremely beautiful woman, and a child. Who are they?' she demanded, preparing herself to grasp the facts as Ursula presented them to her.

Ursula was looking at Lavinia intently, as though to assess the effect of the bombshell she was about to drop on her.

'The child you saw is Maxim's daughter—Lucy.'

Lavinia stared, her hands clenched by her sides, her knuckles white. 'His daughter?' The revelation was excruciating.

'Yes.'

'And—and the woman?'

'Is Alice Winstanley. Lucy's mother.'

Lavinia felt as though she was encased in ice. Every part of her was frozen as she forced her lips to ask the question that sprang to her mind. 'I see. Is she his wife?'

'No, my dear,' Ursula replied, her expression gentle, her voice full of concern. Lavinia's voice was a sound of pain and despair. 'You are his wife. I'm sorry, Lavinia. Maxim didn't intend for you to find out like this. He didn't mean to make you unhappy.'

As straight as a slender slither of steel, Lavinia turned and moved away from Ursula. A terrible, silent stillness descended on the room as she tried to digest the awful truth. At last she knew the reason why Maxim had insisted on an annulment to their marriage. It was to enable him to marry the mother of his child. Why he hadn't married Alice Winstanley in the first place she didn't know and had no wish to. She only knew that by walking in the direction of Rotherfield Hall she had blundered irretrievably into an appalling revelation

'How does he come to own such a magnificent house, Ursula?' Lavinia asked, her voice strained, reluctant to ask about Maxim's relationship with the woman just then. It was much too painful. 'Did it belong to his father?'

'Goodness, no. His father owned a small sailing vessel and made his money carrying coal from Newcastle to London.'

Lavinia's lips curved in a wry smile. 'The house I saw today did not come from plying coal from Newcastle to London, Ursula.'

'No, you are right. Maxim bought Rotherfield Hall several years ago.'

'But—how? Is it true that he's the nephew of the Earl of Brinkcliff?'

'Yes, he is, but he made his money himself. Maxim and the Earl are estranged. His family is an old and noble one and Maxim is untitled by choice. It's a long and bitter tale, Lavinia—going back to before Maxim was born.'

'Will the title pass to the next in line?'

'There is no one else.'

'Why does Maxim remain estranged from his uncle?'

'Because he has been blessed with the same proud arrogance and indomitable will that has marked all the Purnell men before him. He cannot forgive his grandfather and the present Earl for turning their backs on his father and disinheriting him, because he dared to defy his own father and marry the woman he loved—a woman—my sister—the old Earl did not approve of. Oh, she was the gentlest of women, warm-hearted and so very lovely, which were the things that drew Maxim's father to her in the first place. But because she lacked the breeding required of the next Countess of Brinkcliff, she was considered to be most unsuitable.'

'Did Maxim's father ever regret turning his back on his inheritance?'

Ursula smiled. 'No—not for one minute. He was extremely happy married to my sister—making enough money for them to live on. From an early age it was clear to everyone that Maxim had been gifted with a superior intelligence. He learned fast and prospered. Through hard work and determination he owns ships that fly his flag, land both here and in America, where coal and gold are mined. He has amassed the kind of fortune some people can only dream of.'

Lavinia stared at her incredulously, finding the extent of Maxim's wealth impossible to take in.

'My own sons are more casual about life, content with what they have and unhurried about life in general,' Ursula went on, 'whereas Maxim has always been the guiding force. He has a brilliant mind for business and invests his money wisely—although this trouble brewing in France is causing him a good deal of worry. Having capital invested in businesses over there, shipping and such like, he went to see for himself the extent of the trouble.'

Lavinia continued to stare at her in dazed disbelief. Completely unaware of any of this, or the reasons which had taken her husband to Europe—to Venice, where they had met—she suddenly felt very stupid, dismayed and disappointed that he hadn't told her.

'I know Maxim can be a mite overbearing and intimidating at times,' Ursula went on in an attempt to soften her nephew's character, 'but it is not intentional. He works hard and demands too much of himself—and he expects others to have the same drive and determination.'

'But I had no idea he was so rich.'

Finding this difficult to believe, Ursula stared at her. 'He gave you no indication?'

'No, he didn't. It's all so ridiculous, don't you think?' she said with a bitter laugh. 'I thought he was a gambler—a professional gambler, who makes his money going from one gaming hall to the next. How stupid and gullible I must have been.'

At any other time Ursula would have seen the funny side to this—Maxim, throwing his money away at the tables—but she could see how much Lavinia was hurting inside, knowing she was putting off the moment when she would ask her about Alice and Lucy.

'Believe me, my dear, Maxim thinks too much of his money to throw it away at the tables. Oh, I'm not saying he isn't averse to a game of cards or dice now and then, or that he doesn't enjoy it when he does, but he plays purely for enjoyment and is sensible enough to know when to stop. I suppose you could call him a gambler of sorts—thriving the way he does on taking risks on investments, driven by the thrill of the wager.'

Momentarily lost in thought, Lavinia recalled the time in Venice when Maxim had lost such a considerable sum of money at a ridotto to be noticed and gossiped about. Even Robert, who was averse to gambling in any form, had heard about it. But Lavinia felt an unexpected, melting warmth in her heart when she remembered how Maxim had explained that he didn't usually lose such large amounts of money, and how he had told her that it was the night after his meeting with her and he had been unable to concentrate on the game—implying that he'd been thinking of her.

Suddenly Lavinia brought herself up sharp, determined not to let thoughts such as these weaken her. Immediately she brought the conversation back to her husband's relationship with Alice and his daughter.

'What is Maxim's relationship with his daughter, Ursula? Is it a close one?'

'It is. Maxim worships her—and of course Lucy adores him. It's unfortunate for them both that circumstances keep them apart.'

'Circumstances? What circumstances, Ursula? Why didn't he marry Lucy's mother? Was Alice married to someone else?'

'No. Nothing like that. If you knew more about the situation, then maybe you would understand.'

'Will you tell me?' Lavinia asked.

'I'm sorry—I can't. Maxim has to be the one to tell you. He will explain.'

Lavinia was conscious of a sudden surge of despair. In the depths of her misery she recalled her own childhood, of the child she had been who had desperately reached out to be touched and loved by her own father. Unmoved by her longing for affection he had driven her back with a firm hand, and looked at her with eyes which had been unseeing. As she grew older Maxim's daughter would experience those same heartbreaking moments if she was denied the presence and love of her father, and it was unbearable to think that, because of her, it might happen.

A heavy guilt settled upon Lavinia. Maxim had been prevented from marrying Alice by marrying her instead. He should have told her. What he had done was unforgivable. The burden he had placed on her was too hard to bear, and it would be no easy matter pushing him into the arms of another woman.

She took a long, quivering breath. 'If Alice is the mother of his child then he has a duty to marry her. Surely his daughter's future happiness and security is worth that. If he had not met me in Venice he would have returned to England and married Alice, wouldn't he, Ursula?' she said quietly.

Ursula shook her head. 'I believe so,' she answered truthfully. 'But like everyone else I do not know how Maxim's mind works. He is an extremely complex person.'

'Maxim should never have married me,' Lavinia said wretchedly. 'He should have told me all of this.'

'Would it have made any difference?'

'Oh, yes, Ursula, it would,' she cried, quite distraught. 'Were it not for me he would have married Alice. I know he would.'

'Lavinia—you are being too hard on yourself. Believe me, I know Maxim well enough to know that now he has met you, married you, he will never give Alice another chance. He is fiercely proud and accountable to no one. When she told him that she was to bear his child, she hurt and shamed him so much when she refused to marry him unless he adhered to certain conditions. I believe she killed all the feeling he had for her then.

'Before he met you in Venice, if he did think of returning to England and marrying her, it would be for Lucy's sake and for no other reason. If you are in any doubt as to what his feelings are for Alice— just watch his face when you mention her name. He will explain all this to you.'

'I cannot bear to think that everyone here has known about Maxim and Alice all along, that this was behind the knowing looks and secret smiles.'

'No one was being unkind, Lavinia. Maxim asked them not to mention either Alice or Lucy to you until the time was right for him to tell you himself.'

'I feel so stupid. Oh, Ursula, it's all so dreadful.'

'It needn't be.'

Lavinia stared at her. What was she to do? With cynical clarity she knew what she had to do, that she must leave Thornhill and any idea of happiness she cherished with Maxim. She had never realised so acutely as she did now how little she knew about him, and when she thought of what she had just discovered everything inside her recoiled from it with horror.

She could not bear to leave him, but she must. Every time he took her in his arms, kissed her, lay with her at night, she would be unable to put that other woman and her child out of her mind. And she would despise herself for keeping them apart. Her decision became an internal battle, but in the end her conscience overcame her sentiment. She shook her head wearily.

'It's a little late for that.' She softened suddenly, seeing the hurt, pained look in the older woman's eyes. 'I know you mean well, Ursula—and it is only right that you speak up for Maxim, but you must understand how difficult all this is for me. Maxim has a child—to a woman he is not married to. And he should be. It's a situation I cannot accept.'

'I think you might change your mind if you were acquainted with Alice,' said Ursula, sorrow pulling at her heart strings at the thought of Lavinia leaving Maxim.

'Maxim must have some feelings for her—his daughter is evidence of that. And while ever I remain married to him, I am preventing him from doing the honourable thing. Clearly he intended marrying her, otherwise he would not have insisted on an annulment to our marriage when I received my legacy—which I know he told you all about in his letter before we arrived in England. I cannot remain married to him knowing this, Ursula, and I am angry and deeply hurt that he didn't see fit to tell me.'

'But—you do love him?'

'Yes,' she admitted, giving her a sad little smile, feeling a hard lump at the back of her throat. 'I never thought it possible to love another human being so much. I love him so much it hurts. But I will not be lied to or deceived. Maxim married me out of sympathy and pity—nothing more.'

'Lavinia, that is not so!' Ursula exclaimed. 'He married you with the best intentions. He cared enough to marry you at the risk of losing his child.'

'Then he should not have done it,' Lavinia cried wretchedly, biting her lip to hold back her tears, engulfed with anger, humiliation and her own gullibility. 'I didn't ask him to. It is an emotional burden too difficult for me to bear. Had I known he had a child whose mother hoped to marry him, I would never have agreed to become his wife. He should have been honest with me.'

'What will you do?'

'I'm going away—to London,' she said decisively. 'I have friends there—Daisy Lambert and her mother. You remember—they were the people I was in Venice with when I met Maxim.'

'And Maxim?'

Lavinia's expression was suddenly hard and deci-
sive, her tone final. 'He will know where I am when
he files the papers for a divorce.'

'Then take care, Lavinia. When Maxim discovers
that you intend to leave Thornhill, his anger will be
terrible. He's not used to encountering opposition
from anyone.'

'Then it's time he was.' Lavinia's lips parted in a
tremulous smile and her expression softened. 'Don't
worry about me, Ursula. I'll be fine, really. I'll be all
right,' she said with more determination than accu-
racy.

Chapter Ten

Choked by a terrible miasma of loneliness and deprivation—feelings she recognised, having grown up with them—Lavinia shut herself in her room, hoping that no one would intrude. Yesterday she had been buoyed up with expectancy, but now, in the light of all this, her future, as were her prospects, was bleak. With her mind on what Ursula had told her and her journey to London the following morning, she became unnaturally calm, as calm as a block of ice that has no warmth.

After undressing for the night and wrapping a robe round her naked form—discarding with contempt the frilly nightdress she had worn the previous night—mechanically she began to pack her clothes neatly in her trunk. It was her intention to take one bag with her when she left containing a few necessary items of clothing. She would make arrangements to have her trunk collected later. When she heard a knock on her bedroom door she went and opened it, thinking it might be Ursula or Margaret, and was totally unprepared to find Maxim standing there. His face was a hard, chiselled mask, his brows drawn together in an ominous frown as he studied her pale face and strained features before he spoke.

'May I come in?'

Lavinia stood aside and allowed him to enter, unable to do anything else. His words were cold, spoken without emotion, but she wasn't fooled. Maxim was in a fury. In silent dread she watched him move slowly, wordlessly into the room. Having removed his jacket and neckcloth he looked casual, and when he fixed his cold eyes on her she could almost feel the effort he was exerting to keep his temper under control. He was angry because she was leaving. Angry and unforgiving. Ursula had told her he had a vile temper, and she had a strong feeling that she was about to witness it for herself.

Trying to remain calm, Lavinia took a deep breath in an attempt to quell the quivering in her limbs and the gladness she felt on seeing him. No matter what lay between them, she could not stop loving him.

Maxim shifted his gaze to the open trunk. 'You are leaving.' It was a statement, not a question.

Lavinia shot him a mutinous, measuring look. 'Yes. What are you doing here, Maxim? Why have you come?'

Having moved into the centre of the room, he turned and looked at her. His face could have been carved from a block of granite, and there was a hard, ominous look in his clear blue eyes. 'You know why. When Ursula sent word to the hall to inform me that you intend leaving for London in the morning, I came to see what you are playing at.'

'Ursula should have left well alone.'

'Why, Lavinia? Why are you leaving—and without a word to me?' His voice was controlled, angry.

Lavinia's mouth was set in a tight, angry line, belying the passion of which it was capable. 'You know why, Maxim.'

'Do I? Tell me.'

'All right, I will,' she replied, tilting her chin with an air of defiance as she tried desperately to be composed, to still the trembling in her limbs as she faced the cold, dispassionate man in front of her. 'Although I am sure Ursula will already have told you.'

'She has. But I would like to hear it from you all the same. You are angry, I can see that.'

'And with good reason. When I was taking a stroll earlier, quite by chance I happened to come across a house—although being so enormous, it would be virtually impossible to miss—don't you agree, Maxim?' she said, her eyes locking on his and her voice laced with sarcasm. 'I had no idea who owned it until I saw a carriage carrying your guests arrive—and you came out of the house to receive them.' She smiled thinly, showing no sign of the hurt she had suffered, was still suffering. 'That was when I realised it was your home. You all looked very cosy to me—and it explains why you don't want me there.'

'You were watching?' he asked, thrusting his hands deep into his pockets and beginning to pace restlessly up and down the room with brisk, athletic strides.

Maxim would have thought he was incapable of feeling any angrier than he had at Alice's unexpected arrival at Rotherfield Hall, but the explosion of fury and foreboding he'd felt when his cousin Ben had arrived to inform him that Lavinia was leaving for London the following morning, and the reason why, eclipsed that. Clearly what she had seen and what Ursula had told her affected her more than he had imagined it would.

'Yes,' Lavinia replied in answer to his question. 'Although not intentionally. I wasn't spying, if that's what you think. Naturally I was curious when I realised that enormous pile I saw belonged to my husband—and more so when I saw him receiving and kissing another woman before my eyes.'

Maxim was moved to tell her that it had been the other way round, and that if she had looked more closely she would have seen that it had been Alice who was kissing him. But he allowed her to continue.

'She certainly displayed a proprietorial manner towards you, and you did not seem to resent that.'

'I had no idea Alice would decide to accompany Lucy. I certainly did not invite her.'

'Why didn't you tell me about Alice and your daughter?' Lavinia demanded, searching Maxim's granite features for some sign of remorse or guilt, but he gave her nothing but a hard stare that was devoid of all compassion and understanding.

'Would it have made any difference?'

'Of course it would,' she told him, two high spots of angry colour mounting her cheeks. 'Why weren't you honest with me? Despite the knock to my reputation in Venice when you were seen compromising me, knowing this, I would not have married you.'

Pausing in front of her his eyebrows shot up in sardonic amusement. 'But you did.'

'And I regret it. Bitterly,' Lavinia said coldly, purposefully. 'How I wish I could go back. Everything would be different.'

'Despite what you think, it was my concern and loyalty to you that prompted me to conceal the facts about Lucy and Alice. Damn it, Lavinia, I wanted to help you—fool that I was.'

'Yes, you were.'

His blue gaze was mocking. 'Do not forget that it was you who came to me first and almost begged me to marry you,' he drawled sarcastically.

'I did not beg,' Lavinia seethed with angry pride. 'Do you think I wanted to go to you and ask you to marry me? That I liked doing it? How you must have laughed when I offered you my paltry thirty thousand pounds.'

'I did not laugh. I was deeply touched,' Maxim replied seriously.

'When I went to you that day I rejected everything I was brought up to regard as honourable and decent. I could see no other way of extricating myself from a situation that seemed irredeemable to me at the time.'

Maxim studied her, unable to believe her anger. Having left her that morning before she was awake, soft and warm after making love, he found it hard to believe that this virago, with her heightened colour and blazing eyes, was one and the same. She was a different woman to contend with than the serene

Lavinia he had come to know. With a supreme effort he tried to rein in his temper, with little success.

'So you are running away to London.'

'I am not running away. I simply cannot stay here any longer. I'm making it easy for you. Everything is as it was when we married.'

Maxim moved closer to her, watching her, his eyes merciless and unflinching, an almost lecherous smile tempting his lips. 'Not quite.'

Knowing exactly to what he was referring Lavinia flushed and lowered her eyes in mute misery beneath his penetrating, relentless gaze. 'Nevertheless, the bargain we made still stands.'

'In the eyes of the law our marriage is legal and binding. Despite any agreement made between us, by any definition you are still my wife.'

'Nevertheless, it was an arrangement—a temporary arrangement.'

'To hell with the arrangement. I thought we both agreed that the arrangement we decided on when I came upon you in the barn was much more in keeping with our idea of marriage.'

'That was before I knew about Alice. Does she know about me?'

'Of course not.'

'Do you mean to tell her?'

'Yes.'

'How will she react, do you think?'

'Knowing Alice, she'll be furious. But that won't concern you in London.'

'No, it won't. Mrs Lambert and Daisy will have returned from Italy, so I shall stay with them until I have decided what to do next.'

'How do you intend getting to London?'

'I shall take the mail coach from Rotherfield in the morning.'

'That is not acceptable,' he snapped. 'I will not allow it.'

Lavinia stiffened. 'I do not recall asking your permission.'

Looming over her, Maxim looked formidable, invincible. 'Nevertheless you need it. Despite what was agreed between us at the beginning of our marriage, I am still your husband and don't you ever forget it. No matter what transpires between us in private, in public I expect you to behave as my wife. I will not have you travelling in a mail coach like any common traveller and that's the end of it.'

With her nails digging into her palms and her chest rising and falling with each furious breath, blazing anger leapt into Lavinia's eyes as she confronted her husband. 'And I recall you telling me that I am free to do as I choose, to live where I choose.'

'That was before last night,' Maxim said in a terrible, silky voice, his cold, threatening gaze pinning her to the spot. 'Things have changed between us. If you dare venture towards the coaching inn I will have you brought back, and you won't like what I will do. Do you understand me?'

Lavinia paled, flinching at the bite in his voice. This was a Maxim she didn't know. 'You wouldn't dare.'

Placing his hands on his hips and with his feet planted apart, he leaned towards her in an aggressive stance. 'Try me,' he warned softly. Although quietly stated, it had the undeniable ring of a threat to it. 'If you must leave I will send my carriage to Thornhill in the morning. But why you are making such a fuss about Alice is quite beyond me.'

'This is not just about Alice and you know it,' Lavinia argued. 'You should have told me. By making me your wife you have placed a burden on me that is like a stranglehold of guilt. How do you think I feel, knowing I stand between you and marriage to a woman who should be your lawful wife—a woman who is the mother of your child born in an illicit relationship?'

When these last words had slipped from her mouth there was a deep and dreadful silence, threatening and charged with a violent animosity. Lavinia felt the depth of Maxim's fury, saw the strained rage emanate from every inch of his powerful frame. At last he spoke, and when he did his voice was cold and lethal.

'You know nothing of Alice's character or the circumstances that have kept us apart.'

'Ursula told me—'

'Not everything.'

'Then why don't you tell me?'

Maxim stood in front of her, thinking of Alice. Someone as unworldly and naïve as Lavinia wouldn't recognise the type of woman Alice was—self-confident, sexually alluring to every man she came into contact with, never for a moment doubting her power over the opposite sex and her ability to control and manipulate them to her advantage. All but himself. His face tightened, but his voice was ominously low when he spoke.

'I don't think that's any interest of yours. Besides—you have already made up your mind to leave Thornhill, so there seems little point. But what about us?'

'There is no us, Maxim.'

'And you believe that, do you?'

Lavinia nodded, her features strained, her eyes large and full of misery. 'I have to.'

'And are you going to ignore what we discussed yesterday—how it felt when we made love?'

Lavinia's heart twisted agonisingly in her breast, and her emotions told her she could not possibly survive the pain of it. She nodded, a lump of anguish and regret lodged in her throat.

'Yes, Maxim. That's where you made your mistake. You shouldn't have done it. You have a child— a daughter. I refuse to be the one responsible for keeping you from her. Don't you understand? I couldn't live with myself. If you have any conscience at all you will marry her mother—which is what you should have done in the beginning.'

Her words ignited a leaping fury in Maxim's eyes. 'And do you think me so contemptible that I didn't ask her to marry me?' he flared with much bitterness.

'Ursula told me that you did. You will have to ask her again when I am no longer your wife.'

'Alice had her chance to marry me and I will never give her another. There is nothing between us any more. I don't love her. I don't believe I ever have—

and she has none for me. In fact, Alice is a first-class bitch whose ambition and constant scheming sickens me,' he said harshly. 'If you knew her you would know what I'm talking about. When I saw her in London recently I realised I didn't want her any-where near me. That was when I made the decision to keep you with me as my wife.'

Lavinia tensed, humiliated beyond bearing. 'And I will not be kept like your servants and your horses,' she retaliated coldly.

'It was not my intention to keep you like a creature against your will.'

'I'm glad to hear it. You were so sure of yourself, weren't you, Maxim? You came to me like a man bearing a gift, quite unconcerned whether I cared for it or not. But this is not about decision making. It's about your high-handed attitude to assume what I might want. I gave up any idea of an annulment be-cause you asked me to. You didn't consider, you just decided. When you came to me last night you stepped out of line and changed the whole nature of our relationship. You should have left well alone. I cannot stay with you knowing this. As far as I am concerned our agreement still stands and we must abide by it.'

Rage kindled in Maxim's glittering eyes. 'I may no longer want to.'

'Alice is the mother of your child,' Lavinia con-tinued to argue fiercely. 'You should reconcile your-self with her and put your daughter before your own selfishness. What you have done is irresponsible. If you had exercised any decency and restrained your ardour—and I know to my cost how difficult that is for you,' she said with strong reference to what had occurred between them the previous night, 'you would not have found yourself in your present predicament.'

Maxim raised his eyebrows and looked at her in surprise, torn between anger and amusement. 'I cannot change the way I've lived my life until now—and I don't recall you complaining last night,' he said on a softer note, his gaze devouring her face.

His bold, glinting smile and the lazy mockery in his eyes almost proved too much for Lavinia. 'Yes,' she replied lamely, annoyed when she felt her cheeks flush beneath his penetrating gaze. The pull of his eyes was far worse to resist than the frantic beat of her heart. But only an idiot would have succumbed now. She had dared to speak her mind, to let him know how she felt. She must be resolute. 'You can be very persuasive, Maxim,' she conceded.

His finely sculpted mouth curled in a sneer. 'Thank you for that, anyway.'

'I thought you considerate in granting your affection to others—which was the case when you so valiantly rose to defend my honour in Venice—but to hear you vilify the mother of your child, to depict her as some kind of monster, makes me wonder what manner of man you are and if you are to be trusted at all. You speak of her with antipathy—why, I do not know and I have no right to ask. But it's disrespectful and cruel.'

Maxim's entire body stiffened and his metallic eyes snapped to her face. His expression hardened into a mask of freezing rage and they glared at each other, the fragile unity they had shared the previous night shattered. The warm threads that were being woven between them were broken. Maxim's anger made him carelessly cruel and his face became hard with grinding hostility. His voice had a dangerous, cutting edge.

'You, madam, don't know what you are talking about and have said quite enough. You forget yourself.'

His words rekindled Lavinia's receding anger and her eyes sparked like chipped ice. '*I* forget myself? You are the one to have deceived me and yet you have the gall to tell me not to forget *my*self!'

'You go too far.'

Frustration exploded within Lavinia. 'Do I, indeed! I have shocked you, have I not? I have suddenly turned out to be a woman who is not afraid to speak out. Clearly you thought me too naïve and stupid to challenge you. I can see that you don't expect me to think and feel—that you want to do it for me.'

'And I can't see why you are making such a fuss about everything. Perhaps if Ursula had told you about the conditions Alice imposed on me you might understand.'

'Ha! Conditions were imposed on me too, as I recall. The two of you may not love each other, but it seems to me that you have much in common when it comes to proposing marriage. But it makes no difference. Forget your pride, Maxim. Make your peace with Alice. Isn't your daughter worth it? If you don't, you are going to have one very unhappy child.'

Somewhere in the dark caverns of Maxim's mind he slowly began to realise that Lavinia's concern for Lucy's well-being had been brought about by her own unhappy childhood, and that it was why she was hellbent on sending him into Alice's arms. But at that moment he was almost at the point of fury where reason and the ability to think clearly had left him. His features were like granite, the air thick with bitter confrontation.

'I don't like your tone, Lavinia. What gives you the right to sit in judgement?'

'I don't. I happen to be concerned for your daughter.'

'Concerned!' he repeated with insolent amusement. 'I wonder why.'

'Because, unlike you, I happen to believe that a child belongs with both its parents.'

His eyes raked her with a look of glacial scorn. 'Now why is it,' he mocked, 'that after being raised by parents who couldn't be bothered to give you the time of day, I find it strange that you are suddenly such an authority on what you think is best for *my* child. You know nothing. Until you do kindly keep your classifications to yourself.'

Raging furiously inside, Lavinia was incensed by his arrogance. He was cold, colder and harder than she had ever seen him, his face set and remote, watchful and guarded.

'Why—you arrogant, self-opinionated heartless beast,' she flared, breathing hard, her eyes sparking fire as the argument became a battle of unwavering wills. 'You know nothing about what my life has been like. It is precisely for that reason that I do know. I know what it's like to be ignored. I know how it feels to think there must be something wrong with you because you're unloved. So don't you dare treat me like some kind of imbecile.'

'I don't. Lucy is neither ignored or unloved.'

'No—she is more like some pampered pet who can be passed from mother to father while they argue their differences—neither of them doing what is right for the child,' Lavinia flung at him, throwing back her hair and glaring at her husband, who caught his breath, thinking he had never seen her so savagely beautiful. This malleable, tractable young woman he had met in Venice, was changing before his eyes. She was proving to be more volatile than he realised.

'Where are your priorities, Maxim?' she went on. 'Sacrifices have to be made for children. It appears to me that those sacrifices will cause you personal inconvenience—which is evidently too much to ask of you.'

'Damn you, Lavinia, and your narrow, blinkered view of life. You insult me and my intelligence most grievously. But understand this,' Maxim hissed, enunciating every word so they would be indelibly printed on her mind for all time. 'I will not marry Alice. I will never marry Alice. Marriage is not always a foregone conclusion to an affair.'

'I'm beginning to realise that,' she snapped, too angry to quail before the murderous look tightening his face. 'You are a monster, Maxim. A cold and hateful monster.'

His eyes were like ice and cynical. 'You're right. I am.'

'And you have no heart.'

'Exactly,' he replied. 'And you will do well to remember that if you deceive yourself into believing otherwise. I am no poodle to be led by the nose. Alice made that mistake and will live to regret it.'

'I do not like your world, Maxim. You have a distorted view of what is right and decent. In your world it would seem that babies come before marriage. That is not acceptable to the order of things in my life. Maybe you are right and I do have a blinkered view on life, which I can only put down to my upbringing over which I had no control. But I am beginning to realise that perhaps it wasn't so bad after all. At least I was given good principles. I was also taught about decency and the difference between right and wrong—which appears to have been sadly lacking in your own education.'

'I wouldn't go on if I were you,' Maxim warned in a murderous voice, his voice hoarse in his throat, his fists clasped to his sides as he struggled to keep them from reaching out and throttling her.

Lavinia stopped cold, realising that she might have gone too far, but she was too angry to allow herself to be intimidated by him. They glared at each other, neither of them prepared to back down from the confrontation.

'I realise you must despise me for speaking to you like this, but I have to let you know how I feel. You should not have let me find out about Alice and Lucy by accident. You should have told me in the beginning.'

'There was no need if we were to seek an annulment.'

'There was every need,' Lavinia persisted.

Maxim's glare was deadly. 'Have you finished?'

Lavinia drew herself up straight, her face pale and steeled with a resolute, frozen look. 'Yes. I shall leave first thing in the morning. I am quite determined, so do not try to stop me.'

Maxim could almost feel her fury and anguish, but her resolution was firm, solid and unbreakable. Her mind was made up about leaving, he could see that. In the space of twenty-four hours she had developed a newly acquired confidence in herself that was lethal. His clear blue eyes turned to shards of ice.

'Stop you? I'll be damned if I will. Go to London and take your damn sermons with you. I'll even be here to carry your bags out to the carriage and wave you on your way.'

'Don't bother. I can carry my own bags. And where our marriage is concerned, it was never meant to be permanent and can easily be dismantled. I want a husband for life—not until the next woman who takes his fancy comes along.'

'And if I told you that you are the only woman I want?'

'How can I believe that when you have so skilfully hidden so much from me? If you can treat one woman so abominably, how do I know you will not do the same to me?' Lavinia accused, too demolished over his secrecy over this, trying not to dwell on how his eyes were flashing a brilliant, dangerous hot blue in his tanned face, or the snarling smile across his even white teeth, and the tangle of blue-black curls that tumbled over his forehead, making him look like a gypsy, wild and fierce, and so incredibly handsome that it wrung her heart. But she refused to be swayed.

'I have been unhappily deceived in your character,' she went on relentlessly. 'Because we can no longer have our marriage annulled you can go ahead and start divorce proceedings on the grounds of desertion, adultery—whatever you like—I really don't care, just so long as it is over and done with quickly. From what Ursula has told me and what I have seen, you are a wealthy man, Maxim—so wealthy that it makes my thirty thousand pounds seem like a mere tuppence. Use your influence—pull some strings. I'm sure you can manage that.'

Maxim didn't flinch. He merely looked at her with eyes that had frozen over before turning and going towards the door. But with implacable resolve he came back to her with confident, brisk strides, sardonic amusement curving his handsome lips, refusing to spare her. Towering over her, his smile was vicious.

'And what will you do if I refuse to file for a divorce? What if I decide not to let you go and keep you as my lawful wife—to share my board and my bed and bear my children?'

Lavinia stiffened, feeling the colour drain from her face. She didn't recognise the ominous glitter in those ice blue eyes. Behind his sardonic expression was a burning anger. 'You wouldn't do that, Maxim,' she whispered, automatically backing away from him to-wards the bed, overcome with an irrational fear, primitive and instinctive. Never had he looked so tall, so powerful, so coldly frightening.

'I might. I am tempted—especially when I look at you,' he said huskily, only a few inches away. As he let his admiring glance roam freely over her wealth of thick golden hair and slim, restless figure, he noticed she was wearing nothing beneath her robe. He arched a brow and smiled, meeting her gaze.

Reading the sudden glow in his eyes Lavinia was alarmed. The bed blocked her retreat so all she could do was face him. Her breath caught in her throat. If he touched her she would crumble, and after their harsh words which had settled everything between them, she could not allow that to happen. His obvious intention turned her into a trembling mass of rebellion and fear. Swallowing hard she gasped. 'Please don't do this. You can't.'

Maxim moved closer, his gaze focusing on her lips. 'But I can. I am your husband. I have every right. Why you want to torture us both in this way baffles me. Come, Lavinia, admit it. You want what I want.'

'No. Not any more,' Lavinia told him, which was not the truth. She would go on wanting him until the day she died. He was so close she could feel the heat of his virile body.

Maxim experienced a surge of triumphant satisfaction when he saw the flickering weakening in her eyes. 'Then prove it to me.'

Immediately he reached out and Lavinia jerked away from him, but he caught her and drew her closer, his arms going round her and holding her with a crushing force.

'Take your hands off me,' she ordered, infuriated by his obvious intention to weaken her resolve, which he knew he was capable of doing every time he took her in his arms.

'Not a chance,' Maxim whispered as she struggled against him.

All the days they had been together, of wanting her, of frustrating self-denial for the past twenty-four hours—Maxim's need for her had built up to such a pitch that he was almost beyond restraint. All he could think of was shattering her demureness and reserve and laying bare the woman of passion—a woman he had every right to make love to. Bending his head until his mouth found hers and forcing her lips apart, he began kissing her with fervency, determined to make her respond.

Lavinia held herself rigid, her determination not to yield as strong as his own determination to make her. She knew that he wanted her full cooperation, and that if she gave it, it would be more damaging to her pride and their relationship than anything else. Tears gathered under her eyelids and the world seemed to tilt around her and to retreat. She fought the weakness, not wanting to be completely at his mercy, but her body was already beginning to respond with a gross miscalculation of her will.

Powerless to prevent what she knew would happen next, she melted against him and returned his kiss with a silent desperation and a fervour that betrayed her own longing, crushing her soft mouth to his and almost moaning out loud at the sheer pleasure of it. She wasn't made of stone. She was flesh and blood, and her blood was on fire.

The moment she leaned into him and opened her mouth in response, Maxim shoved her back on to the bed. Lavinia gasped when he hurriedly tore off his shirt and trousers and tossed them onto the floor. With a strength born out of fear she turned and struggled to the other side of the bed, but he reached out and caught her, bringing her back and rolling on to her, pinning her hands on either side of her head as his own hovered over her, dark and satanic, desire raging in his eyes.

'Please, Maxim, don't do this,' she begged as he lowered his face purposefully toward hers. The previous night he had been gentle and loving, but now he seemed to want to hurt her. 'Not like this.'

He captured her protests with his mouth, kissing her with a violence that stole her breath away, his fingers searching the soft contours of her body beneath her robe, which had fallen open. They cupped her breasts, teasing her hardened nipples, moving down over her abdomen to the curling mass of golden hair between her thighs, skilfully building her desire.

Lavinia's trapped body writhed beneath him and she tried to fight back the waves of pleasure that washed over her, tried not to respond to the erotic onslaught to her senses. She tensed every muscle in her body to resist the calculating, heartless things his knowledgeable fingers were doing to her, but sharp stabs of desire were shooting through her, melting her resistance, driving her insane with need and want.

When her body became pliant beneath his, Maxim felt a surge of triumphant satisfaction and found her lips once more, kissing her deep and moulding the full length of his body to hers, forcing her to become aware of his raging desire. With her eyes closed, Lavinia felt a warmth begin to seep through her entire body. It brought a soft moan of exquisite, mindless pleasure to her lips, and she kissed him with fierce desperation. Aching desire was building up to a crescendo and jarring through her body. Desperate for release, she wanted him inside her.

Maxim raised his head, his eyes dark with passion, watching her face. 'Tell me you want me, Lavinia. Say it,' he whispered, dragging his lips to her breasts and making small circles on her flesh with his warm tongue. Lavinia opened her dazed eyes and looked at him. Feeling her body tremble with uncontrollable need, Maxim saw the answer screaming at him in her liquid eyes and he smiled. But he held back. He had to hear her say it.

'Say it,' he repeated, covering her body with his own and provocatively moving against hers, deliberately keeping himself in check and controlling his burgeoning desire when she arched her hips.

The fire that had been building inside Lavinia threatened to explode. Unable to stand it a moment longer, the words he demanded to hear tore out of her in a tormented sob. 'Yes—damn it, Maxim. Don't torture me like this.'

The moment she surrendered he drove into her, bringing a moan of pure pleasure to her lips. She received him like an opening exotic flower, wrapping her arms around him and clutching him to her. They moved in unison, each giving the other maximum pleasure, the climax when it came erupting inside them both with spasms of pure bliss.

For a moment only their ragged breathing could be heard, and then Maxim shrugged himself free of her embrace and rolled off her, thrusting his arms and legs back into his clothes. Tucking his shirt into the waistband of his trousers, he looked down at his wife, trying not to dwell on how wounded she looked, how young and heartbreakingly lovely. Having pulled her robe over her naked form, she struggled to sit up, her eyes still dark and sultry with passion, her lips swollen and trembling.

Maxim's hard eyes raked her face. 'You see. Now can you deny that you still want me?' he jeered cruelly.

Clutching her robe beneath her chin with shaking fingers, Lavinia sat up and glared at him. 'Weren't you satisfied with the pain and humiliation you have already inflicted on me without doing that? I'll never forgive you for what you've just done, Maxim. Ever.'

With long strides he crossed towards the door where he turned, contempt twisting his lips. 'I shall make sure your thirty thousand pounds is made available to you within the next few days.'

The door slammed behind him with the cold finality of a death knell.

Trembling violently, all Lavinia's attention was focused on the closed door. Beset by confusion, she was unable to think or feel. She was unable to believe what Maxim had done to her. If he truly cared for her he would not have done that. In the tearing, agonising hurt which enfolded her, she was ashamed, after all her harsh words, at how easy it had been for him to expose the proof of her vulnerability.

She was, in fact, greatly disturbed. It was not what he had done. It went beyond that, and therein lay her confusion. How could she still want him, love him after that? But want him and love him she did. Looking at him standing in the open doorway afterwards, his carelessly thrown-on shirt open to the waist, his gleaming black hair all tousled and an intense look in those clear blue eyes, had shaken her with a desire so strong it frightened her. Remembering him like that was enough to make her forget and forgive anything.

Tears blinded her vision. Lowering her head, she wept for her inability to purge him from her heart, for her lack of will and with a fear for a love she was unable to control. In her fury and ravaged pride, she dashed her tears away and swore she would kill Maxim if he ever touched her again.

Tormented by his callous and cruel treatment of Lavinia and unable to drive out the memory of what he had just done, riding back to Rotherfield Hall Maxim's heart twisted with remorse and regret. She had told him she would never forgive him, and she was right not to do so. She must despise him, but not nearly as much as he despised himself.

Maxim was willing to concede that he had used her viciously, and he would send his carriage to take her to London in the morning. As for her request for a divorce—if she still wanted one, he would give it to her. With his jaw thrust forward and as rigid as granite, anger spurred him on, Lavinia's decision to leave him having put her beyond all limits of his tolerance. The sound of his horse's hooves pounding beneath him took on a deadly finality.

The following morning Maxim lost no time in acquainting Alice with the bare facts of his marriage to Lavinia, without disclosing his impending divorce.

Alice had come to Rotherfield because both Francis Newbold and the Comte de Chemille were out of town. Feeling bored, she thought it might prove entertaining and diverting if she accompanied Lucy to Kent for a few days. Maxim could hardly turn her away. Besides, she had not been incapable of winning his regard once, and she was most anxious to have it now.

And now he had the gall to tell her he had married someone else.

Somewhere in Alice's brain a hot cauldron began to boil and immediately her imagination was seized. The door was blown right open to jealousy and revenge.

'You coward,' she blazed. 'You gutless coward. And you left it until now to tell me. Who is she?'

she demanded in a hysterical tone, envious malice darting from her eyes. 'I demand to know who she is. And why isn't she here with you?'

'She isn't here because I want to settle the matter between us before I introduce her to Lucy.'

Jealousy, hot and fierce, suddenly sprang up inside Alice. 'Never. How dare you make plans for my daughter behind my back?' she spat, her voice shaking with suppressed rage. 'She has no right to even know her. Lucy is mine.'

'Lucy is my daughter too.'

'Who is she, Maxim—this woman you've married behind my back? I demand to know.'

'Demand all you like,' Maxim replied, his voice cold and contemptuous, his expression unmoved. 'You'll find out in time. You don't know her.'

'I'll make you sorry you did this.'

Maxim's forbearance where Alice was concerned was stretched thin, almost to the point of breaking. His eyes became brittle and there was a grim note in his voice. 'Do you dare to threaten me, Alice?'

Alice glared at him, committed to setting Maxim back on his heels because he'd had the audacity to form a firm and permanent union with another woman. 'If you like. Now you are no longer free to marry me I will marry someone who is,' she flung at him savagely, knowing how deeply Maxim would suffer when she took Lucy away from him altogether.

'You heartless, scheming witch. Have you no sense of decency?'

Fire shot through Alice's eyes. 'You're a fine one to talk about decency. If you'd done the decent thing you would have become reconciled with your uncle and married me. Lucy would then have been able to live with her rightful father. But where there is one there is always another.'

Her mocking tone scraped against Maxim's raw nerves. 'And who do you have in mind? Francis Newbold or your French comte?' he ground out.

'The Comte de Chemille will do nicely. Claude has asked me to be his wife so I will accept. He is returning to France very soon. When he does I shall go with him.'

Maxim went white. 'Marry your French comte by all means, but you will not expose Lucy to danger. I forbid you to take her out of this country. Have you no concept about what is happening in France?'

She shrugged. 'It will blow over in time.'

Savage fury ignited in Maxim's eyes. 'Blow over? You fool, Alice. I've recently returned from France, where revolution is apparent in the minds of the people. In Paris discontent is already raised to the point of rebellion, giving rise to bloody riots which have to be put down by military force. I will not stand by and let you take Lucy into that hornet's nest.'

'Try and stop me,' Alice hissed wrathfully, turning from him and flouncing towards the door.

'Oh, I shall, Alice. I shall pull out all the stops to prevent you. I shall get custody of my daughter. I swear I shall.'

'Never,' Alice hissed fiercely. 'You'll never have her. I'd see her dead first.'

'And that is precisely how she will end up if you take her to France.'

Grim-faced, Maxim held a tearful Lucy as she was leaving Rotherfield. She clung to him, her little arms gripping him tightly.

'Please let me stay, Papa,' she begged. 'I like it here. You promised to take me to the farm and show me the ponies.'

It was the first time she had been to Rotherfield Hall, and Maxim had hoped her stay would have been longer. But as things stood, it was best that she remained with Alice.

'I know, princess. But you must go back to London with your mama. I'll bring you back to Rotherfield before too long and take you to see the ponies. I promise.'

Maxim watched Lucy leave Rotherfield Hall with loving but worried eyes.

Chapter Eleven

Ursula arrived at Rotherfield Hall shortly after Alice had left for London. The silence inside the great house struck her and she sighed, shaking her head somewhat sadly. How often had she told Maxim that it was about time he settled down and filled it with his offspring. It was far too big for one man to rattle around in. Maxim was an exacting master who demanded that his house and estate, like his businesses, were run as smoothly as a well-oiled machine. Everyone who worked for him was in awe of this cynical, formidable master and strove to please him.

Mr Perkins came towards her, his expression a mask of aloof formality. He carefully guarded his position of trust at Rotherfield Hall, and performed all his tasks for Maxim with the faultless precision of a well-tuned orchestra.

'Is my nephew at home, Mr Perkins?'

'He is in his study, Mrs Metcalf.'

'And Miss Winstanley?'

Mr Perkins's eyes gleamed and there was a momentary crack in his rigid features. 'Miss Winstanley left with her daughter for London an hour ago.'

Ursula smiled smugly. Now *that* she found particularly encouraging, although she knew how disappointed and dejected Maxim would be feeling following Lucy's departure. The child hadn't been at Rotherfield Hall twenty-four hours before she had been whisked back to London by her mother. Alice's hasty departure could only mean that Maxim had told her about his marriage to Lavinia.

Deeply concerned by recent events, and having become extremely fond of Lavinia, Ursula could not let matters rest as they were. Remembering Maxim's actions over the years where his grandfather and his uncle were concerned, and how he'd succeeded in coldly cutting them out of his life as if he was not of their blood, Ursula knew he would do the same with Lavinia if nothing was done.

When Mr Perkins showed Ursula into Maxim's study, where he was going through a pile of correspondence, he rose from his desk in taut silence and strode towards the window. His expression was hard, his stance like that of a man being stretched beyond endurance by an internal struggle. It was plain that he was concerned about Lucy and already missing her, and he was also feeling betrayed and furious over Lavinia's leaving.

'Alice is threatening to marry her French comte,' he told his aunt, his voice strained, 'more out of spite than any tender feelings she might feel for the man.'

'What do you intend doing about Lucy? You can't let Alice take her to France in the present climate.'

'I don't intend to. Something has to be done to stop her.'

'Would you have married Alice on her terms if you had not married Lavinia?'

Maxim shook his head. 'No. I did consider it when I was in Italy, but when I saw her in London and listened to what Mrs Winstanley had to say concerning her behaviour, nothing could have induced me to tie myself to her for life.'

'So you made up your mind to remain married to Lavinia.' Ursula watched his face. Apart from a muscle clamping in his jaw, it didn't flinch when she mentioned his wife's name.

'Something like that.'

'And you expected Lavinia to go along with it— without any explanation?' Ursula asked, angered by Maxim's ruthless lack of emotion. 'Really, Maxim! That was too bad of you.'

Maxim regarded his aunt's angry face in dispassionate silence as she proceeded to berate him.

'That poor girl has suffered as much as you have. I cannot believe you can be so callous. Because Lavinia's heart is open she gives all of herself, holding nothing back. Don't abuse her goodness, Maxim. Have you given a thought about what's to happen to her when those people who saw you compromising her in Venice spread the gossip in London? No. I can see you haven't. You can't see beyond your own damaged pride. When it becomes obvious that you are estranged, that you have discarded her—'

'I haven't discarded her. Lavinia has discarded me.'

'Well—whatever. Your marriage to her was no secret. People will expect to see you together—will expect you to live together. How will you explain it?'

'I don't have to explain anything to anyone,' Maxim replied with cold indifference.

'Gossip and speculation can be cruel to an innocent like Lavinia.'

'Then she should have thought about that before she ran off to London.'

'You have no choice but to rescue her from that situation. You are her husband. It's your duty.'

'I strongly suspect I am the last person my wife would want to rescue her,' he ground out scathingly.

'I don't believe that. Lavinia doesn't deserve to be shamed. Her connection to you will make that innocent, lovely girl notorious—and that kind of notoriety isn't good. Nobody will want to have anything to do with her. How do you think she will deal with that?'

'Very well, I imagine,' Maxim replied, his voice devoid of concern. 'She told me in no uncertain terms that the agreement we made in the beginning still stands as far as she is concerned.'

Ursula looked at this cold dispassionate man she had known all his life with disbelief. 'It will be difficult having your marriage annulled after sharing her bed,' she said, her voice laced with uncharacteristic sarcasm.

Maxim's expression tightened. 'I'll file for a divorce as soon as I can get to London and see my lawyer.'

'On what grounds?'

'Desertion. Lavinia didn't have to leave. But in doing so she has given me irrefutable grounds for divorce,' he told his aunt with icy finality.

'I see. She will never endure the disgrace of being a divorced woman. That poor girl will be brought low by it.'

Maxim's mouth thinned to an angry line. 'Dear Lord, Aunt! Don't lecture me. Because of this marriage I've more than likely lost Lucy.'

'And Lavinia knows it. She's eaten up with guilt about that. If you can't understand why she's gone to London, I can. No woman would live with a man, knowing she stands between him and his daughter. You can't dismiss her from your life so casually, Maxim.'

'Yes, I can. I have the more pressing matter of Lucy.'

'No one can be that cold, that callous. Do you have to act so dispassionately?'

'What would you have me do?'

'You told me about your talk with Mrs Winstanley when you went up to London. If you want your daughter, take her advice. That Purnell pride and quick temper of yours is a bad combination, Maxim, and you are bringing a lot of grief upon your own head. There's also something else you should consider.'

'What?' he snapped, pacing up and down in restless fury.

Familiar with all Maxim's moods, good and bad, Ursula remained undaunted. 'If you want to gain custody of Lucy, it will be better having your wife with you instead of against you. Otherwise, while you're busy trying to convince the court that Alice is an unfit mother, they just might consider you to be an unfit father. Think about it, Maxim. You failed to marry the mother of your child, and you are in the process of divorcing your present wife after just a few weeks of marriage. What do you expect them to make of that?'

Maxim shrugged, thrusting his hands deep into his pockets and staring out of the window, his brow furrowed with a deep frown.

By no means done, Ursula went to stand beside him, looking up at his granite features, seeing a muscle move spasmodically on the side of his jaw. 'There's more at stake here than your pride and antipathy towards your uncle, Maxim. Your daughter depends on you—and so does Lavinia, if you did but know it. For them you must put aside your feelings and go and see your uncle. With Lavinia by your side, your Uncle Alistair behind you and some influential lawyers to fight your case, you might be able to wield enough power to prevent Alice taking Lucy to France and gain custody.'

Maxim's body went rigid and he stared at her in disbelief. 'Aunt Ursula! How can you tell me to go and see my uncle with a begging bowl in my hand after what he is guilty of where my father and mother are concerned—your sister, don't forget.'

'I don't. And you don't have to beg for anything. And aren't you forgetting that it was your grandfather who was at fault who, by all accounts, deeply regretted doing what he did. I realise how deep your resentment for your grandfather goes, but he is dead. He did relent before he died. I still have the letters he sent, begging your father to return to Brinkcliff Hall. Your grandfather wanted to become reconciled so that he could formally make him his heir, but your father was as stubborn as he.'

'The same letters my Uncle Alistair has been sending to me over the years,' Maxim said scathingly, combing a heavy lock of black hair from his forehead with his fingers and restlessly resuming his pacing up and down the room.

'Yes. Your uncle is a very poorly man, Maxim, and he never wanted the position your father thrust on him. Perhaps it's time you gave a thought to what is to become of the estate when he dies. There is no one else. You are the next Earl of Brinkcliff and there's not a thing you can do about it.'

'I have made it plain to my uncle that I don't give a damn for the estate or the title.'

With a sigh of weary resignation Ursula turned to go. 'Maybe not. But your son might.'

Maxim ceased pacing and glanced at her sharply. 'I don't have a son.'

'No. But after staying at Thornhill the other night, what if Lavinia has conceived a child? I think you should give it some thought.'

Ursula left Maxim in a tormented silence. His mind was locked in furious combat at the thought of having to capitulate to his uncle, but he realised he could no longer remain distant if he meant to gain custody of Lucy. But it would be hard enough to

relinquish his hatred without drawing the old man
into his life as an ally to aid him with his case.

But Ursula had spoken sense. Everything she had
said was true. He realised it would benefit him enormously if the court saw that he had the full backing
of the Earl of Brinkcliff—and his wife. He also realised that he hadn't a cat in hell's chance of gaining
custody of his daughter with a divorce pending.

Thinking of Lavinia, he was torn between torment
and tenderness. When his anger and pain had finally
diminished enough and he could think more rationally, he reconsidered their estrangement. Despite
what had transpired between them the previous night,
with a defeated sigh and unable to lie to himself any
more, he realised he didn't want a divorce, and he
would be damned if he would give her one. And what
if she was with child? He had messed up with Lucy
and he had no intention of doing so again.

Recalling her agonised face when he had left her
last night, how vulnerable and hurt she had looked,
he ached with remorse. How could he have thought
for one moment that he could live without her—that
he could purge her from his heart and mind? In his
fury last night he would have said he could, but now,
in calmer mood, he knew it was impossible.

It mattered to him what happened to this beautiful,
intelligent, foolish young wife of his. For the first
time in his life he had found a woman who was rare
and unspoiled, a woman who had succeeded in touching his heart, which was something all the other
women had failed to do. He had no intention of letting her go, and this had nothing to do with his battle

to gain custody of Lucy. He realised how much he loved Lavinia, and the truth of his admittance didn't really surprise him.

Recalling how severely she had taken him to task over his assumed neglect of his daughter, a smile tugged at the corners of his lips. Her severe dressing down and chastisement over his lack of moral standards had angered him beyond words, but secretly he loved her for it. She was a deeply concerned young woman, to whom strong principles and a high regard and respect for marriage and the rearing of children mattered—a woman who expected the same moral principles from others.

A new sense of urgency banished the anger and frustration that had clouded his thinking since Ben had arrived at Rotherfield Hall yesterday to tell him Lavinia was leaving and why. Resigned to what he knew he had to do if he was to bring some order back to his life, he sat at his desk and began drafting a letter to his uncle.

Lavinia travelled to London alone in Maxim's impressive coach drawn by a team of four handsome horses. She took little notice of the many people milling about both inside and outside the inn where they stopped for refreshment and to rest the horses. It was when she was about to resume her journey that her eyes were drawn to a coach that seemed familiar. It had just pulled into the inn yard and the occupants, three women and a child, were making their way inside the inn. One of the women paused and stared at Lavinia.

Sensing the woman's eyes on her, Lavinia hesitated as she was about to climb inside the coach and half turned in her direction, instantly recognising the beautiful woman with black hair and exquisite features she had seen Maxim receiving at Rotherfield Hall.

It was Alice.

Lavinia's heart almost stopped completely, and then began to pound. For a moment she was unable to move. Their glances caught and locked. An icy chill trickled down Lavinia's spine when she looked into those eyes. They were as hard and ruthless as those of a cat watching its prey.

Why had Alice left Rotherfield Hall after so short a visit? Lavinia asked herself. Was it because of her? Had Maxim told Alice about his marriage? If so, having recognised Maxim's splendid midnight blue coach, Alice would know who she was—and when Alice's savage glare ripped across the yard and tore into her, Lavinia knew that she did.

Lavinia's gaze was irresistibly drawn to the child, Maxim's child, whose features were so incredibly like his that it wrenched her heart. She was dark haired with clear blue eyes and a small dent in her chin. Lavinia detected a sadness about her. Her eyes were red, which told Lavinia that she had been weeping. Raising her eyes to Lucy's mother, she saw her eyes were narrowed as she stared openly. Alice made no attempt to conceal the pure, unadulterated hatred and contempt she felt for her rival. Her look was so venomous that it would have reduced a lesser woman to ashes. Tearing her eyes away from Lavinia, she grasped Lucy's hand and dragged her inside the inn.

Lavinia climbed into the coach, deeply affected by the brief encounter. She felt sick and cold and trembled inside, and she was engulfed by a kind of repugnant horror after seeing the mother of Maxim's child. She was convinced that she had been looking on a woman who believed she had been cruelly wronged and was bent on revenge. And the child had looked so unhappy, so sad. Had she been crying because Alice had taken her away from her father?

With time for reflection, she turned her thoughts to Maxim and questions began to plague her. He had told her he had no intention of marrying Alice once their marriage was ended, and if this was so, how could he hope to live close to his daughter? Ursula had told her how much he adored the child, so surely he would want to play a part in her upbringing. Did he hold his uncle in such contempt that he would rather forfeit living with his daughter than become reconciled? And Alice? Was she so dreadful that he could not bear the thought of being close to her?

If so, Maxim's reasons for not marrying his former mistress might be justified. He had told her Alice had made conditions before she would agree to marry him. What were those conditions? They must have been harsh for a man as proud as Maxim to refuse to agree to them when he was so devoted to his daughter.

Had she been too harsh on him? Lavinia asked herself. When Ursula had told her about Alice and

Lucy she had been too ready to form her own conclusions and judge Maxim, knowing nothing about
his reasons for not marrying Alice. She should not
have done that. She should have believed in him.
After the kindness and consideration he had shown
towards her in Venice, she should have known he
would not shirk from doing what was right by his
daughter without good reason.

Swamped with misery she suddenly wanted to tell
the driver to turn the coach around and return to
Rotherfield, to throw herself on Maxim's mercy and
beg his forgiveness. But when she recalled how cold
and implacable he had been when he had left her
room at Thornhill, and how readily he had agreed to
a divorce, she knew he would not welcome her back.

When Lavinia arrived in London and presented
herself to Mrs Lambert and Daisy at their house in
Stratton Street, they were overjoyed to see her again,
but their delight soon turned to confused shock when
she told them she and Maxim were to divorce.
Feeling that she owed them an explanation, Lavinia
told them the reason why they had parted—about Alice and Lucy—requesting them to keep the whole
shameful business to themselves for the time being.
She refrained from telling them about the conditions
Maxim had imposed on her before their marriage. It
all seemed so sordid and humiliating now.

She heard nothing from Maxim, but true to his
word he made the thirty thousand pounds from her

father's legacy—or his own account—available to her immediately.

She had been in London for two weeks when, after much persuasion and dressed in a satin gown of cobalt blue, she accompanied Mrs Lambert and Daisy to the theatre. They were escorted by Mrs Lambert's bachelor brother, an elderly gentleman who frequently escorted his sister and Daisy to social events.

It wasn't until the curtain had come down, and the actors had retreated backstage during the interval, that she allowed her eyes to idly scan the audience in the auditorium. It was filled with noise and laughter and people moving about to pay courtesy calls on their friends, who received their visitors in their boxes with all the dignity and grace as if they had they been at home.

Lavinia's gaze was idly drawn to a tall, silver-haired, elderly gentleman occupying a box with three other gentlemen across from them on the tier below. She was about to look away when the elderly gentleman rose along with the others to acknowledge a woman who had just entered their box.

Bending forward in her seat better to see, Lavinia's eyes became riveted on the scene and a sick paralysis gripped her when she recognised Maxim as one of the gentlemen occupying the box. The woman was Alice Winstanley, beautiful and vivacious in a sumptuous gown of scarlet and silver lace, her black hair gleaming, her red lips parted in a wide smile of sensuality. When Lavinia saw Maxim introduce her to his friends, and how Alice's fingers wrapped themselves with a possessive familiarity round his arm when she leaned closer and spoke to Maxim, a pain like she had never experienced before almost severed her heart in two.

Unable to tear her eyes away she saw Alice throw back her head and laugh hilariously at something one of the gentlemen said to her, taking a seat among them when the next act of the play began. It was at that moment that Maxim, seeming to sense himself being watched, glanced up at her box and saw her. Across the distance their eyes locked, but then Lavinia looked away and leaned back in her chair, and her husband's view of her was mercifully obliterated by Daisy.

Never before in all her life had Lavinia felt so agonisingly, unbearably jealous of another woman as she did of Alice Winstanley at that moment, or as angry as she was with Maxim. She may have given him her blessing to become reconciled with the mother of his child, but how dare he subject her to the painful, humiliating spectacle by parading his mistress in public so soon after his break up with her?

She gulped, swallowing down the tears that accumulated in her throat and threatened to choke her. Resisting the urge to get up and leave the theatre, she sat through the remaining acts of the play in a haze, deaf to the words and blind to everything going on about her, her only conscious thought being that her husband was close by, dancing attendance on his mistress.

Daisy, noticing her friend's strained profile beside her and sensing that she was not paying attention to the play, leaned towards her. 'Lavinia, are you all right? You're not ill, are you?' she inquired softly.

'No. No—I'm quite well, Daisy,' she replied with a weak smile, preferring to keep what she had seen to herself. 'I have a slight headache, that's all.'

Afterwards, being jostled from every direction by people standing around discussing the play as they awaited their carriages, Maxim stood in the foyer of the theatre, having become temporarily separated from his uncle who had paused to speak to an acquaintance. About to move towards the door where it was less congested, and hoping to see Lavinia before she left the theatre, her presence having taken him wholly by surprise, he halted as his gaze came upon her, standing alone near a tall pillar. She was collecting the attention of most of the men in the foyer—and to his chagrin he had to concede that, dressed in a cobalt-blue satin gown which set off her slender figure to perfection, she warranted such admiring regard.

All his attention became focused on the cool, slim features of his young wife and his brows drew together in a frown. Where he had left her with anger at Thornhill, after discovering just how strong-willed, stubborn and infuriating she could be, he now perceived an air of seriousness about her. She displayed none of the frivolity that was present in all the other ladies present, and there was an intent directness in her gaze as she surveyed the scene about her that told Maxim she was finding it all disconcerting.

Perhaps what had transpired between them on her last night at Thornhill had stripped all humour from her, for she was as cool and aloof as an ice queen, being forced to attend an event she found distasteful. He silently cursed the rift he had allowed to form between them, and Alice's unexpected arrival at his box and her determination to remain for what was left of the play, for he would have liked to have escorted his wife to the theatre himself.

With cool composure Lavinia watched Maxim approach, her eyes fixed on the stony, chiselled set of his features. It unsettled her, especially when those blue eyes locked on to her own and moved with exacting slowness over every part of her. It was only two weeks since she had last seen him, but she had forgotten how brilliant and clear his eyes were. In a strange, magical way they seemed capable of stripping her soul bare. Every fibre of her being cried out for him, but her insulted spirit rebelled.

It was all she could do to face his unspoken challenge and not escape to the confines of the carriage waiting to take them home. There was a change in him, subtle, but still it was there. What it was that had brought it about she had no way of knowing, but little by little the realisation dawned on her that this man was a man she did not know. He appeared able to hold himself aloof and apart from everyone, and yet with his mere presence, dominate the scene around him as he did now.

They stood and looked at each other, each conscious of the anger, the passion, the argument and the strife of their parting at Thornhill.

Having admitted the truth to himself that he loved Lavinia, unable to imagine his future without her at his side, Maxim was eager to reach out to her, to feast his eyes on her again, but something about her stiff manner halted him. He gazed down at her pale face, looking deep into her entrancing turquoise eyes, and he felt himself overcome and gripped by the same coldness that flowed out of her.

But if he had looked deeper into her bright eyes, he would have noticed that they were sparkling with suppressed tears of pain and humiliation; from the moment she had seen him with Alice in the theatre when she had become agonisingly aware of his presence, she was unhappy beyond words, and felt as if she were dying slowly and painfully inside. Even so, she would not humble herself at this man's feet, and pride—abused, stubborn, outraged pride—straightened her back and brought her head up high as she met her husband's steady gaze.

'I did not expect to see you here, Lavinia?'

'Why shouldn't I be?' she replied, her voice strained. 'I enjoy the theatre as much as anyone else.'

'I trust you enjoyed the play?'

He addressed her as if she were a mere acquaintance, his voice cool, matter of fact, and Lavinia's pride ached for some assuaging vengeance. 'Yes, thank you,' she lied tersely, vividly aware of the crisp, familiar scent of his cologne.

'You are staying with Mrs Lambert and Daisy, I understand.'

'Yes. They have been very kind.'

Maxim nodded, regarding her coolly. 'I shall call on you. Maybe tomorrow. You will be there?'

'I might be—but then again, I might not,' she said with a mocking smile. 'I might be driving in the park with Daisy. But you needn't put yourself out, Maxim. There is nothing to discuss.'

'On the contrary. There is much we have to settle between us.'

She arched her delicate brows. There was a saturnine twist to his mouth which made Lavinia want to lash out at him. She seethed inwardly. Didn't this arrogant, infuriating man know just how much he had hurt her, shamed her in front of all these people, by appearing in public with his mistress? His mistress! The mother of his child! These few words stung Lavinia like so many wasps. These people at the theatre tonight may not know who she was now, but they soon would when their divorce became common gossip.

'Was I mistaken? I thought we ended that discussion at Thornhill,' she said with a little defiant toss to her head, refusing to let him see how wretched she felt.

'Then yes, you were mistaken. The argument is far from settled yet.'

Her eyes narrowed. 'If all you want to do is argue, Maxim, then I would appreciate it if you keep away from me.'

Leaving her mother talking to some friends, Daisy came to stand beside Lavinia, greeting Maxim politely, who responded in kind. She smiled brightly in an attempt to banish the crackling iciness between these two, but to no avail.

Maxim fixed his eyes on his wife. 'I am here to-night with some friends—'

'I saw,' Lavinia snapped.

Maxim raised his brows at the angry rebuke, knowing full well she was referring to Alice, but this was neither the time nor the place to explain his former mistress's presence in his box or argue the matter. 'We are to go on to my club to dine, otherwise I would invite you to join us,' Maxim told Lavinia.

'Then I would have to refuse. I have an engagement of my own that I have no wish to break,' she lied, favouring him with a slightly mocking, sweet smile, unable to help herself and wondering why she felt the need to make him jealous. 'Goodbye, Maxim.'

Maxim thrust down the feeling of pique of being brushed off like a mere servant. Watching his wife sweep out of the theatre with Daisy, he was angry, but he could not resist moving towards the door and watching the view of her proud head, swaying skirts and trim back as she climbed into the carriage, the lanterns casting their shifting light upon her lovely face.

Settling herself beside Daisy, Lavinia found it equally as hard to resist glancing back at her husband, and she was startled to find his brooding gaze locked on her with a frowning intensity. As the carriage moved off she released a trembling breath and steadied her nerves, watching the buildings they passed, but in her mind she saw only a startling pair of clear blue eyes.

* * *

Having returned from Europe and hearing from Mrs Lambert when she came to call on her mother that Lavinia was staying with her and Daisy in Stratton Street, Sophia Evesham, as plain and uninteresting as Lavinia remembered, paid them a surprise visit a week after their trip to the theatre. She was aware of Lavinia's marriage to Maxim Purnell in Venice and was eager to know if the rumour was true, and that there really was a rift between them already. She had also come to impart some malicious gossip which she hoped would put Lavinia's back up, unaware that Lavinia had borne witness to every humiliating detail.

Lavinia was unprepared for the renewed jealousy that exploded inside her when Sophia calmly mentioned the theatre incident that the whole of London seemed to be gossiping about. However, despite being in a state of acute misery, with her heart plummeting to the very depths of despair, she was determined not to expose her anguish to this vituperative female who had the nerve to call herself Daisy's friend. She forced herself to hide her annoyance and smile under Sophia's penetrating inspection and unflinching hauteur.

'It was Mama who told me that you have not taken up residence at Mr Purnell's house in Grosvenor Street, and that you are staying with Daisy and her mother. There's nothing wrong, I hope, Lavinia, between Mr Purnell and you. I heard that he left London a week ago.'

Having secretly hoped that Maxim would call on her as he had said he would, and feeling worse than ever knowing he had left London without so much as a note, Lavinia looked at Sophia with a cheerfulness she was far from feeling, folding her hands sedately in her lap.

'Wrong? Of course not. Maxim has pressing matters of business to take care of at Rotherfield, that is all. I expect him to return to London and join me soon,' Lavinia told her, smiling sweetly, hoping God would forgive her this small untruth, but she had no intention of giving Sophia anything to crow about. And as for Maxim owning a house on Grosvenor Street—that was another surprise, she thought bitterly.

'Rotherfield?' chirped Sophia. 'How strange?'

'What is so strange about that?'

Sophia shrugged, the glow of triumph brightening her eyes. 'I heard that he has gone to Oxfordshire with his uncle, the Earl of Brinkcliff.'

Lavinia gave her a tolerant, brittle stare. 'Then he must have changed his mind.'

'Rumour has it that he was at the theatre with him on the night he was seen with his former mistress, and that they have become reconciled.'

'With his uncle, or Miss Winstanley?' asked Lavinia, her soft voice heavily laced with sarcasm.

Sophia gave an annoyingly grating laugh. 'Why, his uncle, of course. Although…gossip has it that he has mended the breach with them both.' Perceiving that her information had hit its mark, she prattled on about other things.

Fortified by her anger Lavinia forced herself to smile and listen, giving nothing away, and only when Sophia had gone did her fragile serenity slip.

'Oh, Daisy!' she whispered wretchedly, her pride well and truly battered. She couldn't bear it. Not when she loved Maxim so much. 'Maxim left town without coming to see me. How could he?'

'Take no notice of Sophia, Lavinia,' said Daisy in an attempt to placate her, while wanting to strangle both Sophia and Maxim Purnell with her bare hands for causing Lavinia so much misery. 'Don't let her upset you. She's just jealous because she'll never be able to catch a man like Mr Purnell.'

The Eveshams were giving a ball and they were all invited. However, not inclined to go out into society after her experience at the theatre, Lavinia immediately declined the invitation, which brought an exclamation of disappointment from Daisy as she was about to write an acceptance.

'How can I possible attend a ball, Daisy, when I'm estranged from Maxim? I have no intention of putting myself forward as an object of ridicule.'

Daisy remained adamant. 'Of course you can. Besides, Lavinia, no one knows about your divorce yet. It's early days.'

Lavinia paled at the mention of her divorce. 'How can you be so sure? Don't forget that Maxim has recently been seen in public with his former mistress, so it may already be common knowledge.'

'I doubt it. Divorce is nothing to be proud of and not the sort of thing one bandies about. In any case, surely you don't intend hiding yourself away until after it's all over. Divorces are rare and it could take at least two or three years before it becomes absolute. Besides, apart from the theatre incident, you haven't seen Maxim since coming to London. Despite what Sophia said, perhaps he thinks you are both making a mistake and wants you back. That may have been his reason for wanting to see you—before you so firmly put him off.'

Lavinia shook her head sadly. 'I didn't mean to. I was just so angry and hurt that he would shame and insult me by parading his former mistress in front of me.'

'But how was he to know you would be there?'

'It makes no difference. After what happened between us he won't want me back. Maxim isn't like that. He's sterner and more unbending than I ever thought. Besides, I'm the one who insisted on a divorce, not Maxim. You don't know him like I do, Daisy. He'll never give me another chance. I no longer exist for him. I realise now that I should never have left him like that.'

'I know, and it was foolish of you, Lavinia. I'm sure the two of you could have worked something out if you hadn't got so angry. Your regrets are written all over your face.'

'You're right,' Lavinia acknowledged honestly. 'But I'm just going to have to accept what's happened and learn to get on with my life.'

'Yes, you must, and you can begin by attending the Eveshams' ball with me.'

'Honestly, Daisy, I don't think I can face anyone at present—especially not Lady Evesham. I still cringe when I remember the look on her face when she came upon Maxim kissing me in Venice—and the malicious amusement in Sophia's eyes.'

'Sophia is only jealous because after all the money her parents lavished on her debut and the trip to Europe, she failed to attract a suitor. Whereas not only were you betrothed to Robert, but you also managed to secure the attentions of the extremely handsome Mr Purnell.'

'Nevertheless, Daisy, if everyone has somehow got wind of my estrangement from Maxim, I couldn't bear the shame of it. How they will gloat. Any decent, unattached bachelor will certainly not want to dance with me, and by the end of the evening I will be a social outcast.'

'All the more reason why you should go. Brave it out, Lavinia. You won't be alone, and by London standards it's only going to be a small gathering.'

'But think of the gossip, Daisy.'

'It's a most unfortunate affair and bound to be much talked about. If your divorce is already common knowledge, then you'll have to face it sometime. Better to get it over with and stem the tide of malice. Contrary to what you think, Lavinia, your success will be greatly increased by your impending divorce to Maxim Purnell.'

'In what way?'

'Any woman who has managed to ensnare a man of his standing and reputation—which I'm only just becoming aware of myself, never having heard of him before he jumped into the Venetian lagoon to rescue you—and then files for a divorce, is bound to become an object of curiosity.'

'My marriage to Maxim, which is to be followed so soon by divorce, may assure me social possibilities, but not necessarily respect,' said Lavinia on a sigh.

'You have not been properly introduced into London society so everyone is bound to want to know everything there is to know about you—and a woman as lovely as you will always cause comment and speculation.'

'And being my first ball, Daisy, I really should be accompanied by my husband. I am certain that if Maxim hears about it he will be furious.'

'Good. It might give him something to think about when he learns his wife is no meek and supplicating young thing who intends hiding herself away from the world in shame and mortification. I intend making sure that you look your best for the ball and have every gentleman in London kneeling at your feet before the night is out. If that doesn't pique your husband's pride and bring him back to London when he learns of your success, I shall be most surprised.'

'That is insane, Daisy. If he'd wanted to see me he would have called before he left London. I'm sure he must despise me.'

Daisy's smile held a touch of cynicism. 'If he does then at least he feels something for you. If news of your divorce has not come out, then you must say that Mr Purnell has pressing matters of business to attend to at Rotherfield and that he hopes to join you in London later. There's nothing unusual in that.'

'Sophia says he's gone to Oxfordshire with his uncle, not Rotherfield.'

'Ignore what Sophia says. She isn't important. You must pretend everything is all right between you and Mr Purnell until something happens to rock the boat. You'll find it easier to live with. My instincts tell me you will be a success and by the next day all the rage—and my instincts are never wrong.'

Taking her courage in both hands Lavinia gave in, but she was uneasy.

Chapter Twelve

The night of the ball finally arrived. Lavinia spent more time over her appearance than usual, having the maid sweep her hair up into intricate, tantalising curls, threaded through with golden ribbon. Her gown was a dream of gold chiffon, with a provocatively plunging bodice displaying more of her swelling breasts than she thought was proper, but Daisy didn't appear to think so. With a twinkle in her eye she smiled with undisguised approval.

'You look splendid, Lavinia. I can't wait to see everyone's faces when you are announced at the ball. But Mother is going to have a fit and order you back to your room to change when she sees how low your bodice is. Here, wrap your stole around your shoulders and don't take it off until you reach the Eveshams.'

Lavinia was unaware that no sooner had society digested the news that Maxim Purnell had married in Europe, when it was followed by his wife's arrival in London without him and that she was to attend the Eveshams' ball. Rumour also had it that she was a dazzling beauty and that she and her husband were not in accord. His presence at the opera in the company of his former mistress had been duly noticed, giving rise to a good deal of interest and speculation.

Entering the doors of the Evesham residence—a large country house on the northern outskirts of London—Lavinia had never felt more terrified in her life. Memories of the last ball she had attended evoked poignant memories, for it had been in Venice and Maxim had swept her off her feet.

The three ladies were escorted by Mrs Lambert's brother. Against a background of music and laughter they were received by Sir John and Lady Evesham, with Sophia standing mute and aloof by their side. After exchanging polite pleasantries they moved off towards the ballroom, where long French windows with velvet drapes opened on to a terrace and extensive grounds. Daisy smiled at her friend.

'There you are, you see,' she said quietly, observing the tension on Lavinia's face, thinking that she looked like a lamb about to be slaughtered. 'That wasn't so bad, was it? Since their return from Europe, the Eveshams have lost no time in spreading the gossip about you and Mr Purnell. Lady Evesham has told me that everyone has been bombarding her with questions about you, and are curious to know why you are in London alone after only a few short weeks of marriage. Already the gossips are talking of a split between the two of you.'

'But no one knows for sure, do they?' asked Lavinia in alarm.

'No. It's no secret that your husband has a daughter, and everyone expected him to marry Alice

Winstanley eventually. His European marriage to you is a mystery they will hasten to excavate. However, no one knows about your separation so relax and enjoy yourself. You are by far the most beautiful woman here tonight, and already everyone is glancing your way.'

Lavinia smiled softly, holding her head high and ignoring the stares as she injected some confidence into her movements. 'They can stare and whisper all they like, Daisy,' she replied courageously, fixing the most ravishing smile on her face. 'I'm not going to let it bother me.'

Daisy smiled at her approvingly. 'Good for you. By tomorrow morning you will be a sensation.'

Moving past huge flower displays and liveried footmen balancing glasses of wine on silver trays in the huge blue and white foyer, they entered the glittering ballroom. Chandeliers dripped their sparkling crystals over the heads of couples dancing to the strains of a waltz. It was a magical scene, of colour and movement.

Feeling she was under inspection, Lavinia had noticed how heads turned her way when she had been announced, which was followed by a buzz of speculative conversation. Despite her assertions to Daisy that she didn't care what people thought about her, she was painfully self-conscious of everyone devouring her with eager interest.

Recalling what Maxim had said to her in his anger on the night they had parted, that no matter what transpired between them in private, in public he expected her to behave as his wife, she was determined to abide by that and do nothing to dishonour his good name. With her head held high and a smile pinned to her face, she moved among the throng, determined that no one looking at her would know how miserable and lonely this mysterious stranger was in their midst, and that her heart was as dead as a stone and as cold as ice. How they would gloat, Lavinia thought bitterly, when they discovered her secret.

She went through the motions of being introduced by Mrs Lambert to people of note, talking and laughing at the right time, protected by an invisible shell that nothing could penetrate. A crowd of young gallants was already forming about her, and she collected her thoughts sufficiently to respond politely to their compliments and to look as if she was enjoying the ball, allowing one of them to lead her on to the dance floor.

From the gallery looking down on to the ballroom, Maxim's eyes were drawn to his wife. Determined to bridge the gap that was widening between them the longer they remained apart, he had returned from Brinkcliff Hall with his uncle to make his peace with Lavinia. Having arrived in town just two hours ago, he had gone directly to call on her, only to be told on arriving at the Lambert residence that she was attending a ball at Sir John Evesham's house.

On discovering that in no time at all his wife had flagrantly launched herself into society, Maxim had experienced a sharp jolt of displeasure. Firmly ordering the servants to have Lavinia's clothes packed and dispatched posthaste to his own residence in

Grosvenor Street, he immediately set off for the
Eveshams' ball.

And now as he stood and watched her, for the first
time in his life Maxim experienced an acute feeling
of jealousy which caught him completely off guard.
It was a feeling he found decidedly unpleasant.
Frowning with furious displeasure, he considered her
décolletage to be too revealing, the neckline cut so
low as to intrigue and tantalise her admirers. He
could not bear to see other men vying with each other
with infuriating persistence to dance with her, cov-
eting her, to watch the admiration and appreciation
in their eyes as they followed and devoured her every
move, leaning forward to allow their eyes to delve
into her bodice.

She was like a young queen holding court. The
loveliness of her smiling face was flushed with dancing and the champagne she drank between dances,
and when she moved her slender, though softly
rounded form floated with a fluidity and grace over
the floor in a swirl of chiffon, the tips of her gold
satin slippers visible as her feet darted to and fro in
step to the music. In the simple elegance of her
golden ballgown, chosen to blend with the soft
warmth of her skin and hair, Maxim's breath caught
in his throat as he watched the irresistible curve of
her lips and the brilliance of her magnificent turquoise eyes as she gazed at her partner.

And yet there was something remote and detached
in the attitude of this dazzling creature. Observing
her closely as she engaged in light-hearted repartee,
he saw there was something mechanical in the smile

pinned to her face. The love, the warmth and the passion that he had roused in her and had flourished, had become frozen into this beautiful effigy.

But he had never seen her look so provocatively lovely, so regal, glamorous and bewitching—and she belonged to him. Lord, how he'd missed her. He ardently yearned to hold her in his arms, to feel her warmth, smell her hair, her flesh. The yearning was like an obsession in his blood. It tormented him all the time. An ache was growing inside him. Never had he felt anything like it, and Lavinia and Lavinia alone could assuage that ache, with her lips, her body.

Unable to endure this torture a moment longer Maxim turned on his heel. His only thought was to get to her and inject some warmth back into her, to take her in his arms and send her persistent suitors packing.

People were still arriving and Lavinia was with Daisy talking to a group of boisterous gentlemen when the butler announced Lord Stannington. The name was unfamiliar so Lavinia took no notice. It was only when the voices around her became hushed and she felt Daisy clutch her arm that she looked at her, following the direction of her gaze towards the entrance of the ballroom. She paled, overcome with shock. Unable to move, her eyes became riveted on a tall gentleman fastidiously tailored in black evening attire. It was Maxim, just as supremely powerful and splendidly and unbearably handsome. When she saw him she felt such a pang of longing and need that she wanted to run to him and fling herself against him.

His commanding presence was awesome. During the time they had been apart she had hoped she had managed to conquer the debilitating effect he always had on her senses, but his potent sexual magnetism was like a palpable force. How tall he was, how lean and muscular, and how her blood stirred at the sight of him. How had she allowed him to do this to her? She was scandalised by the stirrings inside her that the mere sight of him commanded, and she resented this hunger, this need, that held her captive to her emotions.

Lavinia watched him as he talked to Sir John and Lady Evesham. He looked so relaxed, and he spoke to them with such lazy good humour that she could hardly believe he was the same relentless, rage-filled man who had forcibly clasped her to him and made love to her at Thornhill one month ago. It was as if he were two people: one she loved and admired, and one she feared and mistrusted—and, she reminded herself, with good reason.

'Maxim!' she whispered. 'What on earth is he doing here, do you think, Daisy?'

'More to the point, what's he doing calling himself Lord Stannington?'

'I have no idea. I know Maxim cares nothing for titles and that he is estranged from his uncle, the Earl of Brinkcliff. Perhaps they have become reconciled, which would explain his use of the title—being the Earl's heir. What will he do? Do you think he will ignore me? Oh, Daisy—I couldn't bear it if he did that.'

'He won't. Your husband is not the sort to make a scene—and my guess is that he wouldn't be here if you weren't.'

Lavinia was calm as could be to everyone around her, but her heart was pounding and she seemed to have trouble catching her breath. Maxim turned and caught her gaze, and with hope and disbelief springing to her eyes, she watched him cut through the groups of people with deceptive casualness, briefly acknowledging those he recognised, many a feminine eye following him as he advanced towards her.

As he came closer a knot began to form inside Lavinia's chest. He was politely frightening, his eyes like ice, and he bore down on her with the predatory grace of a stalking beast. The music had ceased and people were talking among themselves, but Lavinia was aware that everyone's attention was riveted on them, eager to see what would happen when Maxim Purnell reached his wife.

Holding her gaze, Maxim's eyes were silently telling Lavinia that for the sake of appearances they must both behave as though everything between them was in accord. He had such strength, authority and incredible drive that he would be in control of any situation.

When he stood in front of her he looked searchingly into her eyes, taking her hand and raising it to his lips. 'This is a pleasant surprise, Lavinia. I hope you are enjoying yourself.'

'Yes, thank you, Maxim,' she replied, favouring him with a honey-sweet smile, sensing that behind his chiselled features and air of calm he was furious.

Smiling faintly he swung his gaze coolly over the disappointed faces of the group of young men gathered around her. 'Please excuse us. My wife looks excessively warm after her exertions on the dance floor. I'm sure she will be glad of some fresh air.'

Taking her elbow in a firm grasp, his free hand resting possessively in the small of her back, he guided her towards the French windows somewhat less than gently. A few gentlemen met his eye and, recognising the challenge in his gaze, they turned away. Maxim propelled his wife from the safety of the house on to the terrace, not speaking until they were far enough away from the eyes and ears of everyone, and then he turned, fixing her with the full blast of his fury.

'What do you think you're playing at by coming here? Are you deliberately trying to provoke me?' he demanded with hot, unreasonable anger, the barbs of jealousy pricking him to a painful depth.

'Provoke you?' his wife replied, her eyes wide as she feigned a look of innocence, determined not to let him draw her to anger and cause her to lose her fragile grip on her emotions. 'Why on earth should I do that? We are estranged, Maxim.'

He stepped close, towering over her, and Lavinia almost retreated from those fierce eyes. But she steeled herself and stood her ground before his accusing glare.

'I assure you, Lavinia, that I will have you behave with more dignity and in a manner more befitting your station than you seem concerned about. You are still my wife and you will behave accordingly.'

Lavinia's heart was breaking, but she gave him a ravishing smile. 'I haven't forgotten, Maxim, and there are all sorts of things I remember about being your wife. And don't worry. I will do nothing to embarrass you—and I sincerely hope you do nothing that will embarrass me.'

His eyes narrowed in question. 'What do you mean by that remark?'

She shrugged her slender shoulders. 'What I say.'

'Suppose you tell me why, the minute you are out of my sight, you forget how to behave.'

'My behaviour is quite in order—which cannot be said of your own. I find your manner unreasonable and insufferable.'

He glared at her. She was right. His manner was unreasonable and insufferable, and he didn't even begin to understand it. His blazing gaze was drawn to and froze on the beautiful swell of her petal-soft breasts above the golden bodice of her gown. 'And do you have to display yourself so wantonly to the entire male population of London? How dare you come out in public alone—in that dress.'

Lavinia flinched at the cold, ruthless fury in his eyes as they raked over her. Bravely she tried to hold on to her composure and stop herself exploding. 'I see nothing wrong with my gown. I think it's extremely pretty. And I hardly think you have the right to dictate where I go and what I shall wear under the circumstances. Really, Maxim, if you brought me out here for no other purpose than to berate me, then I shall go back inside.'

Torn between the urge to lash out at him or burst into tears, she made a move to pass him, but his hand locked on her wrist. 'You will stay here and talk to me. I will not have you making a scene, Lavinia. Consider the meal everyone will make when they see there is disharmony between us.'

'Like you considered my feelings when you came to London and paraded your former mistress at the opera for everyone to see?' she flared accusingly, her eyes sparking fire. Bringing the matter out into the open at last, she wanted to fling her hurt in his face. 'How dare you do that to me? Have you any idea how shamed and insulted I felt when I saw you to-gether that night?'

Her words brought Maxim up sharp and he stared at her. He realised that she had seen Alice come to his box that night at the theatre, and the foolish young woman had drawn her own conclusions. Lavinia looked so young, so vulnerable, facing him with those mutinous, appealing turquoise eyes locked on to his, that his anger was defused. His senses were jolted into life by the elusive, perfumed smell of her. Half-smiling, half-frowning, he looked into her eyes. 'I stand rebuked, but that I can explain.'

'I don't want to listen to your lame excuses.'

'Yes, you do,' he said, grasping her arm and forc-ing her to look at him when she spun on her heel to walk away. 'When I came to London shortly after you left Thornhill, it was to see my lawyers and my uncle. I was with him at the opera the night Alice was there. She came to our box to be introduced and it was impossible to remove her without causing a scene. Unfortunately, her visit was long enough to be noted and set the theatre alight with rumours of a reconciliation. Please believe me when I tell you that nothing could be further from the truth.' He smiled, suddenly, his eyes gently teasing, his voice quiet. 'But why all the fuss, Lavinia? I thought that was what you wanted. Wasn't that why you left me?'

'Damn you, Maxim!' she flared. 'Did you have to do it so publicly?'

'I do assure you that it wasn't intentional. I would not have done that to you. And when I told you I was to go on to dine with acquaintances at my club afterwards, it was the truth.' His eyes narrowed, glinting mockingly down into hers. 'Which cannot be said of your own supper arrangement that night. You implied that the company would consist of other men. Were you trying to stir my jealousy by retaliation, Lavinia?'

'Retaliation? How amusing. Do not judge me by your own behaviour, Maxim, or feel you have anything to explain,' she said caustically.

'I don't. I merely thought you would like to know. And the reason I didn't call on you at Mrs Lambert's before I went to Oxfordshire with my uncle was because after your cold reception at the theatre, I considered it best, for the time being at least, to avoid any confrontation that might end as our last meeting did.'

Lavinia's eyes flew to his in blazing fury. 'Whenever we happen to meet in the future, Maxim, it will *never* end like that one, and I would appreciate you not mentioning it again. It is a night I have no wish to recall. Why are you here, anyway?'

'Lavinia,' he said impatiently, taking both her arms and looking down into her lovely face. 'I am here for no other reason than to see you.'

Her ire was ill suppressed as she ground out between clenched teeth, 'You could have done that the last time you came to London, but you chose to ignore me.'

'I have just explained why I didn't come to see you. I did not ignore you. I am here now because there are things we must discuss—that have to be understood between us.'

'I understand perfectly well how things stand between us, Maxim,' she said, turning away.

Maxim moved to stand close behind her, not touching, but near enough to prevent her moving past him without coming into contact with him. 'I'm sorry you were hurt,' he murmured. 'Whatever may be going through that pretty head of yours, Lavinia, I have no desire to return to Alice, and I had no idea she would come bursting into my box at the theatre.'

Lavinia smiled softly to herself, her instinct telling her that his initial anger had been caused by his jealousy on seeing her surrounded by so many admiring young males, and that despite everything, he did still want her. The knowledge warmed her, and made up for a good deal of his abominable treatment of her.

But threads of anger still coursed through her, and she had no intention of letting him off lightly.

Over her shoulder Maxim gazed down at the seductive swell of her breasts and he ached to caress the womanly softness of her, to embrace her and ease the lusting ache at the pit of his belly. Strange lights danced in her golden hair, and her slender shoulders gleamed with a creamy soft lustre. The heady allure of her perfume mingled with her womanly essence, filled his head, stirring and warming his blood.

Lavinia turned and faced him, almost overawed by his nearness, and trying to break the contact he was beginning to stir inside her. She didn't move as he ran a finger along the curve of her lips, trailing it down the column of her neck and along the smooth, velvet curve of her shoulder and down her upper arm. It was a soothing caress that awoke tingling answers in places she tried to ignore. The betrayal of her body aroused vexation in her. His touch burned her flesh and seared into her heart, reminding her how deeply she still loved this insufferable man. It was a hard fact for her pride to accept, especially when they were to divorce.

Maxim lifted a brow as he regarded his wife, and she read in their depths and the heat of his stare what he had in mind. Calmly she met his gaze.

'Cool your ardour, Maxim,' she warned. 'This is neither the time nor the place and most certainly not part of our agreement.' Trying to regain her composure she struck a stubborn pose, the look in her eyes as she silently met her husband's sardonic gaze one of pure mutiny. 'Please excuse me. It's becoming decidedly chilly out here all of a sudden.' Jerking her arms out of his grasp she turned from him and walked quickly back into the house, unaware of his infuriating smile of admiration as he watched her go.

To her husband at that moment, Lavinia was the epitome of a stubborn, prideful woman. Yet for all her fire and spirit she displayed none of Alice's viciousness.

An expression of disappointment crossed Daisy's face when she saw Lavinia enter the ballroom alone. Taking her hand, she drew her to one side, but was prevented from asking what had occurred on the terrace when she became aware that people were looking their way.

Glancing up, Lavinia saw a smiling Sophia bearing down on her, accompanied by an extremely beautiful woman with raven black hair. Immediately she had a premonition of disaster. The woman was Alice Winstanley, Maxim's former mistress and mother of his child, and she watched, sick with dread, as she moved serenely towards her. Oh, why did Alice have to be so devastatingly provocative and beautiful in a rich, burgundy-coloured gown and the body of a goddess? she thought despairingly.

There was a tension as everyone waited to see what would happen when Maxim's mistress came face to face with his wife. Choosing that moment to reappear through the French windows, Maxim saw what was about to happen and sensed Lavinia's distress. Determined to save her from being shamed and humiliated in front of everyone, immediately he made his way to her side, taking her hand and linking it through his arm. She glanced up at him, gratitude in her worried eyes, glad of his support as she watched Alice come closer.

The room began to rock and tremble beneath her, and she was sickened to think this woman knew what it was like to be loved by Maxim, to have her naked body caressed by him, to know how devastating and drugging his kisses could be—for their bodies to be linked as one.

Sensing what she was feeling, Maxim reassuringly squeezed her fingers, which were linked through his arm. He didn't look in the least perturbed that they were about to be confronted by Alice, but the look he bestowed on Sophia, who was taking a malicious delight in a situation entirely of her making, was murderous.

Alice halted in front of them, bestowing on Maxim a smile dripping with charm, whilst eyeing Lavinia like a hostile cat. She had no qualms about meeting his wife, in fact, she was obviously out to relish her rival's embarrassment and humiliation.

'Alice!' said Maxim with a lazy smile. 'As usual you look lovely. No doubt you will have all the gentlemen at your feet before the night is over.' He turned to Lavinia. 'Permit me to introduce to you my wife, Lavinia.'

Normally a man would not introduce his wife to his mistress in polite society, but there was no way Maxim could avoid doing so without making a scene.

Alice's beautiful brows rose slightly when her eyes met Lavinia's. Myriad emotions washed over her face, none of them pleasant. Lavinia returned her stare steadily, trying not to look disconcerted or intimidated. She was aware of every man and woman in the room secretly looking at them with eyes that glittered, above mouths that curled with amusement. She loathed every one of them, furious that, out of sheer spite, Sophia Evesham had put her in this position. Fortified by her anger and her husband's support, she looked directly into Alice's eyes with a quiet, dignified composure which made Maxim proud.

'I'm pleased to meet you, Miss Winstanley.'

'Likewise,' Alice answered, her tone insincere and lightly contemptuous, her look insolent. 'I've been hearing a great deal about you.'

Lavinia gave a delicate lift of her brows. 'So soon? You surprise me, Miss Winstanley. I arrived in town a month ago, and this is only my second appearance in public.'

Alice laughed, a harsh, abrasive sound. 'Gossip is always plentiful in London. That's one thing you can depend on.' She shifted her gaze back to Maxim. 'You really must call some time, Maxim. It's shameful the way you neglect our daughter. You have no idea how much she pines for you.'

Maxim's eyes were like shards of ice. 'Yes, I do. It is my intention to call tomorrow. I trust you will be at home, Alice. There is a matter of some importance I have to discuss with you. Lucy is well, I hope?'

'A little dispirited. But it's nothing a visit from her father won't cure. I'll look forward to your call,' she said with a satisfied smile curving her lovely lips, making sure Lavinia understood the claim she had on Maxim.

In spite of herself, Alice's resentment and jealousy began to rise as her eyes flickered once more over the woman at his side, hating her. She was overawed by Lavinia's cool self-assurance, her casual, confident beauty, and contemptuous of Maxim's open admiration of his wife. She threw Maxim a glare that might once have moved him. Now he was frankly amused. She was hot, suddenly, trying desperately to control her temper for fear of being made to look a fool.

'Excuse me,' she said haughtily, snapping open her fan and using it with verve. 'I am promised for the next dance and I can see my partner looking for me.'

Lavinia and Maxim watched her move on in a relieved silence, the tension beginning to relax between them.

'Thank you, Maxim,' Lavinia murmured. 'I couldn't have endured meeting her alone.'

He smiled down at her, squeezing her hand. 'I dare say you'd have coped admirably.'

The musicians chose that moment to play a waltz and Maxim smiled, a slow, lazy white smile that melted Lavinia's heart. He might be mercurial, unreasonable, demanding and impossible, but he still made her heart sing.

'Every other gentleman here tonight has danced with you. I think it's high time you danced with your husband. Come, dance with me, Lavinia,' he murmured, his voice as soft as it had been on that other occasion when he had asked her to dance at the masquerade in Venice.

Mesmerised by the seductive invitation in his voice, Lavinia let him draw her on to the dance floor, abandoning her waist to his encircling arm. It was as steady and firm as a rock. Maxim was a superb dancer and moved with a lithe, athletic grace. He whirled her into the dance and she seemed to soar with the melody. She gazed at her husband admiringly, liking the way his superbly tailored black coat clung to his splendid shoulders. His face had lost some of the tan he had acquired in Europe, but it was still darker than any other man's present, and combined with his gleaming black hair, his pristine white shirt and neckcloth stood out in sharp contrast.

Maxim felt her tremble and bent his head, giving the impression to all watching that he was paying his wife an intimate compliment. 'We have an audience. Hold your head up, Lavinia. Look into my eyes and smile. Let them see that we are a devoted couple.' He arched a satirical dark brow. 'You may even flirt with me a little if you so wish.'

Lavinia looked at him, utterly confused by his sudden appearance and not knowing what he wanted of her. Had he come because he cared, because he'd missed her and was unable to live without her? Was he sorry for what he'd done and come to make amends? Dozens of questions invaded her mind. There was so much she wanted to ask him, so much she wanted to say to him.

Unable to understand him she searched his sultry eyes, suddenly resenting his easy arrogance in assuming that she would be ready to fall at his feet as if nothing untoward had happened between them. Not at any price would she consent to be treated so. The fact that she had been full of remorse over their parting and her harsh words about his lack of responsibility where Alice and his daughter was concerned, and had considered returning to Rotherfield and throwing herself on his mercy, while praying at the same time that he would come to her and take her in his arms and alleviate her suffering, went out of her mind as her pride came to the fore.

'And if I don't?' she said stiffly in response to his remark.

Maxim saw rebellion beginning to stir in the depths of her glorious turquoise eyes. 'Pretend.' His arm tightened about her waist, forcing her into an awareness of his lithe body. He was perfectly well aware of the effect it always had on her when he held her in his arms, knowing how easily he could bring her to submission.

'I can't pretend, Maxim. Besides, Daisy says that it's unusual for a woman to flirt openly with her husband.'

'I don't give a damn what Daisy says,' Maxim said through gritted teeth, his earlier jealousy on seeing every man in the room undressing and devouring her with their lust-filled eyes still simmering beneath the surface of his calm façade. 'Look at me like you've been looking at all those other doting swains who've been clinging to your side all evening like limpets to a rock—or have you used up all your smiles on them?'

'Of course not, but at least they were civil, their remarks flattering.'

'Every man resorts to flattery when there's something they want from a beautiful woman,' Maxim growled. 'Don't be deceived when they shower you with pretty compliments and speeches. They're all after only one thing.'

'Nevertheless, they were full of charm, every one of them, and told me I'm the most beautiful woman at the ball tonight. What do you think, Maxim?' she asked with mock innocence, looking up at him with her head cocked on one side, her eyes calmly watching for his reaction to her challenging question.

Maxim was furious that so many men had been drooling over his wife, but he swallowed his chagrin and smiled charmingly down at her with half-shrouded eyes.

'What can I say? As your husband I must agree with every one of them.'

'Must? Maxim, I don't want you to feel you must agree with them just to humour me.'

His brows arched in ironic amusement. 'I'm not humouring you. I meant it. You are by far the love-liest woman here—but don't let the compliment go to your head.'

She smiled, satisfied. 'I won't.'

'Now tell me what you're doing here. Not content with attending the ball alone and making yourself conspicuous, you have to make me appear ludicrous by flirting with every man present?' His clear blue eyes held hers, full of accusation. 'Well? What have you to say for yourself?'

With an effort Lavinia retained her composure as they moved over the dance floor, aswirl with couples moving gracefully to the music, lovely and melodic.

'Nothing. When you're in this mood, whatever I say in my defence will be futile. For a start I wasn't flirting. I was merely being polite. And I wouldn't call attending a ball to which I've been invited making myself conspicuous. Besides, I could hardly wait for you to escort me, seeing that we are estranged. What would you have me do? Go slinking around as if I've disgraced myself? We may be divorcing, but that doesn't mean I have to make an outcast of myself. What are you doing here, Maxim? I—I thought—'

'What? What did you think? That I would calmly sit back and allow you to walk out of my life? May I ask what your admirers talked to you about?'

'You may, but I will not tell you.'

He nodded, studying her beneath half-lowered lids with tranquil amusement. 'Do I have reason to call any of them out?'

She smiled, her eyes glowing with repressed laughter. 'Several. But with so many, you would be hard pressed to beat them all.'

'Don't count on it,' Maxim replied, spinning her round with unnecessary force.'

She laughed. 'Maxim, please slow down. You swirl me round so fast I'm beginning to feel quite dizzy.'

'You've drunk too many glasses of champagne.'

She was indignant. 'No, I have not.'

'Yes, you have—four—or was it five?'

His smile was amused and slightly mocking which annoyed her. 'You were watching me?'

'Yes. I had nothing better to do.'

'You could have sought me out earlier.'

'What? And deprive all those besotted swains of the pleasure of your company? You've made quite an impression and, regardless of your marital state, you must prepare yourself to be pursued,' he teased lightly.

'And here I was thinking I would be safe in London,' she quipped.

Maxim caught her gaze, his eyes narrowing seductively. 'Safe? Safe from me? From loving me?' he murmured, his warm breath fanning her face. He smiled infuriatingly at the bewilderment in her eyes. 'What have you told everyone?'

'Nothing,' she replied, totally bemused by his behaviour and wondering what he was leading up to. 'Apart from Mrs Lambert and Daisy, no one knows we are estranged—that—that we are to divorce, if that is what you mean. I must thank you for being so prompt in making the money accessible to me. I have decided to look for a small house somewhere in London.'

'There's no need. There will be no divorce.'

Lavinia's eyes widened in amazement. 'But—I don't understand. What are you saying?'

He smiled down at her, his gaze dropping to the tantalising creamy swell of her breasts exposed above the bodice of her gown, a sight that had enraged him earlier, and one in which he now took lustful delight. She looked incredible, ravishing, he thought, and he was determined to adorn that slender neck with the finest jewels in the kingdom before too long.

'You heard me, my sweet. I don't want a divorce. I have no intention of letting you out of my sight ever again. This last month has been the longest month of my life and I don't intend enduring another like it.'

Lavinia stared at him, reeling from his incredible confession. Afraid to hope, and unable not to, she gaze up at him, her knees quaking so badly that she feared she would stumble.

'Have you considered the consequences of a divorce, Lavinia?'

'The consequences for whom?'

'You. It will certainly be unpleasant.'

'I would imagine divorce is always unpleasant.'

'With a scandalous divorce suit hanging over you, you will become the object of everyone's attention.'

'Surely that applies to both of us?'

'Hardly. Don't forget that I would be the one divorcing you on the grounds of desertion, and it would do you nothing but harm. You would be ostracised by decent society. Could you endure the severe censure and disgrace the stigma of being a divorced woman would bring you?'

'I—I don't know, Maxim. I haven't really thought about it.'

'You will become notorious in a way you do not deserve. What would you hope to gain?'

'My freedom.'

His eyes probed hers. 'And do you want to be free, Lavinia? Of me?'

Lavinia searched his face, feeling her heart turn over exactly the way it always did when he looked at her like he was looking at her now. She saw the glow in his half-shuttered eyes kindle slowly into flame, and deep within her, she felt the answering stirrings of longing, a longing to feel the tormenting sweetness of his caress, the stormy passion of his kiss, and the earth-shattering joy of his body possessing hers. 'No.'

'Thank God for that,' he murmured huskily, impatient for the dance to end so he could whisk her away and make love to her. 'As an experienced man of the world I never would have believed that I would fall victim to a beautiful, innocent young woman who firmly refuses to yield to my authority and blithely incurs my displeasure by leaving me. You, my love, have the power to amuse, enchant, bewitch and infuriate me as no other woman has done before. I only hope that you have been as miserable as I have been.'

The tenderness in Maxim's eyes warmed Lavinia's heart. 'Yes, I have,' she confessed, feeling the music possessing her as her body moved to the melody, melting into his.

'You did miss me?'

Gazing up at him she was happy to see his eyes were serious and devoid of his usual arrogance. She wanted to tell him that she had missed him more than she would have believed possible, that she had missed his presence, his quiet strength, the laughter they had shared and his lazy smile, and the way he was looking at her now.

'Yes,' she admitted softly. 'When I left you everything suddenly seemed so empty and meaningless.'

Maxim's lips curved in a soft, satisfied smile and tenderness washed through him at the sincere honesty of her reply.

'I was too hasty in my judgement, Maxim. I'm sorry. I was upset and hurt that you didn't tell me about Alice and Lucy.'

'I understand that now.'

'Do you?'

'Yes. I should have told you. It was wrong of me not to, I realise that now. I don't blame you for being angry. I want to explain everything to you, Lavinia, but not here. I don't deserve you,' he murmured. 'You're so perfect. When the music ends I have no intention of remaining to dance attendance on dozens of elderly ladies and utter meaningless platitudes for the next few hours. We will make our excuses to Sir John and Lady Evesham and leave soon afterwards.'

'But—we can't, Maxim. It would appear rude.'

'Yes, we can. We'd better leave before I hurl you down on to the floor and ravish you in front of all these people. Do you want to make a scene?'

'No, of course I don't.'

'Then do as I say.' His smile was lazy as his eyes settled on her moist lips with hungry ardour. 'I can think of more pleasurable ways of spending an evening with my wife. In private.'

Hot colour burned Lavinia's cheeks and she ground her teeth with indignation when she recalled the last time she had experienced the kind of pleasure he was talking about. Determined not to let him off lightly for what he had done to her on her last night at Thornhill, she stared defiantly into his eyes, her body stiffening against his as he whirled her over the dance floor, her step matching his with admirable precision.

'Yes, I'm sure you can, Maxim. But I seem to recall that your interpretation of pleasure is not mine. I have every reason in the world to despise you for what you did to me.'

Looking down at her, Maxim's sharp eyes didn't miss a thing, including both her suppressed ire and her nervousness. His expression softened. 'You're right, and I apologise. I realise that some form of atonement for my behaviour towards you is in order.'

With great difficulty Lavinia had to stifle a smile, for despite his words to the contrary, there was a complete absence of contrition on his face.

'I behaved very badly,' he admitted, 'but you did drive me to it.'

Meeting his impertinent gaze Lavinia gasped. The arrogance of his last remark was so typical of him that she almost laughed.

Maxim smiled softly, a warmth entering his narrowed eyes. 'I don't recall you protesting too strongly at the time, either.'

Swamped with embarrassment Lavinia's flush deepened attractively and she averted her eyes, wishing he wouldn't taunt and torment her in this infuriating manner. 'Please, Maxim. Do we have to discuss these things in the middle of the dance floor with everyone looking at us? Have you no shame?'

He grinned, his eyes alight with devilish amusement. 'None whatsoever, my love. But I do agree. I think we should retire to discuss this in private.'

Panic suddenly gripped Lavinia. 'But this is all so sudden. I can't leave with you just like that, Maxim. I came with Mrs Lambert and Daisy. I must return with them. Perhaps we can meet and discuss things in the morning.'

His face hardened. 'No, Lavinia. We leave together.'

The sudden bite in his voice made Lavinia stiffen in his arms. 'You cannot always expect me to bow to your authority, Maxim. I must have time to think about this.'

'I have given you four weeks. Isn't that long enough?'

'A—at least let us stay for the buffet.'

'We'll eat at home if you're hungry.'

Lavinia longed to defy him, but she didn't dare. The music ceased and he led her off the floor.

After making their excuses to their hosts, Maxim escorted his wife out of the Eveshams' residence, aware as he did so of the regret on the faces of several unattached males. He met their eyes with a look that threatened to slice every one of them into pieces if they dared approach her.

Chapter Thirteen

Like every other residence in Grosvenor Street, Maxim's town house was an imposing building. The door was opened by a footman and they stepped into a high, spacious hall with a white marble floor. Lavinia could not restrain an exclamation of approval, which brought a smile to Maxim's lips.

'Goodness, Maxim! You've certainly done well for yourself. Having seen Rotherfield and now this, you have all the trappings of an aristocrat.'

He grinned. 'I knew you would like it.'

Lavinia looked at him steadily. 'Am I so predictable, Maxim? Were you so sure I would come?' she enquired.

'Naturally,' he replied.

'Conceited of you,' she said lightly with a little smile tugging at her lips.

'Life has made me that way,' Maxim retorted.

'Yes—I can see that,' she remarked, looking around her. 'A house such as this is most appropriate for Lord Stannington—the future Earl of Brinkcliff,' she said with a teasing light in her eyes.

An ironic smile twisted Maxim's lips and he scowled. 'I'm glad you think so,' he replied absently.

Lavinia frowned. 'For a man who will one day inherit an earldom and all that goes with it, you don't look too happy about it.'

'I'm not. It makes me damned uncomfortable if you must know. Does it bother you being Lady Stannington—knowing that one day you will be a countess?'

'I confess that I find it extremely daunting, but I think I shall be able to live with it. Ursula told me about your estrangement from your uncle, so I can only assume you have healed the breach and become reconciled.'

'Yes. Ursula pressed me into it. I'll explain everything to you later.' His gaze narrowed on her smiling lips. 'Does the promise of a coronet and all that goes with it make me more desirable as a husband, Lavinia?'

She looked at him steadily. 'Do you seriously think those things matter to me, Maxim? I'm not interested in grand estates or riches. Nor am I interested in a coronet—only the man who wears it.'

'Some women would settle for nothing less,' he said, thinking of Alice.

'I'm not some women. When did you see your uncle?'

'I had a meeting with him three weeks ago here in London.'

Lavinia was still hurt to know he had been in London and hadn't tried to contact her after their encounter at the theatre, but said nothing.

'Come along, let me show you to your bedchamber,' he murmured, eager to be alone with her.

They went up the elegant curving staircase to the landing where they had adjoining suites. Maxim disappeared into his own, stripping off his jacket as he went and leaving Lavinia alone with a fresh-faced young maid. The room was extremely grand and tastefully furnished. the overall colour scheme being midnight blue and ivory. 'My name's Betsy, my lady,' said the maid, bobbing a respectful curtsey. 'Lord Stannington has employed me to be your personal maid.'

'Has he now!' said Lavinia with a wry smile on her lips, her eyes making a sharp assessment of the gowns Betsy was in the process of unpacking from a large trunk. Recognising them as being her own, she felt a stirring of resentment that Maxim had impudently ordered them to be brought from Stratton Street without first speaking to her about it. 'I'm sure we will get along very well, Betsy—' she smiled '—and I must thank you for unpacking my things.'

Betsy helped her new mistress out of her clothes and into a white satin and lace nightdress. She had just finished fastening the tiny buttons at her throat when Maxim strode through the connecting door into the bedchamber, wearing a mulberry-coloured dressing robe and filling the room with his presence.

Casting Betsy a glance of dismissal, he went towards his wife, impatient to have her in his arms after so long. 'Thank God we are alone at last,' he murmured, drawing her close.

Lavinia saw the darkening in his eyes and stalled his kiss by placing her hands on his chest and looking up at him, still annoyed with him for taking the liberty of having her clothes brought here without her say so.

'What is it, my love?' he asked, feeling her hesitate.

'Maxim! When you came to London, were you so sure I could be persuaded to return here with you that you immediately ordered my clothes to be packed up at Stratton Street and brought here?'

'I was,' he murmured, drawing her hair aside and nuzzling her ear with his warm lips.

Lavinia sighed. 'You're impossible.'

He relinquished her ear and grinned. 'We've already agreed that. Are you complaining?'

She looked at him, loving him. 'No. Nothing you do surprises me.'

'Are you still hungry?'

She saw the need, the intensity of his longing, reflected in his eyes, and her stomach quivered in anticipation of what was to come. 'No. Not any more. At least—not for food.'

'Good girl. That's what I like to hear.'

The desire darkening his eyes and the raw emotion in his voice made Lavinia hesitate and draw away from him. 'Maxim, wait. There are things to discuss first?'

'They can wait until morning. We have better things to do just now.'

'Indeed?'

'Yes,' he said, catching her upper arms and pulling her towards him. 'I'm going to love you, Lavinia.' He saw the wary light in her eyes, knowing she was remembering the last time he had made love to her, forcing himself on her. 'I'm not going to hurt you. I give you my word. I would never hurt you, not intentionally. I want to give you the world.'

'I've already told you that I don't want the world. It's not important to me. Why did you come to London, Maxim?'

'Because you matter to me a great deal. Dear Lord,' he breathed, gathering her into his arms, his senses intoxicated with the smell of her scented flesh. 'I've missed you. These past weeks have been hellish. I want you. I need you so much.'

At last his mouth covered hers in an endless, drugging kiss, and his arms tightened around her. Lavinia's heart quickened with pulsating pleasure. Drawing her towards the bed Maxim's questing fingers unfastened the tiny buttons at her throat, pushing her nightdress off her shoulders and letting it fall in a circle about her feet.

Catching his breath his eyes beheld the beauty of her. His fascinated gaze moved over her, having forgotten just how lovely she was. Her skin was as smooth as alabaster, her shining hair tumbling over her shoulders, her brows delicately arched and her sooty lashes thick and curling. Her eyes were like luminous turquoise jewels, her mouth vulnerable, soft, and begging to be kissed.

Loosening the sash of his robe and shrugging out of it, Maxim drew her down on to the bed. He intended to make amends, to give her so much pleasure that she would forget that last time—and as Lavinia moaned beneath him, her body craving satisfaction, she didn't care about that other time.

Later there was satiation and only the sound of their breathing. Lavinia had no basis for comparison, but in bed Maxim was a magnificent lover, both demanding and fulfilling. There was a carefully controlled brutality in his lovemaking, yet there was patience and tenderness and passion. And yet, he might make love to her, but that wasn't the same as loving her.

The relief she felt now he had decided he no longer wanted a divorce was immense, and she smiled into the dark, knowing that even if she still insisted on one, his indomitable will would prevail against any argument she might raise. She accepted that their future was together, and matters concerning Alice and Lucy must be discussed and worked out in a sensible and adult manner. But when the image of Alice invaded her mind, and that of his child, she was troubled.

The following morning, eager to join Maxim for breakfast, Lavinia hurriedly bathed and dressed in a lemon silk gown with a modestly scooped neckline and long sleeves, tying a matching sash about her slim waist. After Betsy had brushed her hair until it shone, she arranged it beautifully into thick curls about her head.

Glancing through open doors into rooms as she went downstairs, Lavinia saw the house was furnished to suit Maxim's excellent masculine tastes. A footman standing in the hall opened the door to the dining room and she stepped inside, seeing Maxim already seated at the far end of a long, extremely grand, mahogany dining table with at least a dozen highbacked, dark green velvet chairs on either side, and two elaborate crystal chandeliers hanging above.

Immediately he rose and came towards her with long strides, looking superbly handsome in tight grey breeches and a shirt of thin white lawn. His hair was brushed back and glossy black, but an errant wave threatened to fall over his forehead at any minute. Arrogance and authority was stamped all over him, but Lavinia was not intimidated by it. As usual there was a strength and vigour about him that brought a warmth to her cheeks, but this morning it seemed more pronounced. He reminded her of a healthy animal trapped in a cage, deliberately restraining his energy.

Enfolding her in a tight embrace, Maxim kissed her lips before standing back and peering with a warm tenderness into her glowing eyes. 'You look wonderful,' he told her. 'Not too tired this morning, I hope.'

She smiled warmly, the pleasant smell of his spicy cologne wafting over her. 'If I am I shall have to blame you,' she teased.

Taking her hand he led her down the length of the table, pulling out a chair across from his own. 'No need to stand on ceremony when there's only the two of us. I'm glad you decided to join me for breakfast. I hoped you would.'

'Thank you. I'd love some coffee,' said Lavinia, smiling at an aloof looking footman who was standing to attention like a soldier close to a large dresser containing platters of food and holding a welcoming pot of delicious-smelling coffee in his hands.

'As long as you don't upset the chef by not eating,' said Maxim. 'André is very efficient and being French, he is extremely temperamental and takes it as a personal criticism if anyone refuses to eat.'

'What! Even you?'

'Even me,' he grinned, spreading a napkin over his knees.

Breakfast was a feast of fluffy scrambled eggs, mushrooms and crisply curled bacon and toast in silver racks, all washed down with fresh coffee. The footman came and went, leaving them alone for most of the time so the two of them could converse in private. Despite her earlier concern as to how deeply Maxim cared for her, Lavinia had never felt so happy and contented. She drained her cup and smiled at him, thinking how relaxed he was. When they had finished eating and their plates had been cleared away, he dismissed the footman, asking him to leave the coffee pot as they would probably want another cup.

Maxim sighed, gazing across at his wife, watching the morning sunlight turn her hair to silver and gold, while he relished her beauty and the keen intelligence in her wonderful turquoise eyes. 'Dear Lord, I've missed you. Do you realise that this is the first morning of our lives together as husband and wife?'

Meeting his gaze Lavinia smiled softly. 'Yes. I find it all rather strange but I suppose I'll soon get used to it. But when you came to London three weeks ago, you could not have been missing me all that much, otherwise you would have come to see me after our encounter at the theatre.'

'I have already explained all that. Besides, my time was taken up with legal matters. Not only did I meet with my lawyers and my uncle, but also with my business managers to discuss the alarming events in France. Unfortunately my investments over there are suffering because of the present crisis.'

'I see. How did your uncle receive you?'

'Like the prodigal son.' He grinned. 'He was not as I imagined him to be. In fact, he bears a strong resemblance to my father and myself. Unfortunately, he is not a well man so he has been unable to enjoy life as he would have wished to—but he did accompany me to the theatre the night Alice decided to introduce herself to him.'

'I think I recall seeing him. Is he a tall, silver-haired gentleman?' she asked.

Maxim nodded. 'He also told me that he never coveted the title and all that it entails, and that it was the worst day of his life when my father left. Did Ursula tell you about the family feud?'

'Yes—at least some of it.'

'Uncle Alistair told me that my grandfather was wrong to treat my father as he did, and quickly came

to realise his mistake when he disinherited him for
going ahead and marrying the woman he loved.'

'Why, after all this time, did you decide to go and
see your uncle, Maxim?'

'Out of necessity rather than any aspirations I
might have for the estate.'

'Why? What do you mean—out of necessity?'

Maxim looked at her steadily. 'One of the reasons
I went to see him was for my daughter's sake. Alice
is planning to marry a French comte and has threatened to take Lucy with her to France. I would not
agree to it at any time, and especially not in the present climate. It is my intention to gain custody of Lucy
through the courts, and I shall find it that much easier
if I have my uncle's backing. I mean to use his influence to block Alice taking Lucy out of the country.
I have contacts in high circles, but my uncle's contacts are even higher. His influence and opinions
carry much weight with people who count.'

Something cold was beginning to wrap itself round
Lavinia's heart. A feeling of impending disaster
seemed to crackle in the air. 'I see. What were the
conditions Alice insisted upon before she would
marry you, Maxim?' she asked quietly.

'That I became reconciled with my uncle. Alice is
a stubborn, selfish woman—and fiercely ambitious.
Her eyes were firmly fixed on the grand title that
would become mine when my uncle dies—should I
bow to her demands and become reconciled with
him, that is. Alice's greatest ambition—or perhaps I
should say obsession—was to become the Countess

of Brinkcliff, and she would not have me without the title.'

'I see. And you refused to concede to her demands, even though doing so would give you custody of your daughter?'

Maxim sighed, absently tracing the rim of his empty coffee cup with his finger. 'I would be lying if I said I didn't consider it—which was the reason why I insisted on an annulment to our marriage. But when I returned to England and saw Alice in London, when I was reminded how vicious she is, how cold and ruthless she can be to obtain what she wants, nothing could induce me to tie myself to her for the rest of my life. Besides, I had made you my wife and already cared for you deeply. My growing need for you made me vulnerable, and it was becoming increasingly difficult to think of parting from you.'

Lavinia was encouraged by his words, spoken softly and with sincerity, but how she wished he had included the word love. 'How confident are your lawyers about you gaining custody of Lucy?'

'Very. With my uncle's influence, some good lawyers to present my case, and you by my side, I am confident that I will be able to wield enough power to sway the courts in my favour.'

Lavinia sat very still, not liking the thought that was forming inside her head. Sitting across from her Maxim looked so relaxed, with a natural elegance that she admired. And yet, she had an odd feeling that behind his calm exterior there was a power, a forcefulness, carefully restrained but waiting. And she had a curious feeling that if she should say one wrong word, make one false move, one mistake, he would unleash that power on her. The first tendrils of fear coiled in the pit of her stomach.

'I can see how it would harm your case considerably if it became known that you were considering divorcing your wife,' she said quietly, her voice strained.

Maxim looked at her, his expression hard, sensing her withdrawal. 'It would be devastating, which is one of the reasons why I cannot allow that to happen. I want to present a settled picture to the courts. It is important that you and I are seen to have a loving, harmonious relationship.'

Bitter resentment wrapped itself round Lavinia like a steel band. So that was it. She saw it all—how his mind had worked with cold, mechanical precision as he had formed a strategy to gain custody of his daughter. He had come to her for Lucy's sake and nothing else. The hurt went so deep she wanted to lash out at him. With heartbreaking clarity, all the pieces of this complex puzzle were beginning to fall into place. The whole picture presented to her was gruesome in every degrading detail. A rock settled on her heart where just a short while ago love had dwelt. She looked back at her husband through eyes of horror, disbelief and dismay, stony-faced, gullible, stupid and naïve.

'You—you were using me all along. When you said you wanted me, that you needed me, they were all lies.'

'No. I have never lied to you, Lavinia. I meant every word I said.'

'What am I, Maxim? Some tender morsel expressly prepared for your enjoyment to take at your leisure?'

'Now you are being ridiculous.'

'Please don't make it worse. This isn't fair. Using me to induce the courts into granting you custody of Lucy—without speaking to me about it first—is—is wicked.'

'It's not like that.'

'Yes, it is. How dare you do this to me? Without consulting me about this, or considering how I might feel, you sought me out and seduced me into your bed because I am a necessary tool in your struggle to obtain custody of your daughter.'

The atmosphere inside the room was quiet. The muscles in Maxim's jaw tightened. He was fuming, and yet he was very much in control of himself and determined to remain that way. He tapped his fingers on the polished surface of the table, his eyes like blue shards of ice as they held hers.

'I admit it. I do need you if I hope to gain custody of Lucy. I can't present a good case if I'm in the middle of divorcing my wife.'

'Thank you for being honest,' she replied icily.

'I need you, Lavinia. Lucy is going to need you.'

Unable to sit still a moment longer Lavinia pushed back her chair and stood up, glaring at him, her eyes alight with bitter, angry condemnation. 'And her mother? Does she not love and need Lucy? For heaven's sake, Alice is her mother, Maxim. You cannot shut her out of her daughter's life. Do you expect her to stand by and watch you take Lucy from her without a fight? Your attitude towards her is criminal and I will have no part of it.'

Like a python uncoiling itself Maxim rose from his chair, flinging his napkin down and placing his knuckles on the table in front of him. He leaned forward, his shoulders squared, his jaw set with implacable determination. He emanated restrained power and unyielding authority Lavinia had always been aware of and feared in him, but she would not be intimidated by him now.

'That is sentimental rubbish. Let me tell you something about Alice you don't know. In short, she is a slut, whose name over the past two years has been linked with an assortment of licentious and depraved men she did not think twice about taking to her bed. She has used every feminine ploy in existence to bring me to heel, but it didn't work. She is also an unfit, unnatural mother, who has no love whatsoever for her daughter and considers her a nuisance.

'Ever since Lucy was born she has hardly looked at her, resenting her because she was not the son she hoped for—which would have made her hold on me complete. When she learned of my marriage to you, she swore to avenge herself and she will—using Lucy as her weapon of destruction if she is not stopped. Now do you see why I want Lucy here with me?'

Lavinia nodded, appalled by what he had told her. 'Yes, I can.'

'You should. In fact, Lucy's upbringing is a scenario not unlike your own, and it is my intention to remove her from her mother's irresponsible care before it runs full term and she is ruined by it.'

Instantly the colour drained from Lavinia's cheeks leaving them ghastly white, but her eyes were so dark they might have been black. Her stiff face was set.

'Please don't make it worse than it is. You take a lot for granted, Maxim. If you think I am going to move into your home merely to protect your interests you are mistaken.'

Icy blue eyes cut back at her, fierce anger knitting his brows. 'Have you an aversion to helping me bring up my daughter?'

'Of course I haven't. I am sure she's a lovely child and will receive all the love you are capable of giving. But she is not my daughter and you must do it alone,' she said, immediately regretting those last few words spoken in anger and not meant. But it was too late to retract them now. 'I shall return to Stratton Street as soon as I have ordered Betsy to pack my things.'

Maxim's face darkened, but his eyes were a brilliant, dangerous blue. 'Like hell you will. You're staying with me and you're going to co-operate and maintain a supportive image. Damn it, Lavinia, you can't run away every time we argue.'

'You're right, I can't, so I shall make quite sure this is the last time,' Lavinia countered, her voice ragged with emotion as she fought to contain her anger, feeling the fragile unity they had shared since the ball beginning to slide down the slippery slope of clashed wills. 'I must congratulate you. What you have done is a brilliant tactical move on your part.

But how could you ruthlessly use me to manipulate things until they happen the way you want them to— if you really cared for me, Maxim, you would not have done this. You deliberately deceived me.'

Maxim turned white. 'Now it is you who insults me. I have an aversion to deceit and would never stoop so low as to use it,' he hissed, clamping his jaw together as he fought to bite back his wrath.

'You've misled me and that's the same thing,' Lavinia cried brokenly, feeling emotionally battered and as if her heart were being torn to pieces. 'I will not live with a man who walks all over people to get what he wants. I'm sorry, Maxim. I am grateful for everything you did for me in Venice, but after this I owe you nothing.'

'No? I disagree. I have given you many things. Let me itemise them,' he said with icy calm. 'I gave you my protection when you needed it, and my name. I also made you my wife in every sense of the word and introduced you to my family and my home. For this I expect you to stand by me on this one, important issue.'

'No, Maxim. You don't expect. You demand it of me.'

No longer casual and relaxed, Maxim was tense, like a panther preparing to spring. He moved round the table towards her with slow, deliberate steps. Looming over her, he forced her rebellious gaze to meet his, cold and implacable. When he spoke his voice brooked no argument.

'If you want to convince yourself that I have deceived you, then do so, but you will do it here in this house. When I made up my mind not to divorce you, not for one moment have I considered letting you go. And if I had, do you think after what passed between us last night I would ever consider it again?'

'Has it not occurred to you that you cannot keep me here by force?'

Maxim's brows arched. 'It has, and I hope it does not come to that. I will not tolerate you doing anything that will jeopardise my daughter's safety. I want your word that you will co-operate with me on this.'

Lavinia's emotions were at war within her. She tried to think objectively, knowing how important Lucy was to Maxim. And if what he said was true, that Alice was thinking of marrying a Frenchman and taking Lucy with her to France, a country that was on the brink of a violent, bloody revolution, then Maxim was right to do everything within his power to try and stop her.

And if she returned to live with Mrs Lambert and Daisy while Maxim remained at his house in Grosvenor Street, everyone would be correct in their assumptions that things weren't right between them. Gossip alone would undoubtedly damage his chances of keeping Lucy in England. She could not do that to him or Lucy.

She nodded. 'Very well, Maxim. You have it.'

Relief flooded his face. He stared at her for a moment longer and then moved away from her with lazy deliberation and poured himself another cup of coffee. Lavinia was infuriated to see he was smiling, a satisfied male smile. He had won, as he had known all along he would. She stood her ground a moment longer, glaring at him with a hard, cold anger that seared through her body, before turning and crossing towards the door. He stopped her with his next words.

'I told you I had more than one reason for going to see my uncle. Aren't you interested in hearing what it was?'

She turned and faced him, the length of the room stretching like a mile between them, waiting for him to speak.

'It occurred to me after you left Thornhill that you might be with child. If so and you bore a son, I realised I had no right to deny him his inheritance. That was when I wrote telling my uncle that I would see him.'

Lavinia stared at him incredulously. 'You—you did that?'

'Yes.'

Her eyes glittered with rage at this final outrage to her intelligence. 'Then I'm sorry to disappoint you, Maxim. There is no child.'

'Maybe not now. But there might be—after last night.'

Fuming, Lavinia left the room, trembling with a rage that possessed her with a hard, merciless force all the way to her room, but if she had looked back, she would have seen that there was neither triumph nor satisfaction on Maxim's face, only an aching gentleness and regret in his compelling eyes.

Left alone an unpleasant and extremely worrying thought was beginning to form in Maxim's mind, one

which, until now, he had not considered. Was it possible that Lavinia did have an aversion to helping him
bring up Lucy, despite what she had said to the contrary? One heard tales about stepmothers who
couldn't stand the sight of another woman's offspring—a child not of their body—and would refuse
to have anything to do with them, especially when
their own arrived.

In the space of a second the realisation that this
might apply to Lavinia stunned him. His body became taut, his face a hard, grinding mask, his hands
clenching and unclenching at his sides as he tried to
bring his feelings under control. Was the sweet drift
of happiness he had felt on finding Lavinia again and
becoming reconciled under threat once more? Dear
Lord, he prayed in twisted torment, don't let me have
to choose between my wife and my daughter.

During the following two days it was as if Maxim
and Lavinia existed in opposing camps. Maxim went
about his business as usual and Lavinia spent some
of her time visiting Daisy and familiarising herself
with the servants and the running of the house.
Mealtimes were to be endured, with neither she nor
Maxim prepared to give an inch—until Lavinia could
stand it no longer.

Tonight they were to dine with Maxim's uncle, the
Earl of Brinkcliff, at his town house in Brook Street,
and she was determined to make a concerted effort
to somehow put things right between them before
they left the house. If it meant unconditional surren-

der on her part, then so be it. She loved Maxim too much to carry on in this ridiculous fashion.

As she dressed with great care for the evening ahead in an extremely fetching cream satin gown, she found herself thinking of Lucy, which she was doing a lot of late as her thoughts became less disjointed and she began to think more rationally. Maxim was hurting, tortured that he might lose his daughter, and Lavinia's heart constricted when she realised that she might have given him the impression that she didn't want the child to have a place in their lives together. That this might be behind his cold attitude towards her melted her heart. Oh, what a fool he was if he thought that.

When she was ready she went downstairs to find him. Having heard him come up to change she knew he would be waiting for her.

'Where is my husband, Mr Perkins?' she asked when she encountered her husband's secretary in the hall.

Mr Perkins cast a disgruntled look at the closed study door, wishing his master would cease behaving like a cross-tempered tyrant and come to his senses. 'In his study, my lady. Would you like me to tell him you're ready?'

'No, thank you,' she replied, heading for the closed door, quaking inwardly at the forthcoming confrontation with her husband. 'I'll do that myself.'

Without knocking she opened the door and went inside, having to repress a smile when she saw Maxim working at his desk, a quill in one hand and his dark head bowed over a column of figures.

Having dressed for dinner with his uncle in a charcoal grey suit with a sapphire blue waistcoat and white shirt, he looked unbearably handsome. He also looked annoyed when he looked up and saw her. His eyes did a quick sweep of her body, lingering briefly on the neckline of her gown, and Lavinia was glad she had chosen to wear a gown with a less revealing bodice than the one she had worn for the Eveshams' ball.

'You work too hard, Maxim,' she said, giving him a brave, tremulous smile, seeing how his shoulders stiffened at the sound of her voice.

'I enjoy working.'

'Yes, I can see that.' When he made no move to rise and cast his eyes down once more to the column of figures, she moved closer to the desk. 'How do I look?' she asked, trailing her fingers absently along the edge of the mahogany desk. 'Do you like my dress? Is it suitable for dinner with your uncle, do you think?'

A wry smile touched Maxim's lips and cracked his granite features. 'I expect so.'

Distracted, he raised his head and studied her from beneath sceptical raised brows, unable to prevent his eyes moving over her shapely form and appreciating the subtle scent of her alluring perfume, which settled over him like an invisible, unrelenting net. His gaze became riveted on her lovely face, the softness in her large eyes and the delectable curve of her soft lips. With a sigh he put down his quill and stood up, her beauty and sensing that she was trying to make peace between them neutralising his anger.

'You seem to have acquired a remarkable collection of gowns, Lavinia.'

'Yes, I have. When you made the money accessible to me, Daisy and I went shopping.'

He arched a sleek black brow. 'I see. You haven't spent all of it, I hope,' he said drily. 'I would hate to think I've acquired an extravagant spendthrift for a wife.'

'Of course I haven't,' she replied, smiling sweetly when he looked ready to argue. 'I hope you will credit me with more sense than that. But, equally, I would hate to think I have acquired myself a miserly husband.'

Unexpectedly an answering smile tugged at Maxim's sensuous lips. He cocked a dubious brow, amazed at the spirit of this woman he had married. He perched his hip on the corner of his desk in front of her, taking the weight on one foot and slowly swinging his other leg, his arms folded across his chest, lazy mockery lighting his eyes.

'So—when you arrived in London and presented yourself in Stratton Street, you weren't pining away for me after all.'

Lavinia's expression suddenly turned solemn and she drew a tortured breath, knowing that if she said the wrong thing he would use it against her. 'I was, Maxim. I was pining. In fact, if you must know, I was quite wretched. I told you how much I missed you at the ball.'

All Maxim's senses collided when he saw the invitation in her imploring eyes. 'You have a very peculiar way of showing it.'

'And you, Maxim, make it almost impossible for me to do so.'

His eyes flickered over her and Lavinia's heart leaped with joy when she saw a warmth and a softening in his eyes, and that he wasn't going to fight her. Instead of suffering in silence she should have approached him in the beginning.

'Come here,' he murmured, his gaze dropping to her moistened lips.

Desire surged through him as she moved closer, heating his blood, as it did every time he imagined her in bed on the other side of the connecting door to their rooms. His body's relentless craving to appease his desire for her had almost driven him insane, and it was pride and pride alone that had prevented him from shattering that door and joining her in her bed. Forcing his hands to reach out and pull her into his embrace, he crushed her against his chest and held her tightly to him, as if he would never let her go.

'Remind me to punish you most severely for putting me through hell. You, my darling, are the most exasperating woman alive.'

'I agree,' she murmured, her lips close to his, her eyes as dark and languid as a warm, moonless night. 'But you do like me a little bit, don't you, Maxim?' she coaxed teasingly.

'More than a little bit, you minx.'

'How much more?'

'I'll show you,' he breathed, unable to resist her a moment longer, wanting to taste the sweetness of her lips, to feel her closeness, the fullness of her breasts pressed against his chest. His mouth locked onto hers hungrily, his kiss searing her lips, and she returned his kiss with a smothered moan of joy. Twining her arms around his neck, she pressed herself close, glorying in his embrace as he deepened his kiss, his arms sliding up and down her back as he moulded her closer to him.

'You little fool,' he murmured when he finally tore his mouth from hers, unable to relinquish his hold on her as he feasted his gaze on her long lashed, turquoise coloured eyes, turned languid and solemn with emotion. 'Do you know what you have done to me? Do you know what you have made me suffer? Do you know what I have been through these past two days? I thought I should go mad. Never do that to me again, Lavinia.'

Leaning back in his arms she looked up at him, loving him, revelling in the simple joy of being held in his arms. 'Do you know why I said what I did, Maxim? Why I was angry?'

'Tell me.'

'Because I was hurt and disappointed. I have always known you to be a man who goes after what he wants, yet the method you have used to win me seems somehow less than honourable. I truly believed you had come to London because you were suffering the same sense of loss as I was. Can you imagine how humiliated I felt when I discovered you had come simply to use me in your custody battle over Lucy—that in your arrogance and conceit you had planned to bring me here to make love to me, knowing perfectly well the effect you always have on me and how easy it is to bring me to submission.'

Shame washed over Maxim in sickening waves when she told him how much he had hurt her. 'I'm sorry if that's what you thought, but in the beginning it wasn't like that. When I made up my mind not to consent to a divorce, it had nothing to do with my custody battle over Lucy. When you left me I was crushed. I could not imagine the rest of my life without you and I was so frightened of losing you, Lavinia. You have become a part of me—like my flesh and blood. I love you. I love you so much. May God help you if ever you run from me again,' he warned fiercely.

Lavinia trembled looking deeply into his eyes, thinking the sound of his voice saying he loved her to be the sweetest sound in the world. Maxim saw it in her eyes, felt it in the way her body melted in his arms, the emotional impact his declaration had on her, and he smiled down at her upturned face.

'You, my darling—you wonderful, infuriating woman,' he went on, his tone husky and deep with desire, 'are the only female alive who is capable of driving me to the point when I am tempted to throttle you or to make love to you until we both expire. You have become such an essential part of my life that I would be desolate without you—and after what occurred between us over breakfast when you argued so forcefully, I envisaged having to decide between you and my daughter. Do you want me to give up all claim on Lucy?'

Lavinia was swamped with shame and her heart contracted painfully when she realised she was right in thinking she might have given him reason to ask that awful question. 'No. I would not ask you to do that. I would never ask you to sacrifice someone you love.'

'Then what is it you want from me?'

'Only that you talk to me, Maxim. There must be honesty and frankness between us. What happens to Lucy does affect us both, you know.'

'And you will be willing to make her a part of our lives together—even when our own children come along?'

'More than willing,' she told him softly, his question telling her that she had been right and that it was this that had been troubling him all along. 'Lucy is your daughter, Maxim. How could I fail to love her?'

'Even if her father is an insensitive brute with a list of shortcomings stretching from here to eternity, with no other thought than to seduce my wife into bed in order to induce a suitable response to my demands?' he chuckled tenderly, sliding his hands seductively down her spine and pressing her closer.

'Maxim!' she laughed. 'I am astounded at your unprincipled determination to get what you want and your absolute lack of contrition. Have you no shame?'

He grinned, a warm glow igniting in his half closed eyes. 'Apparently not,' he answered, his lips claiming hers once more.

So lost were they in their kiss that neither of them heard the carriage halt in the street outside, or the opening of the door when someone was admitted into the hall, only pulling apart when Mr Perkins entered with his usual expression of aloof formality. Maxim

glanced at him, his arms still around Lavinia, unaware of the surge of relief that almost cracked his
diligent secretary's countenance on seeing everything
was back to normal between his master and his wife.

'What is it, Perkins?'

'Mrs Winstanley is here to see you on an urgent
matter, my lord.'

Maxim released Lavinia instantly and his face became a frozen mask. 'Send her in.'.

Chapter Fourteen

The small, dark haired woman swept into the room, her manner agitated, her expression anxious. 'Please forgive my intrusion, but I had to come,' she said quickly.

'Mrs Winstanley, this is my wife, Lavinia. Lavinia, Mrs Winstanley is Alice's stepmother,' Maxim told his wife by way of explanation, trying to stem the tide of terror already searing through his veins, his instincts telling him that Caroline Winstanley was the harbinger of grievous news.

The two women looked at each other, Mrs Winstanley inclining her head politely. Lavinia sensed from her taut expression and anguished eyes that whatever had brought her to this house tonight was a matter of extreme importance and of a serious nature.

'Excuse me,' said Lavinia softly, beginning to move towards the door. 'I'm sure you would like to speak to my husband in private.'

Maxim placed his hand on her arm, halting her. 'No, Lavinia, don't go,' he said, his voice raw with emotion. 'I would like you to stay and hear what Mrs Winstanley has to say.'

She looked at him. His face was tense, but seeing a softening, a pleading in his eyes, she nodded and stood quietly with her hands folded in front of her, waiting for Mrs Winstanley to divulge the purpose of her unexpected visit.

'I have been out of London for two weeks, visiting my sister and her husband in Surrey, Mr Purnell,' she said, ignorant of his reconciliation with his uncle and that he was now addressed as Lord Stannington. 'When I returned I discovered that Alice married Claude Lauriston yesterday and has gone with him to France. I'm so dreadfully sorry.'

Something exploded inside Maxim, shattering his emotions from all rational thought. He stared at Caroline Winstanley as though she had taken leave of her senses, shrinking from asking the question that was uppermost on his lips, but knowing he must. 'And Lucy?'

'She—she has taken Lucy with her,' she told him quietly.

Savage fury ignited in Maxim's eyes. Never had Lavinia seen a face of such dark, menacing rage as his was at that moment—rage at his own weakness and inability to have prevented this happening after all his efforts. For the first time in his life Maxim tasted bitter defeat. His fist came crashing down onto the polished surface of the desk, sending papers fluttering to the floor, the sound vibrating about the room and crashing against the walls as his formidable anger grew.

'Dear God, I'll make her pay for this. I was so close to stopping her—a week at the most. Damn her to hell. She knew what I intended when I became reconciled with my uncle. Knowing I had married someone else, she knew I had healed the breach for one reason only—that I intended to wield enough power to sway the courts in my favour to obtain custody of Lucy. The bitch. The conniving, amoral bitch. This is the revenge she planned when I refused to marry her. I should have foreseen it.'

'She—she did leave you a note,' said Mrs Winstanley, fumbling in her reticule and handing it to Maxim.

He took it and broke the seal, his eyes scanning Alice's untidy scrawl. His face went white. 'Good God!' he exclaimed when he had finished reading.

Lavinia went to him instantly. 'Maxim! What is it? What does it say?'

His tortured eyes locked on to his wife's. 'That she will grant me custody of Lucy for a settlement of one hundred thousand pounds.'

Lavinia was stunned, shocked. 'You—you mean she thinks so little of her daughter that she will sell her to you—as—as though she were a parcel?'

Maxim's eyes were like blue chips of ice, his lips twisting with contempt. 'I tried telling you what Alice is like, what she is capable of. Now do you believe me?'

She nodded slowly, trying to comprehend what this was doing to Maxim. 'Yes—yes, I do. But it's obscene.'

'Claude Lauriston belongs to the French aristocracy,' Mrs Winstanley explained quietly to Lavinia, 'but he is impoverished. He is also past his prime. Having a beautiful wife by his side will boost his ego no end—not to mention replenishing his family coffers should your husband agree to Alice's demands. He has no desire to be saddled with Alice's illegitimate daughter, so her demands do not surprise me in the slightest. He is a greedy man and as amoral as she is. I have no doubt that he put her up to it.'

'And will you give her what she asks, Maxim?' Lavinia asked, unable to imagine the sheer magnitude of the sum Alice demanded.

'The money means nothing to me. I will not argue over the amount when Lucy's safety is at stake.'

This was stated firmly and without emotion, bringing home to Lavinia the sheer magnitude of her husband's wealth. A hundred thousand pounds would be like a drop in the ocean to him. 'What will you do?' she asked him in some confusion.

'I have no choice but to go after them,' Maxim answered, his voice harsh with urgency, his face white and tense with anxiety and pain.

'But—but they will have left England for France by now.' Suddenly, realisation of what he intended doing made Lavinia's heart slam against her ribs. 'Maxim! You can't go to France.'

'I have to, Lavinia,' he said with a cold, controlled calm, sitting at his desk and hurriedly writing a note. That done he strode to the door, throwing it open and handing the note to Perkins who was hovering outside in case he was needed. 'Have this delivered immediately to my uncle and instruct one of the grooms to have my horse saddled while I change,' he commanded. 'I want to be away from here and on my way to Portsmouth within the next half hour.'

Maxim mounted the stairs two at a time, leaving his wife to show Mrs Winstanley out. Overwrought, she then hurried after him with the hope of dissuading him from embarking on his reckless, foolhardy venture, pacing up and down as he changed his clothes, watching as his valet silently put items of clothing that he might need into a small leather bag.

'Maxim, please don't go,' she begged, fraught with anxiety. 'People are being killed all the time in France.'

'I know. And it's precisely for that reason why I must go. Try not to worry, Lavinia,' he said, deftly fastening his shirt buttons. 'The peasants' grievances are against their ruling lords, not a visiting Englishman.'

'But the revolts are taking place with hysterical savagery—with violent men wandering all over the countryside.' She followed him to a chair where he sat to pull on his boots. Putting her hands on the arm of his chair she knelt beside him, her voice anguished, her wide eyes full of appeal. 'Please listen to me, Maxim. They won't care who you are if they think you have money they can steal. And why would the Comte de Chemille return to France now—at this time, with wholesale looting and the burning of châteaux? Why hasn't he remained here in England where it's safe?'

Maxim's finely chiselled lips twisted with grim irony. 'Perhaps the Comte de Chemille has had a touch of conscience and is concerned about his family holed up in his château in Normandy. He has a younger sister and brother, I believe, from his father's second marriage. Neither of them are married. He will want to keep the mob at bay if he can.'

Lavinia sat back on her heels. 'You seem to know a great deal about the Comte de Chemille, Maxim.'

'I was afraid that something like this would happen so I made a point of finding out as much as I could about him, other than what I already knew—that he is a blackguard, a gamester and a drunkard—a man who has never bothered to hide his contempt for the industrious lower classes. Like every other nobleman in France he thought his lands, his feudal dues, and a hundred other things that maintain his indolent, arrogant breed, would last forever.'

'Then why did he not find himself a noblewoman to marry? Why sully his ancient line with the blood of a commoner?'

'The answer is simple. He is impoverished, and what better way of maintaining his châteaux, his stables and his dissolute lifestyle than by marrying a woman who was my mistress and bore me a child. Whatever else he is, the Comte de Chemille is no fool. He knows what I am worth, and through Alice he will also know how much Lucy means to me and that I am seeking to obtain legal custody of her through the courts. He is confident that I will pay dearly for my daughter.'

'The man is a monster,' Lavinia said, getting to her feet when Maxim rose to put on his jacket. She watched in horror when his valet opened a long leather box and handed him two pistols, which he shoved into his belt ready to defend himself if need be, ramming home to her the enormity of what he was about to do. In speechless horror she looked at his face, which was rigid and sterner than she'd ever seen it before, and she was frightened.

'Please don't go, Maxim,' she whispered, her eyes wide with fear. 'I'm so afraid that you'll become caught up in the insurrection and not come back. It's dangerous to be even known as an associate of anyone who has fallen out of favour. If the people should decide to take direct action against the Comte de Chemille and you are seen going to his home, you will be assumed guilty by association and will be shown no mercy.'

Maxim raised his head, his eyes burning into hers. 'Don't you think I know that, Lavinia? Which is why I must get Lucy back. What kind of father would I be if I sat back in the comfort of this house and let the mob attack her—a defenceless child? I would despise myself. How much respect would you have for me then?'

Grasping his bag and enveloped in a long black riding cloak, he turned from her and strode out of the room. Hurriedly Lavinia ran after him down the stairs and into the street, where a groom was waiting with his horse—the poor animal having no notion of the gruelling journey ahead of him. Maxim would stable him in Portsmouth and hire another when he reached

Le Havre. After securing the bag to the saddle he
turned and swept his wife into his arms. Lavinia
closed her eyes and a sob broke from her. She clung
to Maxim with all her strength, feeling his arms holding her tightly, his breath on her neck.

'Forgive me, Maxim. Please forgive my weakness—my selfishness. I am so afraid for you, that is
all. You are right to go and I am so proud of you. I
wouldn't expect you to do anything else, and I would
be disappointed in you if you didn't go to save your
daughter. But please take care,' she implored desperately. 'If anything should happen to you I couldn't
bear it.'

'I will,' he said, his voice raw with emotion. 'I
promise you I will.' With his mouth close to her ear
he tightened his hold. 'I love you, Lavinia. Be brave,
my love. I will soon be back—with Lucy.'

'I love you, Maxim. Please come back safe. Both
of you.'

He stopped her mouth with a kiss, infusing into it
all the passion of his love for her, and then he released her and flung himself onto his horse's back,
galloping along Grosvenor Street and into the night.

In her agony of their parting, the sense of what
had happened scarcely penetrated Lavinia's mind,
and she stood in the street looking into the darkness
which a moment before had swallowed up her husband. She hardly noticed when a coach came to a
halt outside the house and a tall man with silver hair
stepped out. He came to her and touched her arm,
and only then did she look at him, with tears coursing
down her cheeks. Understanding her anguish, the

Earl of Brinkcliff placed his arm about her shoulders and took her back inside the house.

'So,' Alistair said, when Lavinia had dried her tears and they were seated across from one another in front of a cosy fire, 'you are Lavinia—Maxim's wife.' He was not unaware that there had been an estrangement between his nephew and his lovely young wife or the reason why, and he was happy to discover they had reconciled their differences. She really was a lovely, captivating young woman.

'Yes,' she said softly, responding to his warmth with a smile.

The Earl of Brinkcliff was almost as tall as Maxim, and his features bore a startling resemblance. There was also that same proud arrogance that marked Maxim, and his eyes held an alert sharpness she had expected in such a powerful man. Despite his gaunt look and deeply grooved face, in his mid-fifties Alistair Purnell was still a striking-looking man. She wondered why he had never married, thinking that perhaps it might have something to do with his ill health.

'I apologise for my behaviour earlier. I don't normally cry like that in the street.'

'It's not every day your husband rides off at a moment's notice to set sail for a country where revolution is about to explode at any minute. Believe me, my dear, I do understand,' Alistair said, a warm tenderness glowing in his eyes. 'I hope you don't mind me coming here, only I know how deeply Maxim cares for his daughter.'

'I'm glad you came. I couldn't bear being on my own just now. Besides, I'm sorry we had to cancel dinner. I've been so looking forward to meeting you.'

'Thank you. Poor Maxim. This has come as a terrible shock to him.'

'I do so hope he takes care,' Lavinia said quietly.

'Don't be afraid. I am sure he'll be all right. He's sensible, and I'm immensely proud of him—proud that he's my nephew. You know, I've followed his amazing progress since my brother died. My only regret is that we didn't meet until recently—when he decided to accept what is rightfully his. Oh, I know what urged him to do it, but I was happy to receive him whatever the reason. I've waited for this for longer than I care to remember. I look forward to receiving you at Brinkcliff Hall. The old place has been empty far too long.'

Lavinia found herself thinking of Ursula and her large, happy brood of children and grandchildren at Thornhill, and she realised how lonely this man must have been all these years at Brinkcliff Hall, devoid of his family. Alistair was watching her, and did she imagine it or was there a pleading in those sharp grey eyes? Whatever he gave Maxim, it was less than what Maxim could give him—a lonely man in need of the freedom to die with absolution and in the warm embrace of his family.

'I shall look forward to it,' she smiled.

'Thank you, Lavinia. Maxim has told you the cause of the estrangement between us?'

'Yes.'

He shook his head solemnly. 'It was an unfortunate business. When my father disinherited my brother, he realised he had made the biggest mistake of his life. He tried to repair the damage, but my brother—stubborn and stamped with the same Purnell pride as most of our forebears—refused. Not being in the best of health I didn't relish taking on the role of the next Earl—but I don't think I've made too bad a job of it,' he chuckled softly, his grey eyes twinkling with humour lightening his features.

'And how are you now?' asked Lavinia, having noted his breathlessness, his gaunt, grey face and slightly stooped back.

'Since Maxim came to see me my health has never been better. However,' he said, rising with the help of a walking cane, 'I tire easily—so if you will forgive me I will leave you now. And try not to worry, my dear,' he said, noting how worried she looked and seeing the fear for her husband lurking in her lovely eyes. 'Maxim will be all right. I'm sure of it. You'll soon have him back in London with his daughter.'

'I don't intend waiting in London,' Lavinia told him calmly, having made up her mind what she would do.

'Oh?'

'Mr Perkins is to leave in the morning to await Maxim's return in Portsmouth. I shall go with him.'

'Is that wise?'

'I think so. I couldn't bear the suspense of waiting here in London. Besides, when he arrives in

Portsmouth with Lucy after a long ride across France followed by the channel crossing, the poor child will need me.'

'Yes, my dear. You are quite right.'

Having reached Normandy, it was the glow in the midnight sky that Maxim saw first as he rode through dense wood. A sickening dread gripped his heart as he watched it grow redder and brighter the closer he got. He urged his horse into a gallop when a huge flame leaped up into the sky quickly followed by another. The closer he got the higher the flames became, and when he at last emerged from the darkness of the trees, his eyes became riveted on the horrific spectacle spread out before him.

Death and destruction wreaked by the mob surrounded the once-beautiful château of the Comte de Chemille. Some still danced and laughed like wild, crazy savages, drunk on blood and the Comte's wine. Burning torches were still clutched in their hands, some brandishing knives and axes, anything that would serve as a weapon. The blood-soaked bodies of loyal servants littered the ground, and the magical beauty of the flower gardens had disappeared beneath trampling feet.

The château was a blazing inferno, the fire feeding greedily on the precious treasures it housed, the flames penetrating higher and higher into the night sky. The heat was intense. Smoke smarted Maxim's eyes and burned his nostrils, and the noise was like the huge, angry roar of an enraged beast. Above it all could still be heard the agonising screams of those who hadn't got out of the château and were being incinerated alive, and those who managed to escape the scorching, searing heat were set upon and slain by the mob.

Maxim stared transfixed at the horror confronting him. Suddenly there was a thunderous crash of falling timbers as part of the upper floors gave way, sending a fountain of sparks upwards. Their work done, the mob began to disperse. The awful truth that his daughter might have perished in the blaze entered Maxim's soul and panic clutched at him.

Feeling it safe to do so when the last of the mob had disappeared, flinging himself out of the saddle he began searching among the dead and dying scattered over a wide area. In the midst of all this carnage he singled out a woman lying in a pool of blood face down, the fine quality of her emerald green silk gown distinguishing her from the rest. The expensive material was torn and muddied, and her hair was spread out on the grass like a shining black halo. Quickly he went to her, going down on one knee and gently rolling her onto her back.

It was Alice.

Her chest rose and fell in shallow gasps, and he thanked God she wasn't dead. When he touched her hand her eyes flickered open. They became dilated, her mouth a crimson slash across her face whiter than death and already the texture of wax. When her eyes became focused on Maxim she grimaced. It was obvious that she was in great pain and close to death.

'Maxim! You should not have come,' she managed to gasp, and seemed to gain sustenance from his presence.

'Did you think to escape me?' he said gently. Hardened as he felt towards her, there was no longer any anger in him, only an immense pity which welled up from the bottom of his heart for this woman he might have married. 'Did you think I wouldn't come to France and find you at the risk of my life?' He would have raised her, but with a feeble movement of her hand she stopped him.

'Don't, Maxim. It's too late. I know I'm dying.' Her sigh which followed her words gave an impression of extraordinary resignation.

'Lucy? Where is Lucy? Dear God, Alice, don't tell me she is dead.' The acute anguish and pain he felt that this might be so was almost too much for him to bear. Mercifully, Alice's next words brought him immeasurable relief.

'No. She is safe. When the mob came some of the servants escaped into the woods. Lucy is with them. Look for her, Maxim. Find her and take her back to England. You will find her at a village a mile north of here. She is with a family by the name of Laurens.' She closed her eyes as she fought for breath, and a froth of blood appeared at the corner of her mouth. 'Would you have given me the money, Maxim? Would you have bought your daughter?'

'Yes, I would. You know that.'

'Then she is fortunate. She has a place in your heart I could never have,' Alice said, the effort to speak almost too much. Her smile was cynical. 'I never thought I would be envious of my own daughter.'

'Alice—' Maxim uttered, knowing he should hate her, but in these final moments of her life he couldn't. He was unable to go on because a hard lump appeared at the base of his throat, shutting off his words. Tears formed in his eyes and glistened. She saw them and smiled.

'You weep for me,' she whispered, 'after what I have done? How odd.'

'Not really, Alice,' he managed to say, taking her limp hand in his own. 'I know you will die—as we all do in the end. I weep for the small miracle we created, what we once had, what we might have had, if your ambition hadn't got in the way.'

'I know that. I learned my lesson too late. I wanted you to honour me with riches, titles and everything I've always dreamed of, and I became a victim of my own greed—but,' she whispered, a sudden gleam entering her eyes, 'I did become a countess, didn't I, Maxim?'

Maxim swallowed hard, unable to answer.

'I wanted to hurt you because you spurned me. I regret that—and I do not ask your forgiveness for what I have done. Poor Claude. He died trying to defend his château. They are all dead—as I shall be soon. But I'm not afraid of dying—and it's better I go now before I'm old and undesirable.' Her smile was beautiful. 'When you think of me, Maxim,' she whispered with great difficulty, the dazzling brilliance of her green eyes falling on his face for the last time, 'I shall be forever young.'

Beyond speech, she fell silent and gazed at something beyond Maxim. Her eyes glazed over and she breathed her last.

Leaving her lying where she was, his heart almost too heavy to support, Maxim mounted his horse and rode north, towards the village where Alice had told him he would find Lucy. He found her with a servant woman, and with her tiny, warm body nestled close to his beneath his cloak in front of him on his horse, he rode back towards Le Havre.

The following day when Maxim embarked on the Channel crossing to England with his daughter, it was Tuesday, the fourth of August 1789, and it was the dawn of a new revolution in France. Later that night the National Assembly made sweeping reforms, demolishing the feudal regime and all the burdens which had oppressed the people for centuries, making sure it would be impossible for them ever to be reintroduced.

In mounting tension and sick with worry, Lavinia waited three days in Portsmouth for Maxim to return to England. Fate seemed to be taking a malicious pleasure in making her wait. Reports about what was happening in France arrived with every vessel, and were so worrying that she was frightened her husband would not come back.

She was constantly under Mr Perkins's quiet, watchful gaze, for Portsmouth was a busy port with ancient buildings crammed against each other, all fighting for space. It teamed with all manner of disreputable characters of every conceivable shape and colour—beggars and half-naked street urchins and drunken, bell-bottomed sailors who had not seen land for months, poured out of the many taverns and liquor shops bellowing their curses, with hard-faced, gin-sodden women hanging on to their arms, willing to allow any perversion in exchange for the price of more gin.

With her cloak wrapped tightly about her, Lavinia walked along the quay, gazing at the masts and rigging of the merchant ships anchored in the Portsea dockyard, flags and bunting dancing gaily in the breeze. Not one vessel moored without undergoing her close inspection.

Unaware of the sounds, sights and scents that surrounded her, in her solitude she gazed out to sea, watching the bow of a small vessel plowing its way through the green-brown water. It moored not far away from her and she watched with no particular interest, having seen so many come and go in the last few days. It wasn't until she saw the tall figure of a man with a bundle in his arms step on to the deck, that all her senses were jolted into awareness.

Her relief was enormous and her eyes became riveted on him, unable to believe that it was Maxim, but it was. His unshaven face looked haggard beneath the shadow of his hat, and the small bundle in his arms was Lucy. Wild with joy her heart soared, but her recent succession of hope, fear and grief, had taken its toll of her resistance. At first she was frozen, and all she could do was stand and watch as he climbed ashore.

It was then that her body came alive and she was running, tumbling headlong into his one outstretched arm. For a long moment they clung together, a bewildered Lucy trapped between them. Lavinia felt Maxim's lips on her brow, her cheeks, and she was too deeply moved for speech. After what seemed like an eternity she pulled away and looked up at him and smiled, her eyes moist with tears.

'Thank God you're back, Maxim,' she whispered, gazing anxiously into his pain filled eyes. They were bloodshot, his lids heavy, stark evidence of his nights without sleep.

'Alice is dead, Lavinia.'

His eyes were like windows through which Lavinia could see the unspeakable horrors he had witnessed in France. She wanted to know what had happened, but she wouldn't ask him, not now. There would be time for that later.

'I'm sorry, Maxim. Was it very bad?'

He towered over her, his lean, hard face full of torment as he remembered how Alice had died. 'The worst.'

'Tell me later. I can only think of one thing at the moment—that we're together. You're alive, and we'll never be parted again. I couldn't bear having to wait for you in London so I came to Portsmouth in the carriage with Mr Perkins. As soon as you and Lucy are rested we can leave.'

Lavinia looked at the little girl clinging to Maxim like a small, frightened shadow. She was an ex-

tremely pretty child in a sad, resigned kind of way.
Her black hair had a blue sheen and fell in gentle
waves about her oval face, which was pale and delicate. Her pale blue eyes fringed with sooty black
lashes were replicas of Maxim's, and she was looking
at him pensively. Shifting her gaze, Lucy glanced at
her out of the corners of her eyes and Lavinia smiled
softly, gently touching her cheek, hoping to put her
at ease.

'Don't be afraid, Lucy,' she said. 'I won't hurt
you.'

'It's not you she's afraid of, Lavinia. It's the up-
heaval. She's confused about everything that's happened and doesn't understand it.'

'I know. Perhaps Lucy and I can make friends on
the journey to London.'

Lucy's face was serious, her eyes searching Lavinia's intently. Lavinia sensed that she hadn't known
much kindness in her short life—only that shown to
her by Maxim. And he was right. Lucy was confused
about everything that had happened to her, and she
didn't understand the significance of this strange
woman's relationship to her father. But her presence
and her soft words had a comforting effect on her
and she smiled, her soft pink lips opening like a tiny
rosebud.

From Rotherfield Hall Lavinia often walked over
to Thornhill with Lucy, strolling hand in hand down
the lane where she had walked the day she had first
seen her stepdaughter—the day she thought her life

had ended. How wrong she had been. She and Maxim were together now. Alice and the awful events leading up to her terrible death in France were in the past, and Lavinia had found a great joy in getting to know Alice's daughter.

They had recently returned from Gloucestershire where they had been visiting Edgar, feeling free to do so now Robert had finally done the honourable thing and married Julia and she no longer resided at Welbourne House. Edgar, who was a fine young man, who admired Maxim and his business acumen enormously, had finished his education and was excited about continuing in his father's business. He was also looking forward to taking his brother-in-law up on his offer on how best to invest his money.

Thinking of her brother Lavinia smiled, looking forward to the time when he would visit them at Rotherfield. Lavinia loved Rotherfield Hall, with its elegant rooms and beautiful grounds, a house into which Welbourne House would fit a dozen times over. She was so proud to think that Maxim had achieved so much through his own endeavours, although she was still having difficulty coming to terms with his vast wealth. When he had to go to London on business he always took her with him. He would show her off like a precious jewel, wanting her to enjoy the position of prestige she was entitled to—being the wife of the next Earl of Brinkcliff.

Sometimes when she stole a glance at him and realised she bore his name, a sharp thrill would shoot through her. He never ceased to amaze her. He was so sophisticated, so elegant and full of charm, but he was forceful too—a power held in restraint, and a man with a strong sense of his own infallibility, a man with many diverse and complex shades to his character.

He was also a man who was meant to dominate, and he often found it irritating that the gentle, naïve young woman he had plucked from the Venetian lagoon, a woman who had been ignored as a child and had been reared in a sheltered, austere environment, had a mind and will as strong as his own and had not been born to be dominated. The way it looked it was evident the two of them were not likely to lead a docile life.

But whatever their differences—which they always overcame in the nicest possible way—their love was undisputed. They knew they were meant to be together, and the joy and happiness they found in each other was complete.

Today, ten months after Maxim had brought Lavinia to live at Rotherfield Hall, the sky was pale blue and cloudless, with the gentlest of breezes blowing over the paddock at Thornhill. Almost the whole family had come to watch Lucy make friends with her new pony, a little bay mare which had been passed on to her from David now he was too big to ride it himself. David was nine years old now, and Lucy adored him.

In fact, Lucy adored everything about Thornhill. Having so many children to play with was a new experience for her, and after her initial shyness had worn off, she had surprised everyone by responding to all the fuss and attention with a startling vitality, which poured from her like heat from the sun. She was such a happy, bright child, and charged with energy. But her inquiring mind, the playful devilment in her nature and the teasing light in her eyes, reminded Lavinia so much of Maxim.

Having lifted her into the saddle, Maxim leaned on the fence, watching with a look of immense pride as David led her round the paddock, laughing along with everyone else when an arrogant flock of geese was sent cackling out of the way of the pony's hooves, causing Lucy to give vent to a peal of happy laughter. Leaving Ursula's side, Lavinia went and stood beside her husband, placing her arm around his waist when he drew her close.

'Who would have thought she could look like this,' murmured Lavinia, her eyes fixed lovingly on her stepdaughter. Lavinia loved her as she would a child of her own, and Lucy returned her love a thousand fold. She was such an affectionate, pretty little girl, with her black curls and the determined thrust to her round chin.

Maxim looked down at his wife, his eyes as clear and blue as the sky above, crinkling with a smile. 'She is quite amazing, isn't she?' His gaze became intent on Lavinia's upturned face, her free flowing hair gilded by the sun's rays. He was impressed and intrigued, and would never cease to be amazed at some new character of this woman he had married. With each day's passing, their knowledge and understanding of each other increased. 'Lucy adores you, you know that, don't you? It's wonderful what you've done for her.'

A slow flush crept delightfully over her cheeks. 'She's done a lot for me too. Look at her, Maxim. She's as pretty as a picture and as merry as a magpie on her pony.'

'So she is. I am fortunate to have been so blessed,' he sighed, his arm tightening about her shoulders, his gaze dwelling warmly on her upturned face. 'What more could a man want.'

'What more, indeed,' Lavinia said, with a glow in her eyes.

She said it in such a way that Maxim smiled softly, knowingly, having suspected for a while, from the dreaminess in her eyes and the fact that he had never seen her look more beautiful, that she had something on her mind, that there might be something she had to tell him.

'Lavinia, have you something to tell me that I should know about?' His voice was warm with love and humour.

Lavinia's lips curved in a sublime smile while her eyes grew dark and sultry. 'Only that I am with child.'

There was an unusually bright glitter in Maxim's eyes when he took her in his arms, and he had difficulty swallowing. 'Thank you,' he said, his voice low and husky. Drawing back and seeing a sheen of tears in her eyes, he cradled her face gently between both his hands, gazing down into their misty turquoise depths. 'Are they tears I see in your eyes, my love?'

'If they are then it is because I am so happy.'

With a laughing sigh Maxim pulled her back into his arms, hugging her tightly. 'Do you remember what you said to me in Venice when we agreed to marry?'

'Remind me,' she whispered, her cheek against his throat, his chest warm and hard beneath the thin fabric of his shirt.

'When you agreed to those ridiculous conditions I imposed on you regarding our marriage, you told me it was like a masquerade which would lose its magic when the mask was removed.'

'Yes, I remember.'

'Well? Has it?'

Leaning back she tipped her head up to him, her eyes aglow with love. 'No. And the Carnival of love is not such a tragedy after all.'

* * * * *

A ROGUISH GENTLEMAN
Mary Brendan

Viscount Stratton's reputation preceded him: an adventurer and dare-devil, he was renowned for his beautiful mistresses. Owed money by Lady Elizabeth Rowe's family, his only hope of repayment was through her sizeable dowry—but he would have to marry her to claim it!
Lady Elizabeth had no desire to wed such a rogue, even if he was as handsome as sin. Already a wealthy man, why had Stratton actually agreed to marry her? Particularly as her own reputation was sullied by scandal! Was it for love…or revenge?

THE WESTMERE LEGACY
Mary Nichols

Isabella's grandfather, the Earl of Westmere, is insisting she take a husband—and she's to choose which of her four second cousins it's to be! In desperation, Bella turns to Robert Huntley, the cousin with whom she's shared many a childhood scrape.

A distinguished captain of the Hussars, Robert finds himself agreeing to her outrageous suggestion of a pretend engagement. He's told Bella he has no desire to be shackled in a loveless marriage, and their engagement must end once she's had a Season in Town. Why, then, is he tantalised by thoughts of what marriage to Bella could mean?

Available in August 2001

MILLS & BOON®

A PENNILESS PROSPECT
Joanna Maitland

With no dowry and unremarkable looks, Jessamyne Calderwood sees herself as a penniless country mouse. But her spirit is strong and this stands her in good stead when her grasping family attempt to marry her off.

Determined to escape, Jamie takes on the guise of a simple gardener's boy, working on the private estate of Richard, Earl Hardinge. She remains undetected until Richard rescues her from an attack and, to his astonishment, finds he's not holding a boy, but the soft body of a delectable young woman...

THE DOLLAR PRINCE'S WIFE
Paula Marshall

Gauche, unloved Lady Dinah Freville finds a champion in Cobie Grant. He can see that beneath her drab exterior is a lively and original mind. They share the taint of illegitimacy which the rich and handsome Cobie has overcome. And he is equally determined to see Dinah blossom.

Tricking Dinah's feckless half-brother into allowing them to marry, Cobie then sends his wife to Paris to be groomed. The lady who returns is a beautiful, assured woman. But he's already made it clear to her that he'll never fall in love...

Available in September 2001

MILLS & BOON®

HISTORICAL ROMANCE™

LARGE PRINT

LORD FOX'S PLEASURE
Helen Dickson

With the monarchy restored, the exiled Royalists were jubilantly returning home. For wealthy landowner Lucas Fox it was a time to take stock. Where once he'd been a pleasure-seeker, now he was ready to settle and take a wife.

Proud, impulsive Prudence Fairworthy spiced his interest keenly. With her suspicions over his motives and the mystery surrounding his past, Lucas knew she would not be easily won over to the idea of marriage. But there was untold pleasure to be found in the art of persuasion...

The Restoration of Charles II
...secrets, intrigue and conquests...

A TRACE OF MEMORY
Elizabeth Bailey

When a bedraggled woman accosts Charles Clevedon, Earl of Wytham, in his woods, claiming to have lost her memory, his first cynical thought is that it's yet another ingenious matrimonial ploy.

While he remains suspicious of her, he is safe. But somehow the combination of her beauty and vulnerable state is becoming an increasingly alluring mix. Should they give in to their longings when each unfolding memory seems to suggest that she could belong to another man?

Available in October 2001

MILLS & BOON®

HISTORICAL ROMANCE™

LARGE PRINT

THE ABDUCTED BRIDE
Anne Herries

Deborah Ann Stirling is about to become betrothed when she is taken captive by a roguish privateer. Nicholas, Marquis de Vere, has vowed vengeance on her future husband, and Deborah is the bait to lure the murderous Spaniard from his hiding place.

She is dismayed at how easy it would be to give way to her persuasive captor's charms. But what if it's part of Nicholas's revenge to seduce and then discard her?

THE HONOURABLE EARL
Mary Nichols

Lydia Fostyn is being coerced into marriage to an odious older man when Ralph Latimer, Earl of Blackwater, returns from exile—and stirs up painful memories.

Ralph is responsible for the tragedy which has brought about her family's hard times and decides he must do the honourable thing by her. But, as drawn to Lydia as he is, how closely should he get involved with a woman who appears to be aiding and abetting smugglers on his land near the Essex marshes…?

Available in November 2001

MILLS & BOON®